Love Out of Time

by
Joyce Zeller

Published by Joyce Zeller

Dedication

Thank you to the Northwest Arkansas
Writers Group for seeing me through this
book and all the technicalities page by page.
As usual, my eighth grade English teacher at
John Reynolds Junior High in Lancaster,
PA, gets the credit for teaching me to love
the English language and all it's
possibilities.
I must give credit to Herman Melville's
magnificent book on whaling in the
nineteenth century, *Moby Dick,* for
providing the flavor of the times in an 1860s
whaling village, and the Time-Life book,
The Whalers, for the harrowing picture of
the life of a Whaler and the true sense of
what whaling in the 1860s looked and felt
like, and the story of "The Stone Fleet."

This book is pure fiction, and the characters
and events therein are totally a product of
my imagination. There actually was a Stone
Fleet, and other events contained in the
book are drawn from research on the
Internet.

Cover art by Dreamstime.com ©Fenias

Chapter One

She remembered, well enough, the night her life shattered, torn to shreds by a simple declaration. "I'm leaving you, Sara. I don't want to be married anymore. I've already filed for divorce."

While the SUV she drove lurched and careened down the New Jersey county road, on her way to the Atlantic coast, the memories flooded back. The words had come out of nowhere, with no warning, while she and her husband of twenty-two years were settled in the living room for a quiet drink before dinner. The four words rocked her world, without any hint of disaster.

A wave of fear swept through her. Stunned speechless by his announcement, she struggled to say something. All she could manage was, "What? Richard, I don't understand." He looked the same—a large, physically fit man, mid-forties, who projected self-confidence and success. What had changed? Her heart screamed in denial.

This can't be happening to me.

She'd tried to be the poster-perfect wife and mother. Had done it all. She watched her weight; she dressed well, had a reasonably good appearance, shoulder-length chestnut hair, polished nails—all received regular attention. How had she failed?

Until that definitive moment, Sara Burkhart thought her marriage solid and secure. She and Richard had an impressive home in exclusive East Partridge, a New York suburb, and two well-adjusted children getting ready to leave for college. They lived in comfort, with an active social life and good friends, and all the usual amenities. There were never any serious problems, financial or otherwise—until that moment.

"There isn't anything to understand, Sara. I've been thinking about this for a while. The decision is made. I don't want to be married anymore. I want out."

No debate. No discussion. Simply—I want out. Typically Richard.

Her frozen mind refused to think the "D' word. It skittered around the edges, sensing the pain to come.

Get hold of yourself, Sara. Good advice born of experience. If she lost it, she knew from long experience, he'd react, with disgust and walk out, and she'd never know why.

The jolt when the car hit a gully, pitched, and leaned precariously, demanded her attention. When she gained control again, she breathed a sigh of relief and calmed enough to recall her dumbfounded reply—one that still sparked her anger. "But what's wrong? What have I done?"

Dear God, how typical of her. So conditioned to accept blame. Tedious, predictable behavior embedded during years of placating and compromise. How pathetic was that? She'd watched Richard's impatience flare, a characteristic reaction when pushed to defend one of his declarations.

"This isn't about you, Sara. It isn't anything you've done or anything you can fix. I'm tired of our life, this town, and the people in it. I'm moving on to something better."

He continued, his voice flat, devoid of any emotion. "We're set financially. In two months. Jenny and Dick, Jr. are leaving for college. It's time to end this."

Wordlessly, she stared at him. He spoke so calmly. He didn't lie. He'd been planning this for a long time, and she'd had no clue. He might have just said, "I'm going to the gym."

Though still speechless, she struggled to find a rebuttal, but the words deserted her.
Panic, like an acid pool, burned in her gut—robbing her of her ability to think. Richard waited, his expression resolved, daring her to comment.

What brought this on? There couldn't be another woman; she would have sensed it. Frankly, Richard had little patience with any woman. His public image was that of a maverick, ruggedly independent. He preferred the company of men. He disliked social occasions, seldom wore a necktie, lived in an assortment of golf shirts, and still remained a revered executive among his peers, commanding their respect, much sought after for speaking engagements. In a word, he had reached the pinnacle of success.

So say something, Stupid, her mind pleaded. Don't let it end here in predictable mild acquiescence.

"I don't understand. Do you have a plan? Where will you go? What will, you do? What about Jenny and Dick Junior?"

The tone he used mimicked one he'd use explaining facts to a small child. "They're provided for. They have their own funds. You won't have any financial problems. I've taken care of it. You can have the house." He raised his hand, palm out, forestalling argument. "It's over, Sara. I'm moving to Florida. I've sold out of the company and bought a small business down there."

"Why, for God's sake?" There was no point in mentioning love or marriage vows. Richard had no patience with 'women's sentiments.'

His expression changed to a mix of anguish and despair. "You don't get it, do you? You're so complacent, with your groups and your clubs, and committees. You think this is all there is to life. Well, it isn't enough for me."

"But, what do you want?" Could that be her voice escalating to near hysteria?

"What do I want?" He roared at her, rigid with anger, impatient at her inability to comprehend. "I want passion in my life. I want to care about something." He paced the floor, shaking his fists, clearly searching for words. "I want to wake up each morning eager for the day, glad to be alive."

His eyes bore into hers. He stared her down, his expression reflecting frustration born of months of consideration. "Do you even have any idea what I'm saying?"

Her shock began to give way to anger. "I'm trying, Richard, but you're right; I don't get it."

With a sad smile and regret in his voice, he said, "Remember the way it used to be? Remember the thrill of just starting out, the struggle, the good times we had when we were young and poor? I want what we had, Sara. I want to do it all over again."

"You want to be poor?" She couldn't keep the echo of rising panic out of her voice.

"Don't be obtuse," he raged. "I want the struggle. The uncertainty. I want the thrill of taking risks and not knowing how it'll turn out. Hell, I want mind-blowing sex the way it used to be. We have nothing. Damn it, Sara, I want to feel young again, and now I can afford to do it."

Her brain numb, she stared at him.

My God, I've killed my marriage by boring my husband to death.

Finally the rising anger broke free of its restraints. "Damn you, Richard." The words exploded, shocking her. She never used obscenities. "It isn't my fault you're getting old. I can't make you young again. No matter how we try, we can't hold back time. We get older. Our knees get bad, our bodies sag, and there isn't much we can do about it."

He looked at her, disgust and pity shaped his expression. "It's over, Sara," he said, and walked out.

The van hit another gully, reminding her of the rutted road. She fought the steering wheel, regained control, and slowed to a stop. Driving an eroded and sandy Jersey Shore road was not ideal activity while reliving traumatic moments. Her journey's end would provide a well-deserved vacation, alone, where she'd have time to think.

New Kensington-by-the-Sea, her final destination, a small coastal settlement on one of the barrier islands south of Atlantic City largely ignored by tourists, beckoned her. It was briefly popular as a vacation resort in the early 1900s, but went into decline years ago, abandoned, and depressed when bypassed by the new highway. She smiled at the irony of it. But then, so was she—isolated, abandoned and depressed—so she'd fit right in.

Letting the engine idle for a bit while her nerves calmed, she allowed her thoughts to return to the changes forced on her.

Would she ever be able to replay that night without experiencing the heart stopping fear and despair, when she realized what went on with her husband couldn't be fixed? She couldn't give him back his youth. She'd lost her appeal, and was about to be replaced.

She felt a new a kinship with the television images of those tornado and flood victims who stood blank-faced and defeated, surveying the destruction of everything they'd had. Such scenes weren't supposed to happen to women who followed all the rules and did the whole wife-mother-homemaker thing to perfection.

Oh, yeah, I'm a regular June Cleaver. I can make a killer soufflé, knock off a dinner party for eighteen, make Christmas happen like clockwork, but I can't hold a marriage together.

Her friends' husbands had mid-life crises, but they bought a motorcycle, or joined a gym, or had plastic surgery—bought a toupee, for heaven's sake. Leave it to Richard to make the grand gesture. The bitterest disappointment proved to be the reaction of her son and daughter who took it in stride with barely a comment—a sad commentary on what her years of devotion to the family meant.

Their apathy was the ultimate betrayal she'd never forgive. In a moment of clarity she'd realized their family had split into two parts years ago. Her husband and her children had formed an alliance, leaving her out there alone. She'd been demoted to the equivalent of hired help, content with performing the duties attendant to the role of housekeeper and mother, admittedly not complaining too much because she enjoyed the comforts of living there.

Well, okay, maybe that was a little harsh, but on the other hand, she received no recognition of her contribution as a mother who had devoted years to creating for them a home that afforded them every advantage. It was a taste of bitter fruit, indeed.

As far as Jen and Dick Jr. were concerned, they really didn't care. Her children were going off to an exciting college adventure and probably wouldn't spend much time at home anyhow, so what did it matter? Since Richard's announcement, two months ago, they'd spared her barely a moment of sympathy or understanding. The anger and abandonment she felt in response to their attitude festered deep. So, her errant ex-husband traipsed off to a new life in Florida filled with challenges and probably young females named Tiffany, or God forbid, Bitsy, leaving her with no option but to join the ranks of the forty-something single females.

The taste of it fouled her tongue. Was that all the last twenty-two years had meant to them? Apparently the traditional contributions to the family well being expected of the mother/wife were valueless. All the memories were no more than the inconsequential residue of no meaningful activity, no longer needed, so goodbye. Resentment on behalf of housewives everywhere churned to the surface, bringing dark anger with it.

We can't all become cupcake titans incubating businesses in our kitchens. Some of us think it's enough to simply do the job we thought marriage required, content with being taken for granted, and overlooked as an important contributor to the success of the family. It hurt, damn it. She'd learned some hard truths in the last few months. Not anymore. To hell with them all.

Playing the victim in this macabre scene, like some weak character in a Neil Simon play wasn't getting her anywhere. So what cheering advice did her other self, the one lurking beneath the failed character of wife/mother/homemaker have to offer when life threatened to defeat her?

For sure, one thing about divorce hits you instantly. Women you thought were friends avoid you without shame. Suddenly, you have a contagious disease that might rub off on them. You aren't part of a couple anymore; you are the "extra person." You'd changed, and become the dreaded unattached female, suspected to be on the prowl for a replacement. Men you'd always been comfortable with became predators.

I will get through this. So I'm not the mother in charge of Thanksgiving and Christmas every year. No loss, apparently. I'll build a new Sara and I'll go on from there. First stop: New Kensington-by-the-Sea. Satisfied to have a destination, sort of, Sara tackled the rutted shore road once again. The real estate office in the small town held the key to the rental property, and would close at four o'clock.

Her housing choice, selected from photos on the Internet, appeared suitably isolated, built on a dune overlooking the ocean. The weatherworn, shingled, two-story Cape Cod Victorian type, more than a hundred years old, survived as a relic left from the days when New Kensington was a whaling village. It had been added to and remodeled over the years, and offered as "weekly rental." The website had a "virtual tour" option, that revealed a working kitchen, a sparsely furnished living room downstairs with a wall of ocean side windows and a porch beyond, conjuring visions of outdoor meals, with lounge chairs for watching the sunrise. There were three bedrooms upstairs, fresh linens provided. She could imagine being comfortable there, and responded to the photos immediately, with a sense of recognition, as though she'd been searching for the house for a long time. The house called to her.

The road took her across a short bridge, into New Kensington, and dead-ended at the town dock, where a narrow pier ran by the boat slips, each one with a weathered and worn boardwalk, looking like it had been there a hundred years. The tangle of masts and lines from a dozen pleasure sailboats berthed in the small cove, rocked back and forth on a restless sea. They shared the skyline with flocks of screaming sea gulls, ever alert for anything thrown into the water. The approaching bank of clouds on the horizon indicated some rainy weather in the offing.

A narrow, hard sand street, bordered by a sidewalk, ran parallel to the beach, fronted by some gift shops, an old board shack selling fish tacos through a front window, and a grocery store with a faded real estate sign swinging from an overhang.

Sara parked under the sign and entered, noticing not only shelves of groceries, but also some small tables with assorted chairs in the corner under a wall sign said, *Fresh shrimp. All you can eat. $5.99.* The bare board walls and floor indicated that seawater drenching during storms was not uncommon.

"How can I hep ya?" A weathered but robust man, near retirement age, glanced up from behind the checkout counter, and greeted her. His overalls were whitened with age, his bald spot surrounded by a fringe of grey hair.

"Uh, I'm here to pick up a key?"

"Caro," he bellowed, "Somebody's here."

A short, buxom woman about the same age, bustling with energy, emerged from a back room, wearing an apron over blue jeans, her hair in a net. Even from a distance, she smelled of fish.

She offered her hand. "I'm Carolyn Arthur and he's my husband Henry," she said, nodding and smiling pleasantly. "I own the real estate rental office."

The hand was chapped and callused, and covered with small, undoubtedly painful nicks. Caro was a multi-tasker of some sort.

"I'm Sara Burkhart. I've arranged to rent the Stuart House for two months?"

That information earned her a thoughtful gaze and a firm comment. "The house sleeps six. The contract is for a single renter. Don't get many of those, so if anybody else shows up, it'll cost more."

Not used to being regarded with distrust, Sara offered a broad smile she hoped would instill confidence. Maybe single tourists could be a devious lot. "I'm not married, both my children are away at college, and I didn't want to be in an empty house, I decided I'd spend some time at the shore. It'll be just me. If it's okay with you, I'll take the key and get going."

A wide grin split the woman's face, exposing more creases and crannies than Sara would have thought possible. This face belonged in an oil painting, or a black and white portrait by Stieglitz.

Moving behind the counter to a pegboard loaded with keys, she removed one and handed it to Sara. "You lose this it'll cost you," she said. No doubt a somewhat regular occurrence. She presented a copy of a hand-drawn map, adding, "Here's directions, but it isn't hard to find. Go one block down this street and turn towards the beach at Stuart Lane. The street dead-ends at the house. Linens are at the house, utilities are turned on, but you'll need groceries."

"Thank you. I stopped and got the basics on the way."

"Well then, there's a town over on the mainland that has one of them big organic stores, but you might want to wait until tomorrow. We have some bad weather coming in later tonight." With a casual "Enjoy your stay," Caro turned and left the room.

Organic grocery? Sara smothered a grin. I must have a yuppie look about me.

When she was in the car, about to pull away, her landlady hurried toward her smiling shyly, offering a plastic bag filled with ice and raw shrimp.

Maybe her rush to judgment had been too hasty.

"Take 'em for your supper. They just came in. I took the heads off."

That explained Caro's worn hands with the nicks. The storeowners processed their own shrimp. Grateful for the gesture, she smiled and said, "Thank you, Caro. What a generous thing to do."

"You take care now. I think you and the house will get along—no trouble."

Get along? Sara took off in too much hurry to question the odd remark, eager to experience the smell of fresh sea air mingled with the rank, fishy odor of salt backwater, a sure sign the ocean was near. It had been a few dozen years since she'd been near the Atlantic, but childhood memories of better times came rushing back in a restless wave—the eagerness to get a tan going, taste real crab cakes and salt water taffy, and search for the perfect sea shell.

Stuart house, although not large, inspired awe. Like most beach houses, it sat on stilts to allow waves to flow underneath. Patriarchal came to mind to describe the way it sat, a good distance from the houses on either side, like a ghostly sentinel keeping watch, timeless, indestructible, weathered nearly beyond endurance—a lonely survivor on this long stretch of beach. It beckoned Sara with its primal presence, alive, with a soul.

Here lies safe haven and comfort.

The words were there, in her mind—not a voice, exactly, but a welcoming presence. She shivered. Goosebumps crept along her arms.

It made sense now—Caro's remark about the house getting along with her. "What memories must live within your walls," she said. "For more than a hundred years you've taken whatever the ocean delivered and you're still here."

Stuart Lane ended as a hard packed sand driveway alongside the house, with room to park right next to the kitchen door. Though there were only a few steps to climb, unloading all her luggage was going to be tedious business.

In no mood for making decisions before leaving home, she'd packed everything including her computer, printer, and clothes for every occasion, although, after seeing the rustic character of the town, what occasions there might be presented a mystery.

The late harvest season had reached its peak in the truck gardens lining the interstate, and fueled her enthusiasm for fresh fruit and vegetables. In minutes, she had the small kitchen crowded with groceries. Too tired and hungry to deal with the largess, she piled it into the small refrigerator, with a promise to get to it later. Lunch had been hours ago. Hunger had her craving food, and Caro's shrimp with sweet corn was the fastest way to ward off starvation. Quickly she emptied a couple of bottles of beer into a pot and set it to heat on the stove, making do until she could find proper shrimp boil.

The porch, as advertised, had a table, rustic chairs with fat cushions, and two well-padded, oversized Adirondack lounges, apparently designed for larger humans. By the time she had newspapers on the table for the shrimp, and set out sliced tomatoes, butter and salt, the beer had come to a boil, ready for the shrimp and corn, which took only a few minutes to cook.

An hour later, blissfully satiated, she relaxed on the lounge with another beer. She listened to the constant beat of the ocean waves, and slowly unwound from what had seemed like a non-stop, frantic rush, the last two months, finally reaching this place of completion. She needed this escape from everyday reminders a lost life—the sympathetic phone calls devoid of genuine sympathy that only opened fresh wounds to more bleeding.

Dusk turned to dark, bringing a rising wind, precursor to the approaching storm brewing to the northeast. Her gaze drifted over the restless waves. Their angry motion matched her mood. Way in the distance, the lights of two freighters following a shipping lane, signaled in the darkness. Millions of stars, invisible near cities with bright lights, filled the sky with star shine. Overhead the intermittent blink of a satellite competed for attention with the flashing signals from a commercial airliner.

Inevitably, her mind returned to her situation. It was over. Twenty years of marriage, her identity as Mrs. Richard Burkhart, comfortable, suburban wife with all the attendant amenities and social obligations—all of it gone. So now what? The question gave rise to idle memories, like the last phone call she'd made to her best friend before leaving town. Grace's criticism, totally unexpected, caught her by surprise.

I don't understand why you need to be alone. You should be here, getting your life back together. Learn from your mistakes. John has a single friend you might like to meet. I could have you over for drinks.

Learn from her mistakes? The betrayal she felt at the remark still rankled. Her firm belief in her innocence had kept her going. So much for loyal friends.

Forget it, Grace. I'm not looking for another relationship. Maybe never.

That's crazy. The sooner you find someone else, the sooner you'll get back to normal.

Normal? The memory of that comment still raised her ire, making her realize what she'd truly lost. She wouldn't be accepted back into her old crowd without restoring the façade of a normal marriage. The call ended with her grief for a friend lost forever, and anger at a lifestyle that didn't accept any variation of the rules. If she wanted to avoid becoming an outcast to her friends, she'd have to find another man and fill the same spousal role as before. Well, they could take their rules and stuff them. With half her life to live, who says the second has to be a mirror of the first? Forty-five is too young to become old.

The hypnotic rhythm of the waves opened a door in Sara's mind—one she'd slammed shut months ago. Was she to blame for the fiasco of her marriage? Should she have fought back—changed the outcome? To be absolutely honest, she knew the excitement had gone out of their marriage the last couple of years. She and Richard had financial security, and a house in the suburbs, raised two children to be happy and self-sufficient, and acquired like-minded friends, but shared no common interests on which to build a future. They lived separate lives. She became totally involved in her amateur theater group, took on projects, and went shopping. Richard had his business and his golf buddies. They had become a cliché: ships passing in the night. She knew Richard was unhappy. She felt it. The company had lost its appeal for him. It had become an exercise in everyday tedium. He hated his life, and had no interest in hers, and she didn't have the courage to confront him with the problem. Their marriage had gone past the point where they had any meaningful conversations about anything.

I was too comfortable to face the reality of a stalled marriage, like treading water in a vast lake with no destination in sight. I liked living in the biggest house on the block, having money, a comfortable group of married friends. I didn't want to change anything, so yeah, I guess I share the blame for the divorce. I'd left it up to Richard, forcing him to take the lead and admit the dead end. I knew he hungered for more, but I couldn't face what came next.

So I let Richard carry it all, and played the role of the wronged woman. But damn it, he deserved it. He had no right to handle it the way he did, simply dumping the load on me and leaving me to deal with the pity and speculation. That was his punishment—forcing me to face the silently voiced accusations alone. I must have done something wrong to have it end. The familiar lump in her throat meant tears were imminent.

Geez, I'm really sinking into a depression here.

Her hand held an empty beer bottle. Should she have another or go inside?

The wind had increased with the incoming tide without her notice. Strong gusts hit the waves, blowing spindrift into the air with enough force for some of it to hit her in the face. The moon and stars were gone, yielding to the stygian blackness of storm clouds.

Sara gazed at the sea, wondering, how bad would it get? Did she need to think about windows breaking or salt water flooding the house? She stared anxiously at the restless ocean, waiting for some flash of wisdom that would allay her fear.

The awareness came slowly, making her heart pound.

Though there were no sounds of a door opening, the substance of the air changed, as though another person had entered the room, taking up some space. Startled, she looked around. Nothing, but yet she couldn't deny the feeling she was not alone. The sense of another presence felt oddly comforting.

"Oh come on," she said, liking the sound of her voice. "The house has been here at least for a century, so there are bound to be creaks and groans."

The wind spooked her, but she tried to relax. A blast of sea spray hit the house, carried on the wind. She'd have to get used to bad weather while she spent time here. This wasn't a hurricane, just a storm. The waves came closer with the tide, probably bringing dead things, or whatever, onto the beach.

She doubted she'd end up with a shipwreck in her front yard—maybe some driftwood, but nothing worse. How bad could it be, considering all the storms the house had survived 'til now? She made a dash for the kitchen, slammed the door behind her, and headed for safety in the second floor bedrooms.

Wrapped in a blanket, she lay in a twilight zone before sleep, while the wind howled, and the house shook. For what seemed like hours, she listened to the creaks and groans of old timbers. Sleeping in a strange house in a strange place, alone, should have been frightening, but, oddly, for the first time in months, she felt at peace. She had no sense of an intruder, but in those final moments before sleep claimed her, she knew something, some presence in the room, watched over her.

In the far corner a faint cloud that could have been humidity, lingered a while, then dissolved into nothing.

Chapter Two

A soft breeze drifting through the open bedroom window awakened her gently right after dawn the next morning. Its salty moistness touched her skin. The raucous sound of sea birds assaulted her ears. When she looked from the open window, the ocean appeared calm. Waves rolled gently onshore with hardly a whitecap anywhere. The memory of last night's storm brought her fully awake. Anxious about damage, and expecting the worst, Sara pulled on a t-shirt and some shorts and rushed downstairs to get morning coffee and venture outside to check the house.

All appeared normal in the kitchen; everything on the porch was in place and already dried off, as though nothing had happened. Apparently storms like the one last night were nothing unusual. She settled on a lounge and let herself sink into lethargy.

The retreating tide had left behind some interesting debris about twenty feet in front of the house, including what looked like a pile of clothing. Peering intently, she saw it move, and wondered if something was caught underneath, maybe some crabs. Shocked, she watched the pile roll over, revealing it to be a man now lying spread-eagled, on his back, either unconscious or sleeping.

Ohmigod. A boat must have sunk. Somebody had been in an accident. Did New Kensington have 911? Probably not, but regardless, she'd better check to see if she needed to call for help. Her bare feet slowed her progress in her frantic race to reach him, but when she finally did, she noticed, with relief, the man's ruddy color, and regular breathing. He hadn't drowned—he only lay deep into the sleep of the exhausted, which made sense, if he'd had to swim ashore from a sinking boat.

He looked odd, his clothes strange—not something a local would wear, like jeans or coveralls. His dress looked like a costume—one she knew from her work with her theater group. His close fitting trousers of natural broadcloth, almost like leggings, ended just below his knees. A loose-fitting shirt with bloused sleeves, made of unbleached linen, covered his broad chest.

It had been a while since she'd seen a man as muscled as this one. His legs and feet were bare, though not tanned as the rest of him. He must have had shoes and stockings at one time. A vest of the same cream color, maybe sateen, with a double row of brass buttons down the front, suggested this was some sort of uniform.

Good heavens, on closer look she realized all the clothes he wore were handmade. Sara recognized hand sewing, and, with her years of experience in theater, recognized costuming from the 1800s. He had to be from a film set nearby, but then why had he been out in a storm wearing a costume?

Groaning, the man tried to sit up, but stopped, bracing himself with one arm while he tried to brush the sand from his eyes.

"Don't move. I'll get you some help. Keep your eyes closed until I get the sand cleaned off your face."

"What place is this?" His voice had the funny twang of a native New Englander.

"You're on the beach right outside my house, so you'll be okay."

To help with the sand, Sara gently brushed away the dark, thick hair, curling around his face, in a style she knew, from pictures of historical costuming, as "The Brutus." He had a deep brow and strong chin. His deeply tanned, weathered skin had the faint shadow of a beard.

"If you hold on for a minute and keep still, I'll get some water to wash the sand and the salt from your eyes."

"Speak, woman," he demanded. "Where am I?"

Startled, she stammered, "Uh, the Jersey Shore, I mean, New Jersey, near New Kensington. I guess you were in the ocean and you ended up on the beach." Excitement caught at her breath before she could continue. "Hold on a minute until I get back. We'll call someone for help."

The dash to the house to grab a sponge, a bucket, several bottles of water, and her cellphone, took only minutes. When she returned she found him as she'd left him, too dazed to move without aid.

A large and undeniably attractive man, he appeared, from the looks of his long, lean body and broad shoulders, to lead an active life. He looked to be about her age but strong, like an athlete. In her mind she saw him swinging like a monkey from the rigging of a pirate ship. Maybe a stunt man cast in a movie about pirates? It took all her strength to pull him upright.

"Just sit still. I'll get you cleaned up."

Dazed, he submitted to her ministrations until he opened his eyes. They were the deepest shade of green she'd never seen. The powerful force radiating from his gaze told her he lived by his physical strength and his wits, but would be a cruel taskmaster and not hesitate to wreak vengeance on those who denied his authority. Her perception of him changed. This was no ordinary hired actor. Besides, he had a body to kill for. Shocked, she realized despite her fear, she felt an attraction toward the man.

Dear God in heaven. How could she? He was half dead, for crying out loud.

"I have some water," she managed to say, handing him the bottle after twisting off the top. "You must be thirsty. It's pure spring water, no chemicals," she added, in case he was an athlete and health conscious. His expression filled with wonder when he examined the bottle, looking through it and squeezing. "What manner of vessel is this? It is not glass."

Who talked like this? Were his senses rattled? Did he think he still played a scene? "It's plastic. Not environmentally correct, but all I had."

"Most unusual." He drank all the water and gave her the bottle. "You are beyond kind, Madam." Obviously confused, he studied the shore. "I know not how I arrived here."

"Some kind of boat, I'd guess. We had a bad storm last night."

Though he struggled, he couldn't quite manage to stand.

"Take it easy. You'll be yourself in a couple of minutes." She began to worry. He should be talking normally about now, unless he had a head injury. Did he think he was some character playing a scene?

"Be myself? Your speech is strange. Of course I'm myself. Again, I must beg your indulgence, Madam. Where am I?"

Cautiously, she repeated, "You are on a beach in front of my house in New Jersey."

"Impossible. What house?" He got to his feet, stood a little unsteady, and looked around.

Oh, my, he was tall—a few inches over six feet. She'd barely reach to his shoulder. If he turned aggressive, she'd be in trouble. "My place," she ventured cautiously, "its behind you." She pointed.

"Yours?" Looking around, he said, "Hardly. A navigational miscalculation, perhaps." With a groan, he sank into a sitting position.

This was getting weirder by the minute. If he didn't think he still played the scene in his movie, then something very strange had happened. There'd been enough turbulence in the ocean last night for a small fishing boat to wreck, but who went fishing dressed like that?

"Uh, maybe you better rest before you stand up. My name is Sara Burkhart. What is yours?"

"Thomas Stuart, recently of New Kensington, Massachusetts, at your service, Madam."

"Oh. The family who owned this house in the 1800s was named Stuart."

"Of course they are." He struggled to stand, and this time, he made it.

With Sara helping him, they managed to climb the stairs to the porch and she settled him into one of the lounge chairs, not saying a word, while she went to the kitchen to get some food, figuring he must be hungry, after spending the night in the ocean. She'd find him some clothes later. For the present, what he wore appeared to be drying and not too sandy. Returning with some cheese, bread, and left over shrimp on a plate, she placed it on the table along with a fork, which he examined curiously, more interested in the fork than the food. He'd never seen a fork?

He waited until she retired to the other lounge before asking; "I have need of information, Dear Lady, if you would be so kind?" He paused, waiting for her nod, and then began, "You alluded to former owners of this house from the 1800s. The remark suggests this is no longer 1860. Furthermore, your seeming unconcern at your outrageous state of undress is most disconcerting. I have never seen such clothing worn with such disregard for propriety."

Stunned, Sara said, "Oh my word. You have amnesia. You don't know where you are, do you?"

"Begging your pardon, I know exactly where I am. There seems to be some confusion as to when, however. Pray tell, Mistress, what year is this?"

He wouldn't like the answer. Cautiously, she said, "Uh, 2014," and shrank back into her chair waiting for his reaction. No way could she handle this giant of a man if he got upset. It wasn't long in coming.

He leaped to his feet and shouted, enraged, "A hundred sixty years? What bloody hell is this?" What happened next went way beyond her ability to understand. He began to fade. His legs were disappearing, from the bottom up.

"What is happening to you?" she cried, terrified.

When his arms dissolved, the rest of his body followed while she watched. Only his face and hands were left. Then they too vanished in a flash.

The fork remained and fell to the floor.

Fear, such as she'd never known, held her paralyzed.

What just happened?

Had any of this been real? Her mind groped for an explanation. She was still on the lounge, so she must have been asleep, or maybe hallucinating or it was a daydream.

Yes, of course. I think I'm awake, but I'm dreaming. I'm still in bed but, if I'm in bed, how come I feel the chair under me? I'm sitting down. It's a good thing, because I'm shaking too hard to stand. Please, God, this didn't happen, not to me.

Goose bumps covered every inch of skin. Stress and exhaustion from all she'd been through was messing with her mind. Damn Richard. All this was his fault after what he'd put her through.

Something else hovered in the room, something near her— that presence again, taking up space. It told her not to be afraid, though she heard nothing. Another spirit? She was in worse emotional shape than she thought. She was too overwrought to even try to deny it, but what did that say about her sanity? She'd read books about ghosts, seen the movies, enjoyed the stories, but they weren't real.

I'm just a simple suburban housewife. We don't have hauntings in East Partridge.

She wouldn't believe it, but then, how to explain the man? He'd been an illusion, but he'd been here, insisting he came from somewhere back in time.

While her nerves settled, her common sense returned, and, as much as it violated everything she'd believed up until now, she became convinced. Somehow, in a semi-sleeping state, she'd maybe seen a ghost—an honest to God supernatural being. He might never appear again. He'd indicated some terrible mistake made him appear at all.

At first, disappointment flooded her, and then she started to laugh. Was this the aftermath of adrenaline rush? She should be running, screaming, from the scene, but why? Her nerves had calmed, so she could look at this rationally. So she'd met a being—not a real man—who talked to her, and then she watched him fade away, disappear before her eyes. If she believed that, then it wasn't much of a reach to believe she lived in a haunted house—albeit a friendly one—with two spirits. Okay. She could go with that. It certainly added a new dimension to this vacation. She continued with her rationalization.

The house welcomed her, willing to share secrets hidden within its walls. In someway she believed this. How incredible, but what happens next? The image of herself as the middle-aged, discarded wife reformed when she imagined dealing with a couple of ghosts and became more exciting, more interesting. Whoa! Hold on. If her ravaged self could so easily feel sexual attraction to a spirit, she'd better stay away from real men.

How easy it would be to become that most pitiful of females, so afraid to be alone she became caught in a net of futile, unrequited love. She had plenty of time to decide who to be and where her life would go for the next couple of decades. Adding a couple of spiritual visitors to the mix might be bizarre, but a one-time experience.

Coffee. A healthy jolt of caffeine would help her focus, and something to eat would fuel her brain so she could deal with this. Besides, unless Thomas reappeared, the excitement for the day had ended. What more could happen? She headed for the kitchen.

Before long, she sat, content, back on the porch, enjoying the kick of the caffeine and the food she'd offered her guest, remembering every exciting moment with her handsome visitor, the salty scent of the ocean from his clothes, with smoky hints of tobacco, and far off lands, and deep sea mysteries. Why not? She could use a little fantasy as long as she maintained a grip on reality. Who would know she imagined hooking up with one of them? Hooking up? Well, maybe that went a little too far, but experiencing closeness with a man, even a barely there ghost, would be nice. And safe, she added, because he wasn't real.

She remembered the early years with Richard, the tenderness, and being held and touched and nurtured—memories she kept firmly behind a closed door in her mind. They brought forth yearnings better left alone. For the last ten years her marriage had followed a fixed routine with little meaningful conversation and even less intimacy—a given part of her life, but one she didn't share with her friends, who were all, more or less, solidly married couples, though the males surfed steadily for casual sexual encounters. Of course there had been opportunities for affairs, some dangerously tempting, but to her, marriage was a commitment. Still, the longing surfaced when she saw couples connecting, showing their love for each other.

Like all her friends, she didn't question the quality of her life. She'd been born to the upper middle class, attended the right schools, fulfilled parental expectations to make a good marriage, be the ideal housewife, and have the two children expected of her.

Yeah? And how did that turn out?

When it all came crashing down, and she had a chance to look back with a critical eye, she realized she hadn't lived—she'd occupied space.

I have no interests outside family, East Partridge and my little theater group—no political awareness, or, for that matter, no awareness of anything outside my small world. Forty years of my life gone and I have nothing to show for it.

Bitterness threatened to drown her in a black morass of depression. The kitchen door opened from outside, jerking her out of her reverie. Somebody had walked, uninvited, into her house. Who would do this? A real person? An intruder? Before she could panic, she heard someone ask, "Hello? Anybody home?"

A female voice preceded her uninvited guest, who strolled casually onto the porch from the kitchen, as though she had every right to be there. "I'm sorry, I didn't mean to scare you. Peace be with you."

"Uh."

A woman looking unlike any she'd ever met entered, or rather, sauntered casually into the room. She was tall and rail-thin, with sparse, shoulder length, straight brown hair going to gray, simply parted in the middle. A face devoid of any makeup revealed her to be about Sara's age. Some airy, tie-died material, fashioned into a shift, flowed loosely almost to her ankles, barely covering bare feet clad in sandals Sara recognized as Birkenstocks. However bizarre, she appeared non-threatening. Well, bizarre to Sara, at least, who came from the world of Donna Karan and Michael Kors. Within her circle, women didn't dress like this. It was unacceptable. In all of East Partridge, she'd venture, there were no women who owned and wore such garments during the day, especially, God forbid, without pantyhose.

"Hi. I know you're new here and I figured I'd stop and say hello on my way into town. The energy emitting from here is all-good. I'm Clover."

"Clover?" Hopefully, in another minute she'll have changed gears, recovered from her stunned reaction at having been invaded, and gathered her wits about her. She would speak in whole sentences. Meanwhile, she wondered if this might be another surreal event, but without the haunted stuff.

Her guest flashed an understanding smile. "I'm sorry I startled you. The door stood open, but I forget that city folk are afraid of strangers. My real name, Donna, didn't express my personhood, so I changed it to Clover. Are you a writer?"

Where did that come from? "Uh, no, I'm not anything." The moment she said that, she regretted it. Did she really think of herself as 'not anything?' Pathetic, that's what she was.

Clover's glance sharpened for an instant before she responded. "Oh, I'm sorry." She nodded as though understanding.

That made it even worse.

"Your aura shows a lot of uncertainty there—the yellow suggests underlying strength, but it's overpowered by so much dark blue and red—black around the edges. Very concerning. You have a lot of stress going on in your life."

Auras? There are people who talked like this? Not where she came from.

"Sorry. I'm not familiar with auras."

"Melanie, she works at the spa in town, reads auras. She has a Kirlian camera that photographs them. Anyhow, I saw you sitting there, zoned out, in another place," she said, changing direction before Sara could comment, so I thought I'd stop in. " I know writers who space out like that. You just have to wait for them to come back." She smiled expectantly at Sara. "Is there more coffee?"

Coffee? She was still dealing with auras. Who was this woman? Finally, the synapses firing in her confused brain made a connection. Her guest must be a local who stopped in to meet the newcomer to the neighborhood. Clearly, tourist towns as far out of the mainstream as this one attracted a different type of local resident. She'd have to become accustomed to that.

"Don't mind me. I'm a little slow this morning." She gestured to the lounges. "Sit and I'll get us both some coffee." Play hostess. This she could do.

In minutes she returned to the porch, on a quest for information, determined to find out more about her visitor and this house.

"I just arrived last night. As a child, I used to spend summers on the coast," she offered, "but I'm sure it's a lot different from when I was a teenager."

Clover shrugged. "Different, but the same. Locals still fight over the same stuff they did fifty years ago. The tourists keep coming, although more of them arrive on motorcycles."

Motorcycles? "I didn't get the impression the town was big enough for all that when I stopped to pick up the key for this place."

"You must have been down at the docks. There's not much there. If you'd gone on up the road a bit you'd have seen the real New Kensington. When the town rebuilt, after the 1960s hurricane wiped out everything except the docks, the town moved about a mile north to be closer to Atlantic City. About five thousand people live here year round. The money crowd lives in a new development, Kensington Shores Estates. They don't mingle with the rest of us."

"Rebuilt? I don't understand."

Clover's voice shifted to 'tour guide' mode. "In the 60s we had a bad Nor'easter, a hurricane that took out all the houses except this one, on this part of the beach. In fact, except for the docks, only this house survived as the only thing left standing."

Sara wanted more. "It's odd you should say that. We had a bad storm last night but the porch didn't look like it had been touched. The wind and the waves just went around it."

Clover nodded. "They always do. That's why the rumors started about it being haunted. Sometimes renters complain of noises. There's supposed to be a ghost."

Sara could have crowed with delight. Clover might know something about her visitor. "Do you believe a ghost lives here?"

Her guest studied her before answering, apparently used to being patronized by out-of-towners eager for local lore.

Sara hastened to explain. "I know it sounds dumb, but some things about this house have made me wonder if there's a presence, like a spirit, maybe."

Clover paused a minute, frowning, clearly deciding what to say. Her reaction didn't inspire confidence. "There might be an explanation if you are open to belief."

"I'd like to hear it," Sara said, having no idea where Clover was going with this.

"Since the time of the Prophet Abraham, from whom all modern Western religions originate, the belief has been that humans have two parts: the physical, and the spiritual, which lingers here after the death of the physical." She paused, as though having imparted something profound.

It took Sara a minute to process. "You mean ghosts?"

"Maybe not what you've experienced, exactly, but I believe sometimes the human essence lingers." She paused, considering, politely acknowledging Sara's open-mouthed reception of her words. "I know it may be hard to accept at first," she added, in what Sara considered an extreme understatement.

"Sometimes, you'll experience this through the paranormal. I remember one evening, I was at home, reading, when suddenly a little girl appeared right in front of me, sitting on the floor, coloring in a book. I didn't know her. She wore a dress, knee-length stockings, and Mary Jane shoes, like children wore back in the 1940s. She only stayed for a few seconds then disappeared. I figure she must have been a tourist, on vacation with her parents, staying in my house in another time, or perhaps a parallel universe."

Sara's body chilled. "It's certainly something to think about, but this was more like he had come from somewhere else where he was living, in another time." That was the best response she could manage before she changed the subject. She'd had enough weirdness for one day.

"Is there a library in town? I'm curious about the history of this place. It will give me something to do while I'm here."

"Oh, sure. There's lots of stuff. Many of our visitors are into genealogy. There isn't much else going on. What do you do where you come from?"

"Not much of anything. I take care of the house, and serve on some committees. I belong to a little theater group." Lordy, that sounded lame, she realized with a shock, and no longer true. What did she do? Later. She'd deal with the question later.

The mildly judgmental way Clover looked at her, suggested she was being compared to the Toy Group at a dog show—amusing but without meaningful purpose, similar to how her friend, Grace, thought when demanding she get back to being a wife.

Feeling a little defensive, she tried to make light of it. "In another life, were you, by any chance, a woman named Grace?" She stopped, embarrassed. "Sorry, it's just that you remind me of someone back home. I'm not suggesting reincarnation, or anything."

No, doofus. It's better you sound like a demented idiot.

"Grace?" Clover considered the question calmly, her brow furrowed, as though it were an everyday matter. "No, although I think I might have been Imhotep, the Egyptian adviser to King Dozier, who lived seven thousand years ago. I feel a real connection with him. He was a man of extreme vision. Did you know he designed the first pyramid?" She waited for a response.

Sara, speechless, marveled at the way her visitor said that with a perfectly straight face.

Clover stood. "I have to get going. I work three days a week for Dinette, who owns Lady Chatterley's Boutique, downtown. I sell lingerie. Us locals refer to it as "the dirty underwear store.""

The image of Clover selling risqué underwear to a hefty, leather-clad biker boggled Sara's mind. She rose with her guest and walked her to the door. "Come back anytime. I'll be here," she said, watching her sway down the road. It was the only way to describe that carefree walk, with her dress brushing lightly against her legs.

What would it feel like to wear a dress like that? Why not? Who would be there to judge her? Nobody she knew, for sure. She smiled, imagining Grace's reaction.

Positively, going to town would be the next order of business. Clover had mentioned a spa. A pedicure would be a good place to start. She'd shop for clothes, something more in keeping with the local flavor. Next she'd find the town library, to look for information about the Stuart family, this house, and handsome former residents like Thomas Stuart. Would she see him again? She could only hope. She went upstairs to find some slacks; fairly certain tourists didn't go slogging through the sand in pantyhose and heels.

Chapter Three

"This is more like it." Sara paused and looked at her reflection in the display window of one of the shops on New Kensington's main street. The new Sara stared back at her, looking good. It must have been an attack of makeover syndrome that got her agreeing to a newer, short hairstyle. She'd been wearing her hair in the same long, boring, and old-fashioned side-parted style since high school, like ninety percent of the women she saw on television every day. She'd even been talked into some blonde highlights. Her hair now framed her face with chin-length soft curls and a wisp of bangs. While she relaxed, letting the stylist do her thing, she opted for a manicure and pedicure, going for pale pink nails instead of her usual clear polish—not a drastic change, but going in the right direction, free from the habits of her former life, and ready to explore new directions.

She walked along the main street, reveling in her new look. Chandelier earrings made of multicolored Mardigras beads, a radical departure from the tasteful pearls she usually wore, brushed against the shoulders of the silky tie-dyed blue and green, dress which skimmed her ankles, and floated in a rainbow cloud against her legs, shockingly devoid of pantyhose. Never would she have imagined wearing something like this in public, blissfully bare legged. She felt liberated. Behold the new Sara. Nobody in East Partridge would recognize her.

First off she'd found "Lady Chatterley's Boutique" close to where she parked the car. Her makeover project required guidance, so she sought Clover's advice on where to find a light, floaty, tie-dyed dress. The shoe store close-by offered sandals—not Birkenstocks—she wasn't ready to go entirely native—but suitably beach savvy, after which, she stopped at The Serenity Spa, three doors down, for her makeover.

For years she hadn't thought about how others saw her, but now she wondered how she might appear to a man if she were looking for a relationship, which was, of course, out of the question. The thought of sex and being naked in front of a new man made her doubt her appeal. She shuddered. She'd look old—for sure too old to start over. She'd think about that later. For now, she'd enjoy her new look.

New Kensington offered several blocks of retail shops, and outdoor cafés. It appeared as though women ran a lot of the small businesses in this town. They owned most of the restaurants, the stores, and the bed-and-breakfasts, leaving the banks, the larger properties, and the town government to the men. The doorway she entered was a combination travel agency, real estate, and tourist information office.

"May I help you?" The query came from a woman behind a desk by the entrance. Sara had been hoping for another Clover-type, but this woman, close to her own age, wore a severely cut business suit, very East Partridge. Her greeter clearly lived the comfortable lifestyle Sara had left behind. Familiar territory.

"I'm Sara Burkhart, new in town, renting the Stuart House for the summer. I need a map and information on where things are."

The woman rose and offered her hand. "I'm Adrienne Fowler. You're in the right place. Besides running the travel agency, I'm on the board of the New Kensington Chamber of Commerce." She gestured toward the sign on the window. "My husband is a lawyer and sells real estate. How can I help you?"

"I don't need much. Just directions and a local map showing the way to the library. Oh, and maybe some things to do?"

"We have an excellent golf course at the country club, " Adrienne said, her clear hazel eyes accurately perceiving Sara's usual lifestyle, in spite of her current look.

Sara smiled, wryly amused. She'd been recognized as a potential customer. No doubt visitors from the big city, going native, were a common sight.

"Are you with us for long?"

"I'm renting a beach house for two months, so I'll be around town, but I'm not used to going places by myself, so I'll probably spend a lot of time reading." Now why did she say something so boring? It made her sound pathetic. Footloose. Abandoned. Without male companionship. Dismayed, she watched Adrienne's expression change from interest to sympathy and rushed to explain, to avoid any more questions.

"I'm recently divorced and both my kids just left for college, leaving me alone in an empty house. Some of my happiest childhood memories are of seaside vacations, so I thought I'd give New Kensington a try." She cringed mentally. Why was she confiding all this? Why would this woman even care? She didn't expect the wide smile she got as a response.

"You picked the perfect place to take a time-out. Tourist towns are naturally friendly places. It's how we make our living. We've never met a stranger we didn't like."

Sara relaxed. "And you are very good at what you do. Thanks for getting me through that awkward moment. I'm on a quest for information. I want to know more about the Stuart House and its history."

Adrienne smiled at her, knowingly. "You've felt something in the house."

"Is it that apparent, or does everybody?"

"Common knowledge says it's haunted, but if you've seen something, consider yourself privileged. Very few people have. Occasionally a renter will complain of noises, but Caro is careful to whom she rents. If the wrong people get in there, things can get unpleasant. A couple of years ago we had four members of a rock band run screaming from the house yelling about a flesh-eating sea monster. They never came back."

"You don't seem bothered by this."

"Nobody's ever come to harm. The town loves that house. It's been there for 160 years—proof that life goes on, no matter what. We're very protective of it, and we treasure our traditions; besides, the ghost rumors are good for business."

That remark resonated with Sara. Considering what she'd been through the last few months, she needed evidence that life goes on no matter what.

Adrienne assessed her, clearly with something in mind. "I hope you won't think me too forward, but since you're alone, and interested in local history, you might enjoy meeting some of us locals. Some friends are gathering at my house later on this evening. Why don't you to join us? It will give you a feel for the town, and there'll be some people there who've made a study of Stuart House. They can tell you what you want to know."

Amazed at the offer of friendship, Sara replied, "It's very kind of you, since I'm so new here. Is there something I can bring?"

"Nothing this time. Just come and enjoy. It will be a varied group of people—some neighbors, some business acquaintances, and many from The Village Players, our theater group. We closed our summer production last week and for once we made a profit. We're celebrating playing to sold-out houses."

"Wonderful. I appreciate your offer. Frankly, this is the first time I've gone anywhere by myself and I'm feeling a little at a loss."

"Its just part of living in a tourist town. We welcome everyone. Let me mark a map with the address."

Sara didn't know what to make of this. For sure, it would never happen back home. It simply wasn't done—inviting strangers off the street into your home. Small towns were certainly different. She waited while Adrienne drew on a map.

"Come around eight," she said, handing the map to Sara.

"Thank you. I'm looking forward to the evening. I belong to a little theater group back home. What production did you stage?"

"This time we tried a musical, *Guys and Dolls.*"

"Impressive. I had the stage manager job when we did that one last year. It's pretty complicated and ambitious but has a lot of wonderful parts." Usually local theaters chose plays they could cast from their membership, so this should be an interesting group.

"You'll meet a lot of the cast this evening," Adrienne said, "See you then."

Sara left, excited and looking forward to the party. A glance at her watch indicated the library would have to wait for tomorrow. She had to get home, have some supper, finish unpacking, and find something to wear. She'd indulge in a bubble bath and prepare for her first real social event as a single woman among strangers who had never met the old Sara.

Chapter Four

She could tell, at first sight, The New Kensington Estates couldn't be considered typical of most housing developments. It didn't have that new-just-out-of-the-box feeling. Mature landscaping provided a sense of timelessness to the spacious houses, designed to suggest the Victorian trends of the late 1800s, with shingle roofs, horizontal siding, and bay windows. The Fowler home was a two-story version with dark green siding and brown trim.

Sara found room for her SUV among the parked cars surrounding the place, and walked to the elegant glass paned double-door entrance, where she found a hand lettered sign saying '*Come In*' taped to the door.

With a deep breath and a 'now or never,' she opened the door, not knowing what to expect. She'd dressed in her best version of the old Sara with a modest black cocktail dress, pearls, and heels. Would the men look bored after a glance and the women ignore her? Would she be slipping out the back door after an hour?

"Sara, I'm glad you made it." Adrienne greeted her eagerly when she entered, and led her into a room where a mix of about forty people laughed and talked in comfortable familiarity.

"Everybody's here. Follow me."

Back-home nostalgia hit her as she looked over the crowd. Neighbors and business contacts were noticeable because of their conservative dress, in contrast to the younger guests, wearing jeans. She picked the actors out easily, guessing at their roles played in the musical. The resemblance to similar gatherings reminded her of what she'd left behind, lost to her because of her divorce. Such memories could ruin her evening if she didn't get hold of herself.

She spied a tiny, doll-like blonde who didn't need a Salvation Army bonnet to identify her as the innocent saver of souls who falls in love with the elusive Sky Masterson, professional gambler.

"I'll bet the woman by the piano played Sister Sarah," she confided to Adrienne.

Her hostess nodded. "She did a wonderful job. That's Brittany Wagner. The guy beside her, watching her like a hawk, is her husband, Brian. He dotes on her tiny size, calls her Binki, his own little Barbie Doll, and she hates it." The malice creeping into Adrienne's voice didn't surprise Sara. She'd already discerned that Adrienne couldn't tolerate not being in control, and Brian was definitely the controlling type.

Sara's natural tendency to empathize kicked in. "I can see why. No grown woman wants to be demeaned that way. Who played Sky Masterson?"

"Believe it or not, a real gambler type, debonair and sophisticated. Galen Andrews. He isn't here yet. The role wasn't much of a stretch for him. He works at one of the Atlantic City casinos—a bachelor on the prowl, but when it comes to commitment, elusive enough to be a challenge to any female. You already know Caro," she said, beckoning to the woman approaching them.

"Oh, of course, my landlady." She smiled a greeting. "I must thank you again. The shrimp were wonderful." Without the coveralls and hairnet, Caro emerged as the warm, motherly type.

"Glad you enjoyed them. Nothing like fresh caught seafood, I always say." Caro waved her hand toward the bar. "Henry is over there. You can't miss him. He's the one in the orange, green, and brown plaid suit. Used to be a tablecloth. Can't get him out of it."

Sara spotted him immediately, stunned by his appearance. The old guy down at the docks? He looked positively debonair, but loud, and large, very large.

"Caro does costumes for us," Adrienne explained. "Henry is so taken with the suit she made him for the play, he won't give it back to wardrobe, but Caro only allows him to wear it to indoor parties."

The get-up made him look bigger than life. She made a guess. "Henry played Nicely-Nicely?"

Caro laughed fondly. "Crazy old fool. Makes him look the part, doesn't it? He can sing, too."

It took some imagining, after meeting him as the overall-clad grocer, but Sara could see him as the wily gambler addicted to betting on the horses, strolling across stage, singing the opening number with his cohorts Benny and Rusty, reciting the virtues of each horse in the first race. She loved the characters in this show, the gamblers, and showgirls, the bookies who hung out in the gambling underground of New York.

"I wish I could have seen him," she said. "Who played Adelaide, the lovelorn chorus girl determined to maneuver Nathan Detroit, into marriage?"

Adrienne pointed to a buxom redhead, a foot taller and twenty years younger than Henry. Her boisterous laughter lit up the room; clearly an extrovert at ease in a crowd. "Georgia Eberly. She does a Brooklyn accent to perfection. Her *Adelaide's Lament* brought down the house every night."

"Standing ovations," Caro agreed.

Sara recalled Adelaide, seated at a table, facing the audience, with a huge dictionary in front of her. She launches into a definition of psychosomatic symptoms, blaming her head cold and constant postnasal drip on sexual frustration, Nathan's neglect, unrequited love, and a *"feelin' I'm getting' too old."*

Sara laughed, feeling at home, on familiar turf. She was going to be okay. While her gaze wandered over the room, she decided these were likeable people she wanted to meet.

"Adrienne, thank you for making me feel welcome. I think I'll wander over to the bar and get something to drink, then mingle."

The man behind the bar, wearing an apron proclaiming him the bartender, looked up with a good-natured grin. "What'll you have?" His hand hovered near the wine glasses, clearly expecting her to ask for white wine.

But it was time to party. "Scotch rocks with a little water."

His grin got broader. "There you go. I'm Bob Fowler, by the way—Adrienne's husband. You're the new renter in the Stuart house, Sara Burkhart. I got that right?"

Sara raised her glass in a toast and took a long, appreciative drink. "You've done your homework." She detected a little sparkle there. It didn't mean anything except good hosting, but she'd treasure it like a precious shell found on the beach, and hold it close for a later look.

"Watch out for him," a female voice behind her warned. "He'll sell you some real estate before you know it."

Sara turned and saw the redhead. "I know you're Georgia. Adrienne told me how you stopped the show with your Adelaide."

"Yeah, what a hoot. In real life I own Eberly's Seaside Bed and Breakfast. No need to tell us who you are, everybody here already knows. Small town, et cetera."

"And she's an awesome cook," Henry said, joining them. "Good thing you got away from me, woman. If we'd a married, I'd be twice my size by now."

"You are so full of it, Henry." Georgia laughed. "So, are you with us long?"

"I booked the Stuart House for two months," Sara said, drinking from her glass and surprised to find it empty. So what? She was at a party.

"That could be a little more adventure than you planned for," Bob said, smoothly replacing her empty glass with a fresh drink. By now several more guests had gathered round. Ah, this could be the opening she needed.

"Is it true some people believe it's haunted?"

"Absolutely," Bob said.

"C'mon, Bob. Don't scare her off before we get to know her."

Sara turned. The man who'd made the remark put her on alert the instant she met his assessing gaze. He and the woman clinging to his arm were about her age; she wore just enough expensive jewelry to set her apart from the crowd. Sara knew the type.

They could have been clones of a couple she knew back home. Party-hopping, upwardly mobile opportunists, who belonged to every group in town where there might be money, and used their networking skills to take advantage of the gullible, sometimes causing trouble for their own amusement—a common breed of predator.

Bob, ever the experienced host, caught her hesitation and introduced her, covering her reaction. "Sara Burkhart, meet Steve and Sylvie Costner, staunch members of our group even though we've never been able to coax either of them onstage. Sara is visiting for the summer."

"In your dreams, Fowler," Sylvie said. Turning to Sara, she added, regally, "My husband is the Director of the Congressional Ventures Foundation, headquartered in Washington, DC. He commutes so we can live in New Kensington."

Sara managed to look impressed, even though she'd never heard of the organization, and cared less.

"And Sylvie is into pork bellies," Bob said, an obvious attempt to defuse Sylvie's superior attitude.

"I beg your pardon?"

"Bacon," Cora, who had just joined them, said. "That's what they call bacon at the Commodities Exchange. Bob likes to tease Sylvie. She specializes in predicting price trends for bacon futures." Her flip remark earned her a glare from Sylvie.

"Oh," Sara said, still not understanding. She didn't like the negative vibes coming from either one of them, and moved on. Roaming through the crowd, she mingled, enjoying the party, when Cora approached.

"Come on," she said, taking her arm, and guiding her toward the piano. "You can't miss this. Galen is here and he and Brittany are going to sing for us." With a nod back to the Costners, she said, "To tell you the truth, those two give me the creeps. If you'd stayed there Steve would have tried to sell you a life insurance policy. Bob says it's all on the up and up, but I still think it's illegal deducting life insurance premiums from your income tax."

Sara had no time to process that information. Her attention was drawn to the actor who stood by his diminutive leading lady, gazing down at her fondly from his six-foot height, with her husband glowering at them like a storm cloud. A wealth of gleaming, impeccably styled, dark hair crowned his elegant features, and softened the sharp lines of his brow. His remarkable green eyes roamed the room and conveyed an air of big-city sophistication and sexuality. He was polished perfection—every inch of him. Sky Masterson, smooth-talking gambler, absolutely secure, confident and irresistible, had such a commanding presence he would immediately own any room he entered.

The green eyes were familiar to her, though she'd never met him. Even more remarkable, with shorter hair and a more weathered complexion, he resembled Thomas Stuart enough to be his brother.

She experienced a jolt of de`ja`vu. Somehow, somewhere she'd been in a room with him before, and had caught his glance, exactly like this. The idea lingered at the edge of her mind. Did she imagine chamber music? She shook her head to clear it. Dear God, she was losing it over another good-looking guy. "Wow," she said, "he sure fills the bill as a romantic leading man."

"Yeah," Cora said, "doesn't he ever? He works for a corporation that operates several casinos in Atlantic City, where he spends a lot of his time. I know he has a lot of women there interested, but we never see them. He doesn't ever bring any of them home to that gorgeous beach house he built close by Stuart House." She sighed. "He's a very private person, but he participates in the theater group. He always volunteers when we need him, but he doesn't socialize. We don't really know anything about his life."

To Sara, the elegant cut of his suit and the assured way he presented himself indicated wealth, right down to the Piquet watch on his wrist.

"You'd have to be half dead not to notice him. He's gorgeous. A type generally described as 'eye candy," she said.

Cora eyed her with speculation. "The single women in our group have tried to attract his interest, but he doesn't take notice."

The rush she felt instantly appalled her.

Why is this happening again?

First Thomas, now Galen Andrews. With her divorce final for only two months, she shouldn't be feeling anything for strange men, no matter how handsome. Her reaction produced an unpleasantly needy sensation. Her inner voice hounded her.

I am a mature, and until recently, married woman—a mother of two teenage children, and I'm acting like one of them. So knock it off.

Galen winked at her before turning his attention to his partner. She felt her face heat with a blush.

While the pianist played the intro, the crowd hushed, and in a clear soprano, Sister Sarah began the wistful, "*I'll Know When My Love Comes Along.*" When Sky joined in with his romantic baritone, pure magic invaded the room.

Entranced, Sara listened, enchanted. Her mind drifted to Thomas who had come to her from the sea and her response when they'd met, fantasizing along with Sister Sarah. No guilt there. He was a figment of her imagination. Nevertheless, her heartbeat kept pace with the pulsing excitement his memory created in her gut. So what? She'd felt a little tingle for a man who'd been dead more than a hundred years, who could only be a dream in a fairy tale, but this attraction to a man she'd met five minutes ago wasn't so harmless. It was real.

Galen looked up as the notes faded, and acknowledged the enthusiastic applause. He caught her eye, and started toward her.

She gasped. Her thoughts must have shown on her face. Did he intend to make a move, thinking the yearning was for him? Oh dear, maybe, possibly . . . well, yeah. She couldn't handle this. Sexual attraction to any man, at this point in her life, wouldn't do. In her mind she was still a married woman. Maybe it was okay to have fantasies, no harm in that, but this man was not imaginary. He was very real, with the power to reject and wound. Richard's defection left her unable to trust her emotions. It was too easy to act like a fool. Determined to escape, she turned and collided with Georgia.

"Are you okay? You look a bit strange."

She heard Galen's voice. "Hey, Georgia, introduce me to your friend."

Too late. He was standing close, gazing at her, his eyes amused.

"Uh, I need to sit. I think I drank too much too fast." Lame, but it would do.

"Over here." He took her arm and led her to an easy chair, holding on to her until she was settled, his check for evidence of a wedding band too obvious to ignore.

Feeling stupider by the minute, Sara offered, "Too much alcohol. I started to feel dizzy. I enjoyed your singing. You're very talented. I'll bet you were a great Sky."

Dear God, she was rambling like a star-struck teenager.

Georgia, rendered speechless by Sara's behavior, remembered her role in this little drama and said, "Galen, let me introduce you to Sara Burkhart, who will be a visitor in town for the next two months. Sara, meet Galen Andrews."

"Memories of another Sky?" His smile was amused but, nevertheless, devastating. "Why do I have this feeling that we've met before? Are you familiar with the production?"

"Uh, yeah. I belong to an amateur theater group back home and we did *Guys and Dolls*. The role is compelling. Our lead did a great job."

"Competition, huh? Well then, I'll have to do better. Maybe we can discuss it when I take you home?"

Met before? He felt it, too? Her heart thumped. He *was* smooth. Was she going to react like a sex-starved divorcee` to every good-looking man she met?"

"Thanks for the offer, but I drove myself." That sounded cold, but she was groping for words.

His eyes shuttered; his interest screeched to a halt. "Some other time then," he said, preparing to leave. To Georgia he said, "If you need help at the loft, let me know."

"I think I have it covered. Most of the scenery was stored last week," she replied.

He walked off. Sara was aware of Georgia looking at her as though she'd suddenly acquired horns.

"He's really a nice guy."

"Georgia, I'm sorry if I offended him, but he mistook my interest in his performance for something more than I intended. I'm recently divorced after twenty years of marriage, sudden and unexpected. The wounds are still raw, and his interest blindsided me. I'm not ready for another man in my life like Andrews, who would expect more than I'm ready to give."

"Galen has enough women chasing after him. He could use a little rejection once in a while, but I can understand his reaction. From the look on your face while he sang, you were thinking of somebody who must really be something. Who is he? Your ex-husband?"

"As if. You wouldn't believe me if I told you. Richard is past history. This divorce hit me so hard. I can't trust my emotions. It's made me a little crazy, so that I'm afraid I'll act silly and make a fool of myself. Andrews is a very attractive man, but he's real. I'm not making much sense, am I?"

"What do you mean, 'real?' You mean you're afraid you'll fall at the feet of the first man who smiles at you?"

"Worse than that. This morning I felt attraction for a man who wasn't even there."

Georgia stared at her, clearly intrigued. "Okay, I'm hooked. What's the story?" She gave Sara an encouraging smile. "Hey, I can be a good friend and I know how to keep my mouth shut."

Her friend's ebullient personality gave Sara the courage to confide, and obviously she wasn't going to let this go. Maybe telling someone else would lessen the effect the ghostly encounter had on her emotions and put it where it belonged, in the realm of a female fantasy. In two months she'd be gone from here, so what could it hurt?

"Okay, but it's going to require you to suspend your disbelief. What I'm about to tell you isn't possible. In fact, I could have dreamed it while dozing on my porch, listening to the sea." She paused, took a fortifying breath, and began.

"Early this morning the most gorgeous man I've ever seen, sexy beyond imagining, washed up on the beach in front of my house. He wore old clothes. I mean antique, like a costume from the 1800s—some kind of sea captain outfit. He was handsome as sin. I reacted to him like a hormonal teenager with a mad crush."

"Like Johnny Depp in those pirates movies? Oh, migosh." Georgia looked both entranced and doubting. "Then what happened?"

Okay, so Georgia thinks I'm a little crazy.

"I helped him to the house, dying to know more about him, and gave him some water. He introduced himself as Thomas Stuart, and thought he was at his house, and wanted to know what year it was. I told him 2015, and he freaked out. He thought it was 1860."

She paused so Georgia could catch on.

"As in Stuart House from the last century? A blast from the past?"

"Now that I'm telling it, I'm sure I must have dreamed it. I know I sound thoroughly demented."

Georgia sighed. "Nothing like that ever happens to me. So, what next?"

"After I got him up on the porch and settled in a lawn chair so he could recover his strength, he disappeared. Just vanished as in faded away. I think he might be haunting the house. I can't get him out of my mind. Georgia, for a minute there, I had feelings for a ghost." Sara waited for disbelief, but all she got was a laconic shrug. She decided to confess completely. What could it hurt? "What's worse, for a minute there, I thought Galen resembled Thomas."

"Wow," Georgia said, eyes wide.

"Don't you hear how pathetic it sounds? I'm in some kind of crazed, emotional state. Can you understand why I can't trust myself with any man?"

Georgia shrugged, unconcerned. "Well, I remember an old movie where a woman falls in love with a sea captain who died years ago. It's not the first time somebody thought they saw something in that house. Everybody in town believes that house is haunted."

"Bless you, Georgia, for listening. Keep this to yourself until I get it figured out. Please?"

"Sure," she deadpanned. "I can see where you wouldn't want us to think the new woman in town was a sex-crazed psycho."

Sara laughed, but it took too much effort. Suddenly exhausted, she wanted to leave. "You know, I think I've had enough party. I'm going to pay my respects to Adrienne and head home." She wanted to get back to Stuart house. Thomas might have returned.

"We'll talk later in the week, okay?" Georgia said. "Take care."

Galen Andrews watched her go, not bothering to deny his interest. Her outright avoidance of him, as though he represented some kind of a threat, intrigued him. Alone. Unmarried, and she wore clothes with understated elegance. The dress was couture and the jewelry real. Generally wealthy women of her type responded to him, a fact his casino bosses valued as much as they did his sharp legal mind. Avoiding trouble and keeping the clientele interested were top priorities. He liked puzzles and without doubt, this woman hid something that made her nervous. Stuart House lay half a mile south of his beach house, with plenty of opportunity for a chance meeting.

Relieved at the uneventful drive home, Sara pulled up to the side door, with a tired sigh, and entered the kitchen, feeling the loneliness and wishing she weren't coming home to a dark, empty house.

"I need a pet," she mused, "Maybe a cat. It would be something to greet me and be glad I'm home." Terrific. Now she was talking to herself. She never used to care, one way or the other, and with Richard not being keen on the idea of pets, she never pushed the issue.

Her cellphone sang out, distracting her. She'd left it lying on the table and noticed she'd missed several calls, all from her daughter, Jenny. This couldn't be good. She never called to chat—only when she wanted something and her father had already said no. Resenting this reminder of her old life, and feeling guilty about it, she answered the phone.

"Hi, Jen. What's up?"

"What have you been doing? Where have you been? I've been trying to call you." Jen's voice came across full of accusation, implying she was guilty of indiscretion. Sara's hackles rose.

"What's with the attitude, young lady? I've been to a party."

"You've been to a *party*? How did you have time to meet anybody? You just got there."

Her judgmental remarks conveyed disapproval bordering on scorn. It implied parties were more important to her than being a mother. Anger, backlogged for the last months, surfaced with a vengeance. The lack of sympathy or support from either of her children festered in her soul. "Back off. I resent your attitude, young lady, and I won't submit to interrogation from my own daughter. Where I've been or what I've been doing doesn't concern you. It's after midnight and I'm tired. Why are you calling?"

Wow. Wherever that came from, it felt good. She was pretty sure Richard didn't get phone calls like this, questioning his behavior. She waited for Jenny to settle down, aware of the attitude adjustment going on at the other end. Her daughter was a master at manipulation.

"Mom? I'm sorry."

Okay. Contrite was an improvement. She remained silent.

"I was worried, and Dad wasn't home, and I have this problem."

Ah. So she *was* the second choice. When had her opinion ever mattered? "It's late. What's the problem?"

"I'm coming home. I've decided not to go to college. I hate it here."

Home? To East Partridge? Over my dead body.

The memories of her spoiled-rotten daughter living at home were too fresh. The idea of her daughter living there unsupervised while she lived a couple of hundred miles away, gave Sara the shivers. Jenny was so irresponsible. In a matter of days she and about fifty of her closest friends would have the entire house trashed with the remains of one party after another. A sad commentary on her job as a parent, but true.

"Jen, You can't stay in that house alone. I don't trust you."

"If I can't go home, I'll come there. I don't need to go to college."

"Forget it. Without college you don't stand a chance of having much of a job. You at least have to finish the semester and get the credits if you transfer to another school. We've had this conversation before."

"I don't need college. I'll get a job. I'll do what you did—find a rich guy, marry him and let him support me." The caustic description of her marriage and the cavalier dismissal of any contribution she'd made to the family raised Sara's anger to the next level. Her daughter coming here? No way. This was her life—her new beginning, and she wasn't inclined to share. She needed time alone to get herself together.

"Jenny, leaving school to come home or here is out of the question. It is not an option—not now. I've rented this house for two months, and I need this time to myself."

And what about Thomas? Selfishly, she wanted to keep him as her private adventure. Jenny didn't need to be here.

"Then you have to come home. Mom, this is serious—more important than your vacation. I'm desperate." Jen's voice whined in her ear. "You have to come home now."

Typical. Nothing trumped what Jenny wanted. Well, circumstances had changed, and with them, Sara's loyalties, but that didn't prevent some guilt from surfacing.

"Jen, you can't come here. Stay where you are, at least until the end of this quarter. I know college is an adjustment. It's a new environment and there are rules, but you're going to have to give it some time. When I get home we'll see how you feel. Meanwhile, I have my laptop. We'll Skype every night. We can talk better if we're face to face."

"Mom," Jen wailed.

There would be more coming, but the new Sara wasn't backing down.

After a pause, a subdued Jenny said, "Okay. Mom, I'm sorry I said what I did. It's hard when I think of you going out with another man, but I guess you aren't really that old."

Sara let that pass without comment. It sufficed as an apology of sorts and her mother mode kicked in, not totally unresponsive to her daughter's misery. "Look, New Jersey State College is only about two hours away by car. After you've given this a few weeks to work, you can come visit me. College can be overwhelming at first. Take it slow, and we'll talk again in a couple of days." The tone of her response left little hope of any choice but this.

Jen sighed her defeat. "Okay. Mom, I love you."

"Love you too." Sara smiled when she hung up. The call took some of the sting out of remembering the casual way her kids had treated her during the divorce. Mothers had some use after all. On the other hand, her daughter never gave in so easily. Her "mom" radar activated.

Jenny had a set of keys to the house. It would be just like her very spoiled daughter to move back home without telling her until it was too late to do anything about it. First thing tomorrow morning she'd call a locksmith in East Partridge to replace all the locks on the house, and ask one of her neighbors to make sure they got there.

Upstairs, in her bedroom, she changed into a nightgown, while she thought about her conversation with Georgia about Thomas. She should have kept her mouth shut. How had it made her sound, confessing romantic thoughts about a ghost, for heavens sake?

Poor Sara, so shattered by her divorce she's invented an imaginary lover. It made her want to hide for the rest of her stay here.

When she turned on her bedside lamp, dispelling the moon shadows in the room, her eye caught something on the table that hadn't been there before. It appeared to be a very large tooth. Curious, she picked it up. When she ran her fingers over the smoothly polished surface and turned it over, she discovered it was hollow. A whale tooth. She'd seen something like this before. Sailors aboard whaling ships in the 1860s passed the time by etching pictures on the bones and teeth of whales. Scrimshaw. This one had a beautiful rendering of a three-masted sailing ship.

Thomas. He must have come back. It was the only explanation possible. She didn't have neighbors wandering in and out, leaving valuable artifacts. She savored the anticipation coursing through her. That meant she would see him again. It gave her something to dream about. Smiling, she slipped under the covers, and started to drift off to sleep, certain that this time she'd sleep peacefully.

Chapter Five

Sara had always been a light sleeper, accustomed to lying for hours, relaxed, hovering in the twilight zone between being awake and asleep, so it took a while for her to sense something different about her surroundings. She wasn't in her bed anymore. She stood in her bare feet, on a wet, slippery surface, still in her nightshirt, practically naked, in a public place. She could hear people walking and talking—a crowd. Where was she? This was not like any dream she'd ever had. The physical sensations—the cold, the wet, and her bare feet—were too real. Curling her toes, she felt damp, uneven boards, like a wooden sidewalk.

Cautiously she opened one eye at a time, afraid of what she might find, and peered through the surrounding mist. It was night, and too dark to see much, but the chill air told her she was outdoors. The smell of salt water indicated an ocean nearby. Roughly clad male bodies kept shoving past her, ignoring her presence, impatient to pass. Judging by the shadows of the masts of sailing ships in the distance, the sounds of bells and creaking timber, and the smell of rotting fish and fried food, she was somewhere far removed from her time, to a place by the sea.

Afraid of discovery, she wrapped her arms around her shoulders, trying to hide, praying no one would notice her, until she could get away from this place, to somewhere private.

Strangely, the men passing close by within touching distance were not aware of her. They couldn't see her. She had no substance. They walked right through her, even though she could feel the cold, making her shiver, and moisture from the salt air clinging to her hair. She was invisible. Thank God, she didn't have to worry about being seen half-naked.

Could she be on a dock? Hard to know, surrounded by almost impenetrable fog. The shapes moving by were barely recognizable as men, passing in and out of a doorway right in front of her. It appeared, from the raucous laughter and singing coming from inside, that she stood in front of an old tavern, like a Disneyland replica of a pirate hangout.

Cautiously, still not certain she couldn't be seen, she moved a step closer, to see more of the interior. The crowd inside included a strange mix of men, all races, and all nationalities, in all kinds of dress. Some nearly naked black men, towering bodies covered with tattoos, carried long harpoons like regal staffs. The rest of the crowd all looked like seamen, mostly dressed in rough, well-worn clothing, coarse twill trousers, and loose fitting shirts. Some wore short jackets or coats with rows of buttons, dark blue or black, some sort of uniform. Many had full beards and knit caps pulled over long hair, with an occasional tall beaver hat incongruously out of place with the rest of their attire. Maybe the hat represented a status symbol or an indication of rank? These men were seafarers, and judging from the grimy looks of them, the smells, and the bad teeth revealed in grinning mouths, she knew, for sure, if this were a dream, it was frighteningly real.

Looking up, she saw a sign hanging overhead, *Sounder Inn,* painted in coarse letters with the image of a whale spouting water--the sort of sign one would see over a replica of a seaside tavern in the early American colonies. Only this definitely wasn't a replica. More certain she couldn't be seen, she inched forward and slipped further inside.

I'm not really here. This is a dream. If she told herself that often enough, it would be true. Even though the noise, the odors, and the bright colors were not typical of her usual dreams, she had nothing to be afraid of. Oh, sure. Hold that thought.

Terrified, she pressed her body against the wall of the room, trying to stay out of the way, praying that she'd remain unnoticed until she could return to her own bed. A couple of deep breaths and some of her panic calmed enough to stir her curiosity.

Her first impression was of heat, humidity, a heavy pall of tobacco smoke, the odors of unwashed bodies, urine, and a sour odor of animal and wet wool. The room was large, jammed with heavy wooden tables and chairs, every one of them occupied, with seamen shouting to be heard above the din. Back in a corner, a group of five men sat around a table ignoring the rest of the clientele. Their aloof attitudes held them apart from the others. Their clothing was of finer quality, dressed to indicate their status; similar to ship's officers she'd seen in sea-faring adventure films, suggesting they were a cut above the crowd. They wore navy blue, double-breasted coats with rows of brass buttons, and fancy, ascot ties. The clothes reminded her of Thomas. These men obviously were of more importance.

Fascinated, she took it all in. She was in a dockside watering hole for seafarers and whalers, she supposed, because the walls were covered with various wicked looking harpoons, curved blades on long poles and other lethal-looking weapons obviously meant to wreak brutal destruction on a whale.

A bar stretched along one wall, enclosed in an arch maybe seven feet tall, decorated along the edge with some sharp . . . *dear Heaven, those were teeth.* The arch was made, apparently, from the jawbone of a gigantic whale.

"Coming through."

Instinctively she moved back a step to make room for a harried barmaid, her red hair a wild tangle, weighted down with a tray of assorted glasses and mugs. She saw something odd about the glasses. They looked to hold a half-pint, but the glass walls inside got thicker near the bottom, thus cutting the amount held.

A glance at the bartender, working at pulling mugs of ale with calculating flair, convinced her he was a smooth operator, not above cheating. Physically imposing, with a florid face, a shock of shaggy grey hair down to his chin, he dressed like his clientele in a homespun shirt covered with an apron. His most remarkable feature the profusion of grey hair sprouting from each ear. She shivered with fear.

I've never been in such a place, so why does it look vaguely familiar?

"No." A young voice screaming in pain sliced through the noise. "D-d-d-d-don't." Across the room, she saw a young boy, of about fifteen or sixteen years, being brutally beaten about the head by one of those well-dressed men, who clearly enjoyed tormenting his victim. The boy tried to defend himself, but his tormenter outweighed him by a hundred pounds.

"You clumsy whoreson," the man yelled, not letting up on the blows.

"It's only the dummy," a man near her said. "He stutters so he can't hardly talk."

Outraged at the cruelty, and lost in the scene, Sara cried out, "Someone help him."

One of the group from the corner table stood, disgust twisting his features.

"Hold," he said, his word unmistakably a command, in a voice with an air of authority that conveyed no tolerance for interference.

She gasped at the sheer beauty of the man. His commanding stance revealed a lean but well-muscled body, taller, by at least a head, than his companions. The sharpness of his brow, softened by the wealth of dark hair that framed his elegant features to just below his ears, gave him the look of an ancient Greek warrior. Piercing, green eyes swept the room, seeking a challenge, but none dared.

I've seen him before, but how can that be?

Sara froze, praying no one had heard her.

"Stop now or answer to me." His tone promised retribution if not obeyed.

The room stilled, waiting.

The bully immediately acknowledged the man with a bow of his head.

"Sorry, Sir. Didn't mean nothing." He backed away, and his victim, seizing the moment, fled the room. The boy's benefactor surveyed the crowd, his arrogant expression a warning. When his eyes met Sara's, he smiled and acknowledged her with a nod.

He can see me. They all can.

She froze, sick with fear. Oh, God. She lived her worst nightmare, being caught without clothes in a public place.

"Avast. What strange sea kelpie be this?" A short, wizened old seaman, smelling of stale tobacco and alcohol, leered into her face, his toothless mouth not inches away, his hands reaching out to grab her shoulders.

Scared out of her wits, she screamed. The world twisted around her and turned black. She felt herself falling.

Blindly reaching out for anything to stop the spinning, she grabbed something bulky and soft. When she opened her eyes, she had enough light to recognize the softness in her hands—her pillow. She was back in her bed, still tangled in a web of fear, her throat raw from screaming. Groping frantically, she found the bedside light and turned it on, and sat, shaking uncontrollably, a sheet wrapped around her, while the shapes in the room became familiar.

The nightmare had seemed so real. She could still feel the cold and the fog. Her feet were freezing. Pulling them up to examine, yoga fashion, the fear hit her again. They were wet, with sand clinging between the toes. A painful splinter protruded from one heel, and black, crusty dirt covered the soles. From a tavern floor? Shocked beyond comprehension, she knew it wasn't merely a nightmare. If she needed further evidence, the smell on her gown was enough. Tobacco smoke and stale beer. Somehow, she had gone back in time to an American seaside town. Shaking uncontrollably, and frightened beyond reason, she wondered, bordering on panic.

How could that happen? Is it going to happen again? Something in this house made it happen. Somehow, it had sent her back in time and probably bore responsibility for Thomas turning up on her beach. Could Clover's belief in parallel time shifts contain some truth?

If she had any sense she'd pack up and get out of here now. She couldn't accept the possibility of moving through time, but what if she did? If there's a next time what if she couldn't get back?

She should be terrified by something so far beyond anything in her experience or that of anyone she knew, but her fear gradually ebbed. Somehow she knew she was safe, as though the house, or some presence in it, protected her. She felt it was with her now, in this room. How crazy was that?

For sure, I can't imagine spending the rest of the night in my bed. Whatever had caused the back-in-time experience might still be there.

She needed a shower to get rid of the smells, and the last vestiges of her dream, after which she'd grab a blanket and a pillow and head downstairs to spend the rest of the night in a chair. Maybe when viewed in the light of day, she'd have a better understanding of what happened. One thing for certain, tomorrow she would schedule a trip to the local library to find out more about this house and the former residents.

Chapter Six

Her neck hurt. Her head ached and she had no feeling in one arm. Gradually, Sara took inventory before opening her eyes. She'd been asleep, but not in her bed. Daylight hammered on her eyelids and her nose caught the fresh smell of clean air. Slowly she opened her eyes and searched the space, cataloging familiar items—the chair, the table, the porch railing, and the rhythmic sound of the ocean. Thank God. She was on the porch at the beach house and not in some grungy tavern on the waterfront. She'd survived the night without any more adventure.

Poor Thomas had sounded so confused when he awoke on the beach. No wonder. Remembering last night, she understood the feeling. Could something about this house, some supernatural thing make time shift? Well, a trip to the library and a little serious research would shed some light on the matter.

It took an entire pot of coffee and some toast to get her going, but she finally made it to the tidy brick building identified as the New Kensington Public Library, on the town square.

"Oh, goodness, yes. We have many requests for information on early settlers." The librarian behind the desk, a cheerful, middle-aged woman, hastened to reassure her. Her nametag said Emily Coggins. "The recent craze for genealogy, you know," she said while she prepared to do a computer search. "My goodness, everybody is searching for their roots. I've worked here for ten years so I'm familiar with what we have. Now then, what are you looking for?"

Sara recognized a true history junkie, and if she didn't focus her informer's enthusiasm, she might be here all day. She'd better cut to the chase.

"I'd like some information on the Stuart House. I'm staying there for a few weeks."

The shift in the woman's attitude to one of fascinated speculation couldn't be missed. "I see," she said. "Have you an interest in anyone in particular who might have lived in the house?"

Sara laughed. "Okay. I confess. I'm interested in the haunting I've heard so much about. His name is Thomas, perhaps? I've sort of met him."

After a few minutes searching a file, Emily shook her head, despairingly, clearly distressed. "I'm sorry we don't have more, but the sixties hurricane took almost everything in the archives. The entire building flooded, taking out the basement and most of the first floor. You'll find a few things at the town museum." She paused to take a breath then her face lit up. "Oh, for goodness sakes, I forgot we have contributions of private family papers from local citizens, stored in boxes in a back room. I'll get them out and you can go through them here."

"How exciting that you may have seen a spirit. I can't recall anyone ever seeing him before." With a look of intense anticipation like that of a cat contemplating its next meal, she pounced. "How did he look? I mean, how did he dress? In what time period? It was right after 1860 that Caleb Stuart arrived here. He built the house. You're sure it wasn't him?"

"Emily, I'm depending on you to tell me. I can describe his clothes, although they were waterlogged. He washed up on the beach in front of the house. He had on cream-colored, close fitting breeches of some sort of twill or canvas, a natural linen, bloused shirt and a pale yellow vest that might have been satin before the salt water got hold of it. And lots of brass buttons."

"The buttons could be a clue, although, my goodness, they hardly signify. Victorians loved brass buttons. They put them on everything."

Her confidante had given herself away by using the words *hardly signify,* an expression common to writers of Regency Romance. Sara suppressed a smile. Emily read romance novels, but so did she. It made them sisters of a sort.

"I'd say he was an upper class gentleman," Emily said, "maybe an officer on a whaling ship. The Stuarts were whalers but the major part of the industry was centered way north of here, around New Kensington, Massachusetts in the 1860s."

Disappointed, Sara asked, "Was there any whaling industry here?" She had hoped the tavern she'd seen last night had been local.

"Oh, no. When the Stuarts came here they bought farmland as an alternative to whaling. Cranberries, you know. You might have to go north to find out more, but we do have some books on whaling. Thomas might be mentioned there." Pausing, she turned her attention to a teenage boy who stood next to her, patting her arm. His eyes were bright with intelligence, and he appeared to Sara to be about her daughter's age. He bore a striking resemblance to the tavern boy of last night's experience.

"Yes, Colin. What can I do for you?"

His hands moved rapidly, using sign, which Sara knew well.

"Yes, dear," Emily said. "That was the book I thought of. You can go get it for me." She turned to Sara. "This is Colin Henley. He spends most of his time at the library."

When the boy looked at her, Sara signed, *Hello. My name is Sara.*

"Oh Colin can hear," Emily said. "He's really smart. He just can't talk. He has a severe stammer, so he and I decided to learn sign so we could communicate better." Colin nodded and walked to the shelves in the corner.

Sara watched him go, stunned. He was the image of the boy in the tavern, but that was far north of here. How could this be? She shivered, suddenly cold. Could he be related to the other boy? Not likely, if the tavern was miles away, and separated by 150 years. "What is his story? Why can't he talk?"

Emily sighed. "Poor boy. I've heard the problem started when he was about three years old and his father walked out, leaving his mother unable to cope."

"I can relate to that," Sara said, with enough feeling to get her a curious look from Emily before she continued.

"They put him into foster care and the stuttering began. I don't know how many times he's been in and out of the state facility and how many foster homes. Presently he's living with a distant cousin in town here, but that family is only interested in the monthly check from family services, so he pretty much raises himself."

Dismayed, Sara asked, "Does he go to school?"

"High school senior, though he's nineteen. At first he was held back, the reasoning being that if he couldn't talk he must be retarded." Her expression showed disgust for a system without a clue. "Now he gets passed along because he is so smart. As long as he doesn't have to talk, he manages. He spends his spare time here, reading, and goes home to eat and sleep."

"Does he have any friends?"

Emily laughed. "He's a good looking kid. You'd be surprised at the attention he gets from girls."

"When my daughter was two, she developed a serious stammer, apparently caused by a lot of stress between my husband and myself. A wise therapist told us to show patience, give her time to say what she wanted, and don't try to fix it. He said to tell the school to back off until it cleared up, and advised us to learn to sign."

"What happened?"

Sara sighed. "Isn't it amazing what we do to our children? In this case, the parents start seeing the doctor and the child got better. I worked with Jenny for a few months. When the situation at home improved, she started talking again."

Colin returned with two books, one Sara recognized as one of the Time/Life Series—her kids owned dozens—and a copy of *Moby Dick*.

"Thank you, Colin," Emily said. "I'm afraid that's all we have on whaling, but the industry thrived in our sister city up north, so you might find mention of the Stuarts there."

I can help, Colin signed, taking her hand.

Sara smiled at the boy's eagerness. "Thank you, Colin. I'd like your help." She wanted to spend time getting to know this boy and how he connected to her dream, or what she still tried to call her dream. "Tell you what, it's an hour before lunch time. We'll work until then, and after, I'll take you to lunch. You might even help me find a place that sells kittens, like a pet store. I've decided I need some company in that old house."

"Good heavens," Emily, who had been listening, said. "You don't find cats. They find you with their built-in radar. They know when somebody needs a cat. I'll bet the word is out, and you'll find one waiting for you by the door when you get home."

"Emily, in the two days I've been here, so many strange things have happened that I wouldn't doubt you for a minute."

"You and Colin use that table over there. I'll go get those boxes right away." Emily proved as good as her word. The boxes she brought were full of old photographs that gave Sara a good picture of how things looked over a hundred years ago.

Though eager to learn what she could, the pleasure she felt working with Colin became an unexpected bonus. She experienced a closeness she hadn't had with her own children for years. When had they become "Richard's" with her being the outsider? She squelched a small niggling of guilt that stirred over her hostility toward Jenny last evening. No time for that now.

The more they looked at the pictures and read the lurid descriptions of the hunt and the brutal killing of the huge animals, the more Sara realized that whaling wasn't the romantically adventurous life she'd imagined.

"These pictures are making me sick," she said. "I've never seen anything so disgusting." Was this the life Thomas lived? She shuddered at the graphic depictions of men throwing one harpoon after another into a mortally wounded animal. The harpoons were attached to ropes that dragged the whalers' boat after them for days while the whale bled to death.

She remembered the walls of the Sounder Inn, and the long spears with their wicked looking, curved blades hanging there, and shuddered. "I guess I've never considered what it might take to kill an animal as large as a whale with something so primitive as a harpoon."

The harvesting process, depicted with paintings and drawings, showed the floating carcass tied to the side of the ship, men crawling over it, slicing long strips of blubber to hang from cranes until they could be lowered into boiling water to extract the oil.

"I've always thought whaling was an exciting adventure, but this is the brutal destruction of a magnificent creature."

Colin called her attention to a passage on the page. Sara read aloud. "The stench from the harvesting process could be detected for miles, long before the whaling ship could be seen on the horizon." She laughed. "Wow. Considering that it took weeks to carve up a whale and these men had nothing but salt water to do laundry, I wonder how they ever managed to get clean once they were ashore." She decided she'd had enough whaling for one day.

"I don't know about you, Colin, but I'm about done here. Let's go find some lunch."

She thanked Emily for her help and they left to look for a restaurant. "I haven't the slightest idea where to go."

He pointed toward the docks, signing Fish Shack. "Oh. I know where that is, next to Cora's real estate office. We can walk there."

When they arrived at "Vinnie's Tacos," they found the place besieged with customers lined up at the order window. The single-item menu, on a board hanging by the window, offered *Fish Taco with fries,* simplified ordering. Somewhat hesitant, with images of the whale slaughter still in her mind, Sara told herself, firmly, that the tacos were made with fish, not whale meat, and different.

When they were next in line, she said, "I guess we'll have tacos." She glanced at Colin who eagerly held up three fingers. "Three for my friend here, and one for me, hold the fries on that one, and two large, uh," clearly Pepsi was the only choice, "two large drinks." She looked around her. "Wow. Judging from the traffic, these tacos are really something."

The order taker, apparently lone cook, and likely owner beamed at her, assembling tacos with the speed of a robot. He was a large man who obviously enjoyed his product as much as the public. Grizzled grey hair covered his head, inside his ears, and his chin in the day-old beard he sported.

"Best fish tacos east of Maui," he said. He reminded her of someone, but she couldn't think of whom.

After paying for the meal, Sara followed Colin with the order. He had already placed their drinks on one of the outdoor tables on the sunny patio next to the restaurant. A faint breeze kept the patio pleasantly cool and the ocean had barely any surf. The screech of the ever-present gulls provided the only noise as they competed with English Sparrows for crumbs that might fall to the board deck.

"I've had Maui fish tacos," she said, unwrapping her food, noticing Colin had finished one in three bites and was already at work on the second. "They're a hard act to follow."

She smiled, remembering her son at that age and his constant demand for something to eat. Every half hour he went looking for food. She dug into the large, crispy corn tortilla shell stuffed with grilled white fish, lettuce, tomatoes, black olives and some sort of pink sauce covered with shredded cheese, possibly Monterey Jack. Not quite the Maui version, but tangy and delicious.

"So, what do you think?" The proprietor came up to their table, after the lunch crowd had dissipated, clearly intent on conversation, reminding Sara she was new in town. "I'm Vinnie Rose." Glancing at Colin, he said, "You managing to fill up that hollow leg of yours, Boy? I got more." He smiled at Sara. "This kid eats like you wouldn't believe."

Colin nodded, his hands too full to sign.

"I'm Sara Burkhart, a new visitor."

"Yeah, I heard. You're staying at the Stuart House."

Sara smiled, becoming used to the way information got around.

"You know Colin?" She asked, curious at the easy way the man accepted the boy's handicap. Many people raised their voice to non-verbal people, assuming they were also partly deaf.

"Oh, sure. My daughter, Celie, and Colin are friends. She's autistic and doesn't talk, but she and Colin understand each other. They get along real well." To Colin, he said, "Celie misses you. You haven't been by for a while. Come to the house tonight for dinner, okay?" He laughed at the boy's enthusiastic nod.

Sara smiled. Apparently the entire town knew of Colin's situation.

"My daughter stays at home with her mother," Vinnie said. "She doesn't function too well with strangers, but she likes Colin."

"That must be difficult."

"Yeah." He frowned, thoughtful. "The worst thing is you worry about what's going to happen when you can't take care of them anymore."

"It's something that worries every parent of a handicapped child," Sara said, surprised that he would talk about it to strangers, but people were much more open in a small town.

"We have an insurance policy that'll provide for her when my wife and I are gone. It's affordable because we deduct the premiums from our income tax."

This must be what she'd heard at the party last night. She wasn't a CPA, but working with Richard's books their first few years had taught her a lot about the IRS. Curious, she said, "I've never heard of this. I didn't think you could deduct personal insurance premiums."

"Yeah, Steve Costner, who lives in town here, fixed it for us."

She remembered Costner at the Fowler's party, and recalled her immediate dislike, pegging him as a slick operator not to be trusted.

"I've met Mr. Costner. He's the director of something called the Congressional Ventures Foundation, right?"

"Yeah. They're all in that little theater group together. I'll tell you, it's taken a load off my mind having Celie provided for."

"Well, speak of the devil," Vinnie said, looking past her with a wide smile of welcome.

Steve Costner greeted her like she was an old friend. "We meet again, Ms. Burkhart. I see you're sampling one of our culinary tourist attractions, the fabulous Vinnie's Fish Taco." Something about the man raised her hackles, but years of social correctness prevailed.

"I admit they're a taste delight." She nodded toward Colin. "This is my new friend, Colin Henly. We thought we'd try them out."

Steve glanced at Colin with mild distaste. "You're that kid that hangs out at the library." To Vinnie he said, "I only have a few minutes, but I want to run something by you. Can we talk?" Clearly what needed to be said must be discussed in private.

"Sure, Steve, let's go inside. Take care, Sara. See you tonight, Colin." Vinnie turned and led Steve into the shack.

Sara watched them leave, stunned. Rarely had she ever encountered such rudeness. He'd ignored Colin as though he were nothing, or not important enough to acknowledge. Worse than a snob, his manners were appalling.

The boy's reaction to Steve, however, left her speechless. What on earth? The kid cringed, showing his fear and strong dislike.

"Colin, have you met Mr. Costner before? Has he hurt you?" Sara signed. If he had, she'd tear his face off the next time she met him.

The boy shook his head, "no," but he stood abruptly, gathering up their trash to put in the can nearby, indicating they should leave, right now.

"Okay, I'll walk you back to the library to get my car." There were so many things going on in this town that required explanation. She thought of her MAC sitting on a table in the living room back at Stuart House, and decided to Google Steve Costner and the Congressional Ventures Foundation, to look for information. If he cheated with the IRS a lot of good people could be in a world of hurt. The massive government computers knew everything, crosschecking constantly. All it would take would be a random audit and innocent people would be at risk of losing everything if they had to pay back illegal deductions plus penalties.

When she returned to the Stuart House, the thought of sitting in front of a computer didn't appeal to her. She was also disappointed when she didn't find a cat at her front door. Had she really been silly enough to buy that story about being "found' by a cat? It would have been nice, but at least she took credit for not stopping at the grocery on the way home to buy cat food. Before long this town would be turning her brain to mush.

This late in the season, she knew the ocean would be warm enough to be bearable, so she donned her swimsuit, remembered sneakers, because the sand would be hot, and set out to see what she could find. The tide was out, leaving behind sand dollars, scallop shells and her favorites, the smoothly polished cowries. That most mysterious of all sea animals, a juvenile horseshoe crab, lay stranded, but still alive. Picking it up gingerly, by its round turtle-like shell, she carried it to the water line and watched it swim away, then decided to splash water on herself before tackling the small waves.

"I can help with that." Turning, she saw Galen Andrews smiling at her. Deeply tanned, his brown hair suntossed, making him look impossibly sexy, the way it fell along the side of his face, with the mere shadow of a beard, he sauntered toward her. His brief swim trunks clung precariously to his hips. With clothes on he was handsome; nearly naked he was stunning. Wow. Lethal curb appeal. She wondered if the deep tan continued under the suit. Her reaction to him had her rattled. She said the first thing on her mind and realized immediately it sounded judgmental.

"You're not working today?" A really dumb remark. Why should she care if he kept banker's hours?

His smile vanished. "I handle a lot of work from home. I'm at the casino generally after 7:00 p.m." By his shuttered expression, she was sure; her opinion of men with uncertain work habits appeared judgmental. "I'm sorry. That came out wrong. I didn't mean anything by it."

"What?" he asked, reading her easily. "You suspect I might make my living as a professional gambler? Sorry, I'm legitimate—no Sky Masterson."

She glanced up at him, thinking she could drown in the green pool of his eyes. Something about his grin teased the back of her mind. She'd seen him somewhere, in another setting. If he were dressed like Thomas, the two could be brothers, except that he was one hundred percent real. Her hormone overload left no doubt.

"Well, what *do* you do?" He was an attractive man, not a relatively safe fantasy. She needed to know. It would be easy to get involved.

The way Galen studied her before he answered, his expression a mix of patience, tolerance, and possibly disappointment, had her wishing he would vanish, like Thomas. No doubt he thought her not only predictable, but a snob.

"I'm sorry. I didn't mean to sound presumptuous."

His brief smile offered a mere token of forgiveness. "I'm chief counsel for a corporation that owns several casinos on the East coast. They're my only client, so I guess you could say I'm a concierge lawyer."

"You're a lawyer?" The surprise in her voice didn't enhance the bad impression she'd already made.

"I also play host to our most favored customers and work with security during the evenings." He threw her a teasing grin. "I think the modern term for it would be multi-tasking."

" I can understand the need for security. A lot of money changes hands in a casino."

His smile patronized her, but she deserved it. He appealed to her on such an elemental level, it worried her. She didn't usually sound this awkward.

"You'd be surprised at the people who try to work scams. I guess they think we have so much money we wouldn't notice. Our surveillance makes Homeland Security look like amateurs. As soon as you enter, we have you in a computer, drivers license, probable income, credit history, and within hours we'll know what you drink, what games you like and what caught your eye in the gift shop. Give me a day and I'll know the name of your eighth grade English teacher."

"Kathryn Buckwalter. I'll save you the trouble," Sara said, properly chastised. Time to make amends. "Look, I'm sorry for my rudeness and the bad first impression I made at the party. I don't trust men so much, lately. I'm still in shock from a sudden divorce after what I thought was a perfect marriage. I'm afraid it colors my reaction to every man I meet."

Boy, this small-town attitude was taking her over. When had she ever revealed so much to perfect strangers as she had the last two days? But he seemed like a nice guy and she wanted his approval.

His voice gentled. "I knew something was going on there. When we were introduced I was still role-playing, and I can see where it hit you wrong." He gave her a boyish smile that weakened her knees. "I have to admit, you bruised my ego."

"Oh, please. Now that's a crock."

He threw back his head and laughed, genuinely amused. "Okay, Sara Burkhart, you're somebody I'd like to know better, so let's start over."

"Okay, Galen Andrews, let's agree to be friends."

He started walking along the tide line. She walked beside him, companionably. "So," he said, "how are you getting along with the haunted house?"

"You know about that?"

"Everybody knows there's something in that house. A while back a rock musician and his entourage stayed there and had some trouble. I got a call from his lawyer, a friend of mine who knew I lived here, asking if I could help."

"What happened?"

"By the time I got there they'd trashed the place. All that was left for me to do was make sure Caro got reimbursed for the damages, which were considerable." He laughed. "Whatever they saw, it put the fear of God in them."

"So you've never seen the ghost?"

"I've never been inside the house. Is he giving you trouble?"

Reluctant to discuss Thomas, Sara said, "I'm not having any trouble so far." Searching for another subject, it occurred to her if Galen was a lawyer, he might know something about Costner's insurance business, or, at least, have an opinion. "There's something else I might ask you, though."

"Sure. What is it?"

"What do you know about this group Steve Costner is with, the Congressional Ventures Foundation?" The sudden change in Galen's attitude—the unmistakable warning in his expression—startled her. She said, "What? Is there something wrong?"

"Look, Sara, there are some things you don't want to know about." The urgency in his voice was unmistakably a warning. "You're not part of the town. You're only going to be here for a few weeks and then you go back to wherever you came from. Don't be asking questions about this. The people involved play hardball politics and you'll find yourself in over your head before you can stop."

He was serious. He frightened her, but still, she had to know.

"What could be so bad about a congressional committee?"

"It has nothing to do with Congress. They call it that so people like you will think it's about government and won't ask questions."

The 'people like you' label got to her. Her temper started to heat. "Galen, I'm not stupid and I have a legitimate reason to ask. I know something about the tax code. For years, I was involved in my husband's business. When I heard about a life insurance policy with deductible premiums through this organization, I wondered about it. I doubt it's legal, and I resent the patronizing tone in your voice that women have been hearing throughout hundreds of years of history when they're told they should leave matters to the men."

Galen ran his hands through his hair, apparently frustrated. "Just about everybody in town is in on this and if you don't let it go, you could get hurt."

Incredulous, she stared at him. "You mean that literally? Physical harm?"

"Yes." His expression was grim. He wasn't kidding.

"Do you have one of these policies?"

"No. Leave it at that."

"But what if the IRS audits somebody?" She thought of Vinnie and what that could mean to his plans for his daughter. "It happens, you know. Those giant underground government computers are at it 24-7."

Galen grabbed her shoulders, turning her to face him. "Dammit, Sara, are you hearing me? The world you live in is neat and orderly, untouched by violence, where bad things don't happen to good people. Go back home and forget about this. I don't know how to make it plainer. There's a lot of money involved here. If you keep on, you'll be in more trouble than you can handle."

His green eyes bored into hers. He frightened her. For an instant his autocratic expression and air of authority reminded her of the man in the tavern, but that was ridiculous.

"Let go of me," Sara snapped. "I'm not supposed to care if unsuspecting participants, people I happen to like, get burned? You're telling me I have no business getting involved? I should go back to my harmless little committees and my 'ladies' lunches and not worry my 'pretty little head' about what could happen to innocent people?"

Her bitterness stopped his rant.

"I wouldn't exactly put it that way."

"There's no other way to put it." In a voice loaded with sarcasm, she continued, "No thank you. I've been there; done that; bought the t-shirt. So far I've not accomplished a whole lot with my life. I occupied space, living in my own carefree bubble, oblivious to the rest of the world. Lately I've been forced to take a hard look at my priorities." Dismayed, she felt tears crowding into her throat. She was losing it, and fought for control.

"I'm starting over, and this time my life is going to have some significance. Why is it so hard to understand that I want the rest of my existence to mean something? I want it to matter that I lived and by doing so, my living made a difference to someone. I'm going to pay attention to what's going on around me, and be involved with people."

"Look, I'm sorry. Hell, I didn't mean to be patronizing."

"Never mind," she managed. "My fault. The last two days—no, make that the last two months—have been a bit more than I can handle."

The conversation had taken a serious turn that she wasn't ready to think about. Taking a deep breath, she searched for some meaningless words to end the conversation. She'd revert to her old "platitudinous" self, if that was a word, and not say anything controversial.

"I'd better go in. I think I'm starting to burn."

That did it. His face shuttered completely.

"Take care, Sara. I think I'll go on for a bit."

She knew she'd somehow missed an opportunity, but for what? It didn't matter. Amazing how quickly one became involved in other people's lives by simply caring, or maybe it was because this was a small town and her time here was limited, and things moved faster. Once she returned home it would be forgotten. For sure, she didn't need any more mystery or drama.

***

Galen walked away from her, lost in thought. She was the most unusual woman he'd ever met, and he suspected, was going to be the most exciting—if she didn't get herself killed first. He had to find a way to distract her from

Costner's insurance scam. Costner frequented the casino and was involved with some pretty heavy hitters. Those guys didn't fool around. If they had word that someone was meddling, they'd take care of the problem, permanently.

He wanted her, damn it. Wanted her with an intensity he couldn't remember ever experiencing, unmistakably drawn to her, and, oddly, he couldn't shake the feeling that they'd met before, or that he'd been waiting to meet her most of his life.

I'm going to have her, by God.

This attraction mirrored a restlessness he'd been feeling lately. The time had come to let someone else into his life. He walked on, lost in thought, soothed by the rhythm of the waves.

***

Arriving back at the house, Sara rummaged in the fridge for dinner.

"I need an evening of peace and quiet and no weird happenings," she said. Not for a minute did it seem strange talking to a house because she was convinced she felt a presence here, other than Thomas. "I'm going to have dinner, watch a movie on TV and have a long, dreamless sleep. That's an order."

Laughing at her whimsy, she sorted through the pile of DVDs in the living room, courtesy of her innkeeper, and came across an old favorite, *Adventures in Babysitting*. Perfect. No stress, funny, and it had that great scene in the blues club at the end. She settled down with her sandwich and a bottle of beer, anticipating the evening.

The dream came much later. She'd fallen asleep in the chair with the DVD still on. Its light gave an eerie glow to the room. She became aware of a woman's voice, desperately pleading. It pulled her consciousness up to another level of consciousness. With her feet not quite touching the ground, she floated, past a row of houses on a narrow, unpaved street. The late evening fog, redolent of saltwater mist, hung in the air with an oily tenacity too thick for much visibility.

Dread filled her. No, not again. This would not happen to her again. She would not allow it. She waged a futile struggle within her mind to awaken, but she was in the unbreakable grip of another force.

A disembodied voice cried out to her. "You have to talk to him. He'll listen to you. There's nobody else." The voice pleaded with her, but in the dark, she couldn't find the source.

"Where are you? Talk to who?"

Gaslights, spaced at intervals along the street, cast a yellow glow that barely lit the horses and carriages making their way on the nearly deserted thoroughfare.

"Help me stop this madness. You must. He'll put us all in danger." The voice felt closer, a woman's voice, but where?

Once again she'd found herself in the same seaside town. Simple, two-story frame houses, barely visible in the fog, lined the board sidewalk on her left, all facing the wide bay. Docks occupied every available space on the other side of the street, jutting into the ocean. They provided berths for a gathering of tall-masted sailing ships. Behind these houses, on another street, homes in grander style were set higher on the hill, affording a clear view of the inlet. From their vantage point families could stand watch for the return of the ships bringing loved ones home after years at sea.

She felt she had done this, sometime in the past, in this town, familiar because, in another life, she had lived here.

"Where are you? Who are you?" Could anyone hear her pleas in the dark as she moved along the sidewalk? Surely someone must.

"Felicity?" The voice held the edge of panic, frightening Sara.

"I'm not Felicity, but tell me how to help you."

"He's set his course, bent on this madness. If he proceeds, we're all lost."

"Who?" Sara asked.

"Thomas, of course."

Sara stopped and searched the shadows behind the shrubbery. Urgency gave way to frustration. "How many times I have to explain that I'm not who you think I am. I don't belong here. I just want to return to my time and forget this ever happened, so go away and leave me alone."

The voice wept with despair. "Why do you deny me? How can you leave us to his foolhardiness?"

Sara knew must be something she was supposed to do, but what?

Confused and frightened, Sara tried to escape the voice by crossing to the other side of the street, running as fast as she could. She didn't see the horse and carriage until it was almost upon her. Screaming, she fell and darkness engulfed her.

Chapter Seven

Please don't let this become a habit.

The silent wish crept into Sara's mind while she slowly
awakened to the morning sun. A new day had dawned. Keeping her
eyes closed, she cautiously explored with her hands. Yep. She felt
the blanket, the mattress, inhaled the familiar freshness of morning
sea air. There was no doubt she lay in her bed, with no sign that
she'd been out of her room, except for the lingering echo of that
woman's desperation, and a vague sense of having been in another
life. Probably a dream, but dreams can be a premonition of things to
come, or some catastrophic event that would be the ruin of someone.

Sara no longer had doubts. Her presence in this house had not
been by random choice, although she couldn't recall exactly why
she'd settled on New Kensington and this particular house for her
vacation. She searched the New Jersey shoreline on the Internet,
looking for a small town away from the tourist crowds, and the name
caught her attention. For sure, she needed coffee to solve any more
riddles. She headed downstairs to start the day.

Relaxing on the porch and communing with the ocean while
waiting for the caffeine to kick in had quickly become Sara's
morning ritual. This morning the tide was out, ready to turn toward
shore, with very little wave action. The wind lay quiet. Even the
gulls had found some other beach to plunder. Conditions were right
for some deep thinking. She sat in her favorite chair recalling last
night's dream.

The voice knew her. *How can you ask me that?* What did
those words, spoken by the unseen woman mean? She'd never taken
reincarnation seriously, but the question came begging. Had she
lived another life as someone else? Twice, in a dream state, she'd
gone to this place in another time.

Well, she'd come here because she wanted adventure, but
ghostly trips into a distant past were more than she'd bargained for.
Someone must have some theories about this stuff and some
familiarity with the Stuart family. That woman last night could have
been a Stuart. One of them, apparently Thomas, had been involved

in something illegal, maybe smuggling. This morning she'd find Caro to see what she could learn about the family. There had to be some local history handed down with the house. Henry might know about the insurance thing.

She remembered Galen's warning about Steve Costner. He'd scared her, but dammit, caring for a friend didn't constitute meddling. Shouldn't she be concerned about Vinnie being drawn into something that would mean trouble for him?

"You're very beautiful, Madam, in spite of the bizarre manner of dress you persist on wearing."

Thomas materialized against the porch railing, startling her. This time he appeared flawlessly groomed, garbed as a ship's captain like the pictures from the 1860s she'd seen at the library. Buff cambric pants hugged his thighs; his boots were polished to a brilliant shine. He wore a cream colored vest with a white ascot, and a navy blue coat cropped at the waist in the front with tails in the back. A double row of brass buttons gleamed in the sun. His dark hair, brushed back, curled around his ears, with a casual lock left to frame his face. She regarded him, standing before her, every bit as handsome and appealing as she remembered. Chills chased up her spine.

He isn't real. The constant reminder was necessary, or her fantasy would take over. He's connected to this house and has something to do with those trips to the past.

"Thomas. I wondered if I'd ever see you again. Why are you here? Do you do this often?"

"I know not why I am here, nor who summoned me, since this has never happened before. I, too, am confused by the circumstances. Your presence must signify."

"Did you live here? Was this your house?"

"No. My oldest brother, Caleb, built it." His expression changed to disgust. "Pure folly. He insisted the days of the whaling ships were over, to be replaced by steam powered vessels, already plying the Hudson River trade. With increasing the scarcity of the whales, the whaling industry would be coming to an end."

His face twisted with an ugly sneer. "He came here because he believed the family future lay in agriculture." He paced the floor, becoming increasingly agitated. "Bah. Stuarts had been whalers for more than a hundred years. We descended from generations before us. I am no farmer. I command my own ship. There is no other life for me." He glared at her, arrogance dominating every inch of him.

He expected her to argue? He looked dangerous. His men probably lived in fear of him.

"The war presents lucrative opportunities beyond whaling around us, but my brother will not listen to me. His loyalties lie with the Union." His expression darkened with anger.

Union? As opposed to the Confederacy? He had to be referring to the Civil War. Though she barely remembered high school history, she recalled the sentiments of Massachusetts, one of the original colonies, were allied with the Union.

While Thomas' anger grew, the atmosphere around the house thickened, making it hard to breathe. The sky darkened. The surf grew restless.

Is this what happens when a ghost has a temper tantrum? She didn't want to find out. Possibly she could change the subject? She remembered reading something at the library.

"Wasn't whale harvesting losing favor with the discovery of oil in the ground?"

He turned on her, his face livid. Oh, wow. That struck a nerve.

"What can you know about anything?" he roared. "Women have no head for matters of commerce."

Hold on. Could this tedious old refrain be genetically imbedded in male DNA? Hadn't she heard this very thing from Galen yesterday?

"Thomas, I only ask because I want to understand. What opportunities wouldn't your family support?"

"You have no business meddling. Women should make social visits, provide heirs, and tend to their knitting circles."

He hadn't answered her question or voiced an opinion; he'd issued an order. Disgusted and disillusioned with his chauvinistic attitude, she realized he'd lost his luster, and become an ordinary, garden-variety man. Her romantic fantasy faded, not to return, while her temper came near to exploding. She reined it in firmly, reminding herself that women were not allowed to vote in elections in 1860. "It's plain to me that you fought with your brother about something you wanted to do that he wouldn't go along with."

The wind increased, the sky became blacker as Thomas' anger exploded.

"He didn't know anything about it. He had no business getting involved. It was my idea. I controlled it."

The memory of last night's dream remained fresh in her mind. Thomas must be the 'he' putting the family in danger. "What were you doing that your brother opposed?"

"Silence. Do you never learn, Mélange?" His face grew red with anger. "Stop your meddling before it becomes the death of you, as it almost did Felicity."

Mélange? What meddling? She stared at him, shocked. What did he mean, the death of her?

"Hello? Hello? Are you here, Sara?" Clover's voice, coming from the kitchen, shattered the mood on the porch. Thomas vanished in a flash, the ocean stilled, and the sun reappeared.

Drat. She wished she could continue the moment, but it wasn't to happen. Well, this could be good. Slightly spacey Clover might know about dreams of another time.

"I was sure you'd be up." Clover floated into the room, trailed by yards of tie-dye. "So I thought I'd visit on my way to town."

"I'm glad you did. There's something I wanted to ask you about. Could I offer you some coffee or tea?"

"Iced tea would be nice."

Sara went to the kitchen and returned with the tea and some biscotti. "Here you go." She waited until they were settled before beginning. "Remember what you told me the last time you were here? About lingering spirits?"

Clover beamed approvingly, as she might at an obedient acolyte. "What do you want to know?"

"You're the only person I'm sure won't think I'm crazy if I tell you."

Finally Sara had Clover's full attention. She'd chosen the right approach. Maybe she'd get some answers.

"I was someplace in the past, but I'm not sure I dreamed it. I think it actually happened. I was there. Does this make any sense to you?" She held her breath, not knowing what reaction she might get from her unworldly guest.

Not much, apparently. Clover hardly blinked. "Sure. Did you go there or did they come here?"

So relieved she wanted to hug her, she held back. "Well, both, but could this really happen?"

"It happens to a lot of people. You've had a paranormal experience. They're not all that uncommon, but I don't know anybody who physically appeared somewhere else."

Clover nodded, "Or they were afraid, like you, to admit it. Most episodes last a few seconds, usually when you're totally relaxed and you're mind is open. You dismiss them as a dream before falling asleep and don't talk about it because others will think you're crazy."

"You have that part right." Sara sighed. "What do you think happened to me?"

"You shifted out of time. Maybe you slipped through an opening to another parallel universe, where your life is going on in a different year, although I've not heard of regression to the past. More like the future, and only by a few minutes. I don't know a lot about parallel universes."

"No. It wasn't me. I was an observer, but it was me in my time."

"Well, that makes as much sense as anything." Clover's acceptance gave her the confidence to continue.

"Okay. Here's the story. I've had a visit from a ghost who I believe is Thomas Stuart, a sea captain who lived sometime around 1860. Not once, but twice I found myself in the same time period, first in a tavern and then wandering the streets in a seaside village. I think I might have been in old New Kensington, Massachusetts, where the Stuarts came from."

Clover considered. "I can believe the appearance here, because everybody knows this house is haunted. Could the others have been an especially vivid dream?"

"No way. The first time, in the tavern, I was in my nightgown and bare footed. When I woke up I had sand and dirt on my feet and splinters from the boardwalk. My clothes smelled like tobacco smoke and stale beer. How could that be if I only dreamed it? Last night I walked on a street in this village, trying to find a hidden voice that followed me, pleading for help. It called me "Felicity.""

Still afraid, she avoided mention of Thomas' reference to her death.

"Whoa. This is very heavy stuff." Clover's eyes gleamed with excitement. "You need to talk to the Metaphysical Society. Some of our members are experts on paranormal experiences. We meet once a month, at the church—tomorrow evening, as a matter of fact. You can come with me, be my guest."

"Metaphysical Society?" There were groups who studied this stuff? Why not? "Sure. I'd love to. I'll never get a chance to do this in East Partridge. This whole conversation might be taking place in a parallel universe. What time?"

"Seven." Clover stood, ready to leave. "I have to go before I'm late for work."

"I'll meet you at the church," Sara walked her to the door, and watched Clover's swinging strides carry her down the road before returning to her seat on the porch. She'd wait an hour before leaving for Caro's in a quest for more history on the Stuart house, taking advantage of the natural lull in town business during the afternoon hours with more time to talk.

Meanwhile, she'd boot up the Mac and do some research on foundations and Steve Costner. She might find some answers, even if she didn't like what she learned. Galen was adamant that she should leave this alone or she'd be in some kind of danger.

After an hour of futile searching on the Internet, she decided this would have to wait for another time. She discovered that New Jersey had over 23,000 tax-deductible organizations registered. Her brain couldn't handle more input. One excuse was as good as another, she decided, as she shut down and headed for town to talk to Caro.

Chapter Eight

The streets of New Kensington were quiet on the lazy, late September afternoon, when Sara entered the grocery store. The weekend tourists had headed toward home, and the next wave of weekenders hadn't yet arrived. Caro and Henry seated at one of the tables, enjoying the lull by having a glass of iced tea. They looked so at ease with each other. Henry had forsaken his plaid suit for overalls and was settled comfortably in a chair, looking like he didn't intend to move anytime soon. Cora was in jeans and a clean apron, appearing as relaxed, not appearing to have anything pressing to do.

Sara envied them. She'd had this easy camaraderie with Richard in the early years of her marriage, and then they'd lost it when they drifted into their separate lives.

"Hello there, friend," Caro said, "Come sit down and I'll get you some tea. Unsweetened, right?"

Sara nodded. "How's it going, Henry? It's awful quiet on the street. Ready for the weekend?"

"Yeah. Enjoying the temporary lull. Got me some nice steaks in for the barbecue crowd, if you're interested. Top grade choice, locally grown."

"I'll take you up on it if I ever satisfy my craving for fresh fish. I can't get over the difference between fresh and frozen."

"You're not here to talk about fish," Caro said, returning with the tea, "What brings you to town?" She took her seat, ready to talk.

"I'm here for information about the Stuarts; like who lived in the house when it was first built."

"I'm afraid there isn't much history," Cora said. "Caleb became the family patriarch when his father was lost at sea, because he was the oldest of three brothers and two sisters. He came here first, around 1860, or thereabouts, and built the house. His brother Uriah, and wife Phoebe followed shortly thereafter with two young children. There was another brother who didn't join them, but chose to stay in New Kensington." She turned to Henry. "You remember the story? I think it was Uriah and his wife who built next to them."

"Yeah. At one time there were about a dozen houses on that ridge, all destroyed in the hurricane of 1960, except the Stuart House. The rest simply blew away. Nothing left. Not a single board. That's the strangest thing about that house. Nothing ever seems to touch it. No matter how bad the storm, it never suffers much damage."

"Did everyone survive?"

"Well, there's a bit of a mystery about that. There were about a dozen residents that were unaccounted for and no bodies were ever found. They simply disappeared and no one ever came looking for them."

"Was Caleb a sea captain?"

Caro nodded. "A whaler. The family owned a fleet of ships, but sold everything about the time of the Civil War, moved here and started cranberry farming. Did quite well."

"Then Thomas wasn't here?"

"Thomas?" Caro said, puzzled.

"The ghost I met is named Thomas. I'm sure he and Caleb didn't get along."

"You've seen a ghost? That's strange," Cora said. "I've never heard of any sightings there. I've been renting that house for about ten years, and although guests have reported some strange goings on, nobody ever reported seeing anything."

"Must have been the other brother," Henry said.

"I saw him once for a few minutes, and he identified himself as Thomas Stuart," Sara said. "He was dressed as a sea captain I think, but it was hard to tell. He'd washed up on the beach after the last storm and his clothes were wet. He seemed to think the house was his."

"All I know," Caro said, "is when Caleb came here he didn't own any ships. The War had come that far north, and Confederate privateers patrolled the coast as far as Massachusetts, looking for Yankee vessels. The whalers made easy prey because they were all sail powered. Confederate ships were faster. They had steam engines."

"Drat. I guess I need to go north to the New Kensington Library. They must have some mention of such an important family."

"Not gonna happen." Henry said. "Although the Stuart fleet sailed out of New Kensington, the family lived in a settlement a mile up the coast. They called it Port Kensington. About 1865 or so, a tornado along with a hurricane destroyed the town. Everything was gone, including the residents. Vanished. Nothing remained, not one brick or board."

"Nothing? Not even the people survived?"

Caro nodded. "It's like the earth opened up and swallowed the town whole."

Stunned, Sara asked, "How can that happen?"

Henry replied. "When you've lived on the coast long enough you know that about every sixty years or so, a Nor'easter comes along and wipes out everything. Been going on for hundreds of years."

"What's a Nor'easter?"

"Has to do with cold fronts and currents. The wind turns and comes off the north instead of the usual southern flow. Big time flooding. Wipes out everything."

Cora and Henry exchanged looks. "We're overdue for another," Cora offered. "Been about long enough between storms." For the moment there were no words, until the rusty spring on the screen door screeched, announcing a visitor. Georgia came in carrying something wrapped in a towel.

"I knew I could find somebody to eat this." She unwrapped a deep-dish pie plate with a flourish. "I come bearing lunch, a cheese and mushroom quiche, one of my specialties."

"Well," Cora said, "what's the occasion?"

"It's left over from breakfast. I only had two couples this morning and they were into bran muffins and oatmeal. I never know what they'll go for, but we have a reputation for bountiful breakfasts so I always offer several choices. Most of the stuff I can keep, like the fruit and the baked goods, but quiche gets soggy in the fridge."

Cora shook her head. "I gotta' hand it to you, Georgia, I'm a grouch in the morning. I couldn't do what you do, get up early, cook all that food, and be cheerful at the same time. Bed and breakfast owners are a special breed."

"Nah. You just have to like people." She looked around. "Has anyone seen Colin? He loves quiche."

Sara laughed. "Does the whole town feed Colin?"

"It's like they say," Henry dead-panned, "It takes a village. Galen took him fishing on his boat early this morning. Should be back soon."

"Galen has a boat?" Sara's dismay at being left out surprised her. She hardly knew the guy and the last time she'd seen him, they'd argued. "He never mentioned owning a boat." But then, when had she given him the chance?

"Oh, yeah." Henry said. "A real beauty. A forty-foot motor sailer. He could go around the world on that boat."

Georgia sighed. "I could live on it. It is pure luxury."

"Cost a pretty penny," Henry agreed, "but our Galen can afford it."

Sara glanced up at the sound of the door opening again. Was it chance, or fate by design that the persons under discussion were fated to enter right then? When she saw Colin's face flushed with happiness, she silently thanked Galen for taking time with the boy. She should stop treating him with such suspicion, and consider the possibility that he was simply a nice guy.

"You should see the fish we caught." Galen sounded like a proud dad.

Colin held out his hands to measure three feet.

Galen laughed. "Well, maybe not that big, but a nice size sea bass."

"Them are good eating," Henry said. "What are you going to do with it?"

"I have the day off until late this evening, so we're going to cook it and eat it, aren't we?" Galen winked at Colin, who grinned with enthusiasm.

"You clean it; I'll cook it," Sara volunteered on an impulse, wanting to be part of the happy scene.

Galen looked at the grinning boy. "What do you say, Kid? Should we let her have a go at it?"

Colin nodded, joy lighting his face.

"We'll cook it at my place with my special basil/lemon aioli," Sara said. "I'll need to borrow a pan big enough to bake it."

"I have a pan," Cora said. "Galen, you can clean the fish out back and I'll pack the filets in ice. Now, let's sit down and eat this quiche."

Is there anything better than friends sharing laughter and food? Sara didn't think so. She translated the account of the battle with the fish, which Colin told in sign, embellishing the tale, with outrageous exaggeration. It became an account to rival *The Old Man and The Sea.* She basked in Galen's laughing approval and noticed Cora and Georgia exchange sly looks about something. So what? She was a free woman who didn't have to feel guilty when a man noticed her.

"So, Sport." Galen watched Colin polish off the last bit of quiche. "We need to get moving. You clean the fish while I secure the boat. We'll shower and change at my house and be at Sara's about six." He looked at Sara. "That okay with you?"

"That's fine," she said.

Colin left the room. Galen stood, but paused to speak to Cora and Henry.

"Do you guys have room for Colin to stay the night?"

"Sure," Cora said. "What's going on?"

"When I picked him up at his house this morning, there was trouble. I heard his uncle cursing him and yelling about not getting enough money from the state and that Colin should be working to pay board."

"That's a bunch of crap," Henry said. "I've seen the check he gets every month."

"Yeah, but I have a bad feeling about taking him back there tonight. I'd let him stay with me, but I have to be at the casino for a late shift and I don't want him to be alone in case his uncle comes looking for him."

Sara's mother mode kicked in, big time. "He can stay with me for as long as it takes. I have plenty of bedrooms and besides, I promised him help with his speech. I worked with a therapist to help my daughter, then a three-year-old, who had a bad stammer and she got over it."

"It 's good of you to offer, Sara," Cora said. "His uncle doesn't know you and won't know to come around. We all worry about that boy."

"Does he need to get his things?"

"Everything the kid owns he keeps in an old duffle bag he takes with him everywhere. That way he's always packed and ready to move on."

"The poor kid, not knowing where he'll be from one day to the next." Sara said, near tears, her heart aching for Colin. "I didn't need to know that. May that uncle rot in Purgatory.

"So. You guys do your thing with the fish, and be at my house by six. Don't forget the pan. I'm off to find some lemons and fresh basil. I may even have time to make my special "death by chocolate" brownies."

She left them planning dinner, filled with anticipation, not a small bit of it her happiness at having Colin with her—almost like family. It was a good feeling, having someone who needed her.

Chapter Nine

Sara had everything ready, waiting for the fish by the time Galen and Colin arrived. The kitchen smelled of chocolate and lemons. She had set the table for three with fresh flowers, and added a colorful fruit salad, a soda for Colin, and two iced teas.

Galen entered, his arms full, followed by Colin. "There's enough fish here to feed an army." He handed her the pan and a bag filled with crushed ice and several large fish fillets.

Sara laughed. "Nevertheless, we'll bake all of it. I'm not going to ruin it by freezing half. If there's any left over, I'll think of something." She sprayed the pan with cooking oil, added the fish, covered the filets with the lemon mayonnaise she'd made, and put the pan in the hot oven.

"This will take about twenty minutes, so let's sit down, and start with the salad and breads sticks."

"This is nice," Galen said, surveying the table with appreciation. He took a seat and passed the salad. "I'll bet you're a wonderful hostess at home."

"Thank you." She glowed, reminded of how much she missed having company for dinner. Colin eyed a salad ingredient suspiciously, so much like her son when he was little, who never put anything unfamiliar in his mouth unless he had examined it thoroughly and smelled it. A wave of nostalgia threatened to drown her. "It's kiwi fruit. Tastes like peeled grapes."

He shrugged, popped the fruit into his mouth, and reached for a breadstick.

"Are you expecting company?" Galen asked, peering out the window. "There's a car pulling up."

"No, I'm not expecting anyone." Curious, she went to the door, and watched, in dismay, while her daughter lifted a suitcase out of her car and began dragging it by the handle up the stairs. She wasn't ready to deal with this. Conflicting feelings shot through her, overwhelming her. Anger, intense enough to make her tremble, fought with niggling guilt because a mother should be glad to see her own daughter, shouldn't she?

Damn, Jenny. Anger won out. So, her conniving daughter thought that by showing up here, backing Mom into a corner, she could get out of finishing the semester at college? No way was that going to happen.

"Jenny," she said, opening the door, her expression grim. She was aware Galen watched her, puzzled. Every fragment of emotion she'd just experienced must have passed over her face like a bad drama. "You didn't call to say you were coming for the weekend. That's a long way to drive for an overnight visit."

"Hi, Mom." Her voice pleaded, her voice laden with guilt and doubt. "I thought I'd surprise you."

Jenny stood, uncertain, clearly sensing her mother's anger— alarmed, and embarrassed when she realized there were other people watching.

"Well, you're just in time for dinner. I'll set a place for you. " Sara sighed, resigned, but she couldn't stifle completely the angry resentment, regardless of the maternal instincts that were battering her. "The fish has to come out of the oven right now, or be overdone. Sit and we'll talk later. I'll figure out what to do with you after dinner."

Galen looked at her without judgment, his expression at once questioning and amused, no doubt, because her aggravation was so apparent. The man was entirely too good at reading sign.

"Colin, clear the center of the table and set the wooden cutting board there" Sara said, "I'll take the fish out of the oven, the pan will be hot."

Galen stood ready to help. "I'll get the fish, Sara, you make room for it."

She nodded, grateful for his calm acceptance of an awkward situation, and glared at her daughter who took her place at the end of the table, appearing contrite and a uncertain. Good. It was time she realized her mother was not the pushover she used to be when Richard ran things.

Galen found a spatula and lifted a large helping of fish onto Colin's plate. "Your catch, you get first dibs. Lord, Sara, this smells incredible." He glanced at Sara, winked reassuringly, and held out another serving while she slid her plate underneath. It had turned out perfectly, the rich mayonnaise bubbly and golden. "Jenny, is it?" he asked. "Hold out your plate." Too stunned to say anything, she complied, and muttered, "Thank you."

Man and boy ate with apparent enjoyment, delighting Sara. The mood quieted while the eager diners focused on appeasing their hunger. She and Galen spoke easily on a range of subjects while Jenny picked at her food in silence.

This was not the dinner Sara had anticipated. Though Galen did his best at conversation, time passed awkwardly. After glancing at his watch, Galen said, "I'm being a poor guest and leaving you with the cleaning up but I have to go if I'm going to be at the casino by nine.

"I've never had fish as good as this. That settles it. I'm in love. You have to come live with me." He winked at Colin. "What do you say? Should we kidnap her and keep her here?"

Colin, who'd been staring at Jenny, fascinated, laughed. "Yes."

Sara's smile let him know she understood what it took for him to speak.

Jenny noticed the exchange and, not accustomed to being ignored, demanded, "What's the big deal?"

"The big deal, my insensitive daughter, if you haven't noticed, is that Colin says very little. He has a bad stammer, similar to the one you used to have."

Dismayed, Jenny dropped her glance while her face reddened.

Barely able to control her displeasure, Sara added, "If I were you, I'd hold my tongue and behave with the utmost care until we have a chance to talk. You'd better have a good reason for being here."

"Are the arrangements still on?" Galen asked, with a glance toward Colin.

"Absolutely. Colin, take your things upstairs to the middle bedroom next to mine, then come back down to watch TV or you can play video games." She glanced at her daughter. "You'll have the bedroom at the end of the hall. You can unpack what you'll need tonight, and then wait for me on the porch. We're going to have a serious talk." Jenny's pale face told Sara she knew she'd gone way over the line by coming here without calling, and she turned toward the stairs, leaving quietly.

"Galen, I'm sorry you had to be part of this. My daughter and I have barely spoken for years, but I can read her like a book. She's quit school, probably going home first to East Partridge. When she discovered her house keys no longer worked she came here, thinking I'd have no option but to let her get away with her little scheme."

"Hey, Sweetheart." Galen smiled, placing a reassuring hand on her shoulder. "Take it easy. Murdering children is against the law, especially when they're yours."

"However," she said, her smile thanking him for trying to lighten the moment, "I'm reminded, in the animal kingdom, there are mothers who eat their young. Why does that suddenly appeal to me?" He put his arms around her in a reassuring hug.

It felt good to be held. She leaned into him while her traitorous body reminded her that it had been a long time since she'd had any closeness with a man. He nuzzled her neck under her ear. How could he know that spot was so sensitive? With obvious regret, he drew back.

"As much as I'd like to stay to see this scene play out so I can give you a standing ovation at the end, I have to go." His parting kiss, hard and passionate, foretold of things to come leaving her breathless. When the door closed behind him she turned to see her daughter standing there, her expression shocked and devastated.

"People change. Get used to it. When you come downstairs we'll talk, after I set the kitchen to rights." Responding to her daughter's hesitation, she said, coldly rejecting the plea in Jenny's eyes, "I don't need the help. I need the time alone to think about how we are going to proceed."

Cleanup didn't take long. All the food had been consumed, and there weren't many dishes, but there was plenty of time for her parental instincts to kick in.

Murderous anger faded to irritation, then regret. This was her daughter, in crisis. No matter how they'd gone on before when things were tense between her and Richard, it had nothing to do with the here and now. She had given this child life. She was her mother, therefore responsible. She grabbed a bottle of beer for herself and a can of pop for Jenny and went out onto the porch, giving Colin, playing a video game on television, a nod. Jenny sat on one of the chairs, her knees drawn up, huddled into herself. Sara put the can and bottle on the table and waited.

"Mom?" Her daughter huddled in the chair, looking so miserable, so defeated. Sara recognized a defining moment in her life.

I've done the talk about becoming a new person. It's time to act—time to grow up, and acknowledge, through no fault of her own, her daughter had been brought into this world and needed her mother. Her heart filled with love.

"Oh, Jenny." She pulled her child to her feet and hugged her. "It's okay. Let's forget all the pain and hurt feelings that brought this about and talk. What's wrong?"

Clearly uncomfortable with the unfamiliar closeness, Jenny pulled away, reached for her can of pop, and sat down.

Regret, sharp as a whaling harpoon, pierced Sara, at the rejection.

"Okay, why are you here?"

"Nobody wants me." The tears came, along with a wailing lament. "I don't belong any place. The kids at college don't like me. I don't fit in. Dad doesn't want me; he wants Dick to live with him. You don't want me." She glanced at Sara, accusing her. "I went home, and the house is locked up. I don't have any place to go."

"Sorry about the house. At the time, I didn't feel I could trust you. What do you mean, Dad wants Dick Junior to live with him?"

"For Christmas and next summer. He's going to teach him the new business. Make him part of it." Spite made her spit out the last of it. "Since I'm a girl, I'm not invited."

Damn Richard for his insensitivity. Sara started to reassure Jen with words, however insincere, that her dad hadn't meant to reject her, but that's what the old Sara would have done. Peace at any price, even if it meant a lie.

"The bastard."

"Mom." Jenny stared, shocked.

"Jenny, you might as well face it. You're dad will never grow beyond what he is. I have to be fair. He was a good provider and husband, but he always put himself first, and he'll go for whatever makes him feel good at the moment, regardless of the road kill he leaves accumulating behind. We lived well. You had everything you wanted, except what everybody needs and few ever get—unconditional love."

"How is that different?"

"It's a state of maturity we all strive for, but few attain, including your dad, where we can love something or someone more than we love ourselves, and not want anything in return. Dogs and cats give it freely, but humans? Not so much."

"It sounds nice, but right now, I'd settle for a friend who just liked me. You don't know what it's like to be rejected and made fun of because you're different. It hurts."

"J-j-j-jen."

Colin stood in the doorway, smiling shyly. Cautiously, he reached out and touched Jenny on the shoulder. He signed, *I will be your friend,* and stood quietly, waiting for her response.

Jen shrank from his touch, suspicious. "What's he doing? What did he say?"

"He's signing. He wants to be your friend. Know that it took courage to make that gesture," Sara said. "He knows all about rejection. Though he can hear, he has a bad stammer and many people treat him as though he's retarded. He has nobody, which is why he's staying here for awhile." She held her breath, praying Jenny would at least be kind.

Surprised and relieved, she saw her daughter's smile light up like a Christmas tree. His smile in return reflected near-worship.

Sara rose. "Sit down, Colin. I'll get you a soda."

When she returned, Colin was trying to talk to Jenny, but she wasn't getting it. "This isn't working, she said. "I know." She looked at Sara. "Do you have an extra cellphone?"

"Yes. In the kitchen. If he doesn't speak, what does he need with a cellphone?"

"Mom." Jen looked disgusted, and rolled her eyes. Things were getting back to normal.

"Texting. I have two phones, one with a different number. They're upstairs in my bedroom. We'll text. Come on, Colin." She took his hand and pulled him to his feet. "Grab your can and follow me."

While Sara watched in amazement, a totally bemused Colin, a silly grin plastered on his face, follow Jen out of the room. Later she'd worry about her daughter entertaining a boy in her bedroom, but something wonderful had happened here. Jen had selfishly offered to share herself with another person who needed help. That was a good sign, wasn't it?

She guessed the mother-daughter bonding thing would have to wait. The time had come for her to relax with her nightly porch-sitting ritual, waiting for sleep to come. She needed a tall, frosty glass of iced tea. The salty ocean air constantly made her thirsty. Settling on a chair, her tea beside her, she waited for the soft night breeze to lull her into sleepiness. It had been quite a day. The story of the Port Kensington disappearance had stunned her. What happened to all those people? Were they, as Clover would suggest, stuck somewhere in time? A dozen souls adrift? Nobody, no matter how hooked they were on the supernatural, could believe that. Besides, if that were so, then why involve her? She'd never heard of these people before today.

Had anyone else ever seen the ghost of Thomas? And that dream—she had to think of it as a dream or go crazy—how could she accept the idea that some force could send her back in time and she had no way to stop it? She'd never believed the supernatural was anything but silly superstition; anything else was too terrifying.

Of one thing she was sure; this house was haunted, which meant a larger problem loomed. If Jen stayed here, even briefly, how would she explain ghosts, or even worse, time travel?

The air around her became denser; something crowded her space.

"Who's here? Thomas?" No, Thomas had a different feel about him. This was someone else.

The table beside her chair shook, rattling the glass. Her skin crawled and her heart pounded with fright, something she'd not felt until now.

"You're Caleb, aren't you?" She struggled to muster some bravado along with the fear creeping into her gut. "I'm not really into this haunting stuff. If you're trying to tell me something, get on with it."

Nervously she reached for her glass, and stopped when she saw words slowly appear in the condensation.

It ends here. You must stop him.

What ends? Stop him? Stop who? What?

"If you're Caleb, tell me what you mean."

A piercing scream came from inside the house, turning her to ice. Jenny? Her daughter was in trouble. She dashed to the kitchen and found Jen, in her sleep shirt, white faced and clutching a pan, ready to fight some invisible enemy.

"Jen, what's wrong?"

"A strange man is in the house. He was standing right there, but when I grabbed the pan to hit him, he was gone."

"What man? What did he look like?"

"Some gay guy."

"Gay? Why do you think he was gay?"

"He was dressed like he came from a Ralph Lauren fashion shoot. I mean he had on skin-tight riding breeches and boots and a poet shirt with a vest hanging open. Nobody normal wears stuff like that."

Sara couldn't help smiling. Her unimaginative daughter would never suspect a ghost.

"Honey, there's something you need to know about this house."

Colin burst into the room, fully dressed, wild-eyed.

The poor kid sleeps in his clothes? Probably. In case he has to leave suddenly.

"Calm down. There's an explanation for this. I didn't want to get into it tonight, because it's a little hard to understand, but there's only one way to say it. The house is haunted. Jenny, you saw a ghost."

Jen rolled her eyes. "Oh Mom, no way."

"True. In fact, there might be two. I've never met the other one, but I think it might be the man who built the house back in the 1860s. His name is Caleb Stuart. The one you saw is Thomas Stuart, maybe a relative, a captain of a whaling ship out of New Kensington, Massachusetts around 1865."

"How do you know this?"

"A couple of days ago I found Thomas washed up on the beach, dressed in something like he wore today. I thought he might be an actor with a film company. He was really confused. He said this was his house, but everything, including me, looked strange. He stayed long enough for me to learn he was from another time. He didn't know how he got here, then he disappeared."

"Mom, come on." Jen's intolerance for adult fantasies bordered on disgust.

"He's shown up once since then, but not long enough for me to learn much more, except that he has some issues with the man who built this house. I think the house ghost might be his brother."

"Is he evil? Like a vampire or something?"

"No. He's nothing to be afraid of. In fact, if he did intend harm, I think Caleb would interfere."

Jenny was not convinced. She shrugged and rummaged in the freezer while she thought about it. "Is there any ice cream?"

Sara laughed. Teenagers had their priorities. "No. You forget I haven't been feeding teenagers. I'll stop at the store."

Jen settled for a bag of pretzels, offering some to Colin.

"So, if this is true, what are you going to do? Are you staying here? This is kind of exciting and that Thomas guy is kind of cute." She glanced at Colin, who was frowning at her. "For a ghost."

"Considering the only ones you've seen were characters in the movies."

"Well, yeah. So what do we do now?"

"I want to learn more about the history of the house. I've been invited to a meeting of the local Metaphysical Society tomorrow evening and I hope to learn more about ghosts and time travel and stuff like that. You can come if you like." This was not the time to mention her journey into the past. Thomas was enough to deal with for an evening.

"Okay. Colin and I can hang out here."

"He has classes at the high school. This is his last year. You'll be on your own, because I'm going to drive up to Atlantic City, where they have a much larger library, to research another project about insurance. I'll be back in plenty of time for the meeting."

"Can I come with?"

The idea had some appeal. How long had it been since she and Jen had done anything together? Too long. "Sure. Now, I'm going to bed. I'll see you guys in a couple of hours."

She left Colin and Jenny sitting at the table, communicating with hand signals and words in a way they'd made their own, and would probably stay with them long after Colin was speaking normally, which Sara had no doubt would happen soon.

Chapter Ten

"This was a total waste of time." Sara and Jenny were having lunch in a seaside delicatessen they'd found on the boardwalk in Atlantic City after spending several hours at the local library. "I haven't learned anything useful about the Ventures Foundation." She studied the remains of her shrimp sub sandwich; disgusted, and discouraged with the way the day had gone, so far.

Jenny shrugged. "Well, we got to see some of the town. This is a cool place, a lot bigger than I thought it would be, and this boardwalk is awesome, the way all those stores and hotels are on one side and the beach on the other."

"The boardwalk has been here since 1890. I remember it from when I came here as a child. My parents liked to visit the auction houses along the walk, so they'd give me some money, and I would spend hours sightseeing."

"So, where do we go from here?" Jen, ever impatient, asked. "What is a 501(c) 3 anyhow?"

"It's a Federal tax designation. If you have it and are a charitable fundraising organization, there are tax benefits and contributions are tax deductible. You get larger donations."

"So what's different with the Congressional Ventures Foundation?"

"I don't know, yet, but I think they're operating illegally. They raise money for several causes, but more importantly, they allow other charities to operate under their charitable status to fund their own activities. How they make money off this, I haven't yet figured out, but they take in a lot of cash."

"Duh," Jenny said. Considering this guy Steve Costner is the chairman, his wife is co-chair, his mother is the treasurer, and his father is the only board member, that can't be good. The money stays in the family. Even I'm not so dumb I can't see the possibility of some kind of a scam going on."

Sara laughed. "You are far from dumb, my dear. A little wet behind the ears, but not dumb."

Jen's slyly calculating expression alerted Sara to an attempt to manipulate her.

"You know, you don't need a college degree to know how to make money."

She waited for Jen to go on.

"If you're not a Mark Zuckerburg or a Bill Gates you can start a 501(c) 3. Or, there's this guy I know at school—a regular geek—who says there are three ways to get rich in this country without too much effort; you start your own religion, or a labor union, or an Internet company, and people give you money. He must not have known about this."

"Forget it. We're not going down that road. You're going back to college next semester."

"Geez. Colleges just teach you how to be an employee. I don't want to work for someone."

This was not the time for that argument. "I have an idea how we might go on from here. There is an FBI office in town. I think we'll pay them a visit and ask about these charities."

"The FBI? Mom, you just can't go waltzing into the FBI and ask about crime. I mean, they'll think you're a terrorist, or something."

Sara laughed. "Don't be so paranoid. I'm a taxpayer and I need information."

Jenny looked at her, puzzled. "What's happened to you since Dad left? You never used to want to get mixed up in stuff like this. You never thought about illegal stuff. You sure never went looking for trouble, and you would have never stayed in a house with a ghost. You'd move out rather than have your vacation spoiled."

Though Jen painted a bleak picture, she'd asked a legitimate question. Her daughter deserved some kind of answer. Could she explain changes she didn't completely understand herself?

"Remember life at home, with you kids and your Dad? My opinion hardly mattered, and you never sought it. I might as well have been invisible. Your dad controlled everything and left all the caretaking to me. I cooked the meals, did all the housekeeping. My opinions weren't considered, but I didn't care. I did my job well, and avoided family dissension. I kept the peace. I found ways to be a person outside the family, like with my theater group and all the committees."

Jen didn't deny any of this, but her silent agreement confirmed an accurate picture of her mother, and it hurt, damn it.

"The divorce set me free from those constraints, and now you're meeting the real me I've always been. The one I kept hidden to avoid argument."

Frowning, Jen took her time before replying. "I never thought you were invisible. I just thought you weren't interested." Her expression, however, admitted the truth. She paused, considering, and then said, "I kind of like being together like this. I'm getting to know my mom and I'm thinking maybe she's pretty neat."

Something wonderful was happening. She and her daughter were bonding—getting to know each other. Sara could have remarked that nobody had ever cared what she thought, but she didn't comment. Instead, she smiled. "Well, thank you. Same here. I'm beginning to think you're a pretty neat daughter." Maybe something good would come out of this trip, after all.

Bringing herself back to the problem at hand, Sara said, "It's all past history. Come on, let's go find the Feds."

Although she'd spoken with confidence about approaching the FBI, she couldn't believe it when they were actually ushered into an office and greeted by a young man dressed in a suit and a tie. A brass plate on his desk identified him as "Mark Walther - Consumer Affairs." He listened patiently to their story after informing them they were being recorded.

"What did you say was the name of this organization?"

"The Congressional Ventures Foundation," Sara said.

His sudden, intense interest surprised her. He pressed a button on his phone and the young woman from the outer office appeared with a notebook and pencil in hand.

"Miss Pace is going to be taking some notes while I ask you some questions."

Jenny asked, "Does this mean, this could be something?"

Walther frowned. "Tell me, Ms. Burkhart, is it? How do you know of this organization?"

"I'm vacationing in New Kensington By-The-Sea, south of here. The chairman of Ventures belongs to a little theater group I've met socially. In fact, his wife is also in the group."

"What caught your interest?"

"He's selling large, as in a million dollars, life insurance policies to members through the organization, telling them the premiums are tax deductible as a contribution to charity. I'm worried that this might be illegal, and I'm afraid some of the friends I've made are going to get into trouble following his advice."

Walther peered thoughtfully at the pen he held. "Although there are too many of these groups for us to monitor closely, once in a while one will stand out because of their activities. This is one of them. Their client list extends to other parts of the country. We've received several complaints, and we've been keeping track of them for several years, but when we get too close, they dissolve and surface as another group. It's a common way to avoid scrutiny."

Sara asked, "Could my friends be in trouble?"

"With the IRS, no doubt. However, what the foundation is doing is allowable. Their clients send the amount of the insurance premium plus a hefty fee to the foundation as a charitable donation, with a receipt recording the transaction as such. Congressional Ventures buys a policy in the client's name. Each year the annual renewal fee is handled the same way, as a charitable contribution."

"Then the client is the one breaking the law by deducting the premium."

"Exactly. It is their decision to do so. These groups also profit by allowing small fundraising groups to temporarily borrow their non-profit designation when filing for their own is too expensive or too complicated. Checks are made out to the foundation, cashed, a fee deducted, and what is left is returned to the client."

"They're getting away with this?"

"Probably. The ones who will suffer are your friends."

Her disappointment growing, Sara said, "So what you're saying is that I should look the other way."

"There's a long history of suspected fraud here, Unfortunately, sometimes it's safer for an amateur like yourself to stay out of it."

"Funny. A friend told me the same thing."

"If you decide to file a formal complaint, I'll help you, and the Bureau is appreciative of your vigilance. Whatever you decide, keep in touch with us. If you hear anything that will help the investigation, call me." He handed her a business card.

"Unfortunately, that is all I can do for you at this time, but I must warn you to be careful. These are clever people and they are not going to give up a lucrative business like this one easily. Good luck, Ms. Burkhart. Miss Pace will see you out."

As quickly as that, the interview ended, and Sara and Jen were on their way out of the building.

"Wow, they sure know how to get rid of someone," Jen said.

"At least we know the Costners are up to no good, and we're onto something, so the day isn't a total waste, and we have plenty of time to get home for the meeting of the Metaphysical Society tonight."

"Mom." Dismay, mixed with disbelief and some scorn. "You're really going to go to that thing?"

That tone could only mean an argument. Jen was her father's daughter—a linear thinker, totally left-brain, without imagination— not ready to accept a bunch of people speculating on the unknown.

"I think you should go with me," Sara said, on impulse. "You've seen Thomas. Are you denying that it happened, even though you can't explain it?"

"Well, no. Are really weird people going to be there?"

"No weirder than us. We believe we live in a haunted house."

"What is metaphysics anyway? Like magic, or stuff?"

"I looked it up on the Internet. As far as I can tell, it involves discussions of things that can't be explained logically, or scientifically, or factually. In other words, supernatural stuff, including ghosts."

At Jen's expression of doubt, Sara chose her words carefully, not wanting to sound too crazy, but the evidence couldn't be denied. Something beyond explanation happened in that house.

"Before the Hubble Telescope allowed us to see beyond our world, we thought we had it all figured out. We believed we were the only life in a galaxy within a universe, on a planet revolving around the sun. Now we know there are universes beyond us with galaxies and planets, and worlds almost beyond our imagination. The vastness of space is something very few of us can grasp or begin to understand. There is more to life than what we know."

"So why do we have to know anymore? Can't we leave it at that?"

96

"Because, every day, events happen. We experience things we can't explain, like ghosts of those long dead suddenly putting in an appearance—like visions of the future, or glimpses of another world."

"But that's just superstition. It isn't real."

"Then who did you see in the kitchen last night?" Jenny's face wore a frown. It fascinated Sara to watch her daughter awaken to something beyond herself, and become engaged in coming to term with new thoughts.

"But if some of this stuff is true, it changes everything," Jenny said. "What else is out there we don't know about?"

"Well, that's what metaphysics is all about—looking for what else is out there." "Okay. I'll go with you, but only to make sure you don't get too weirded out. This new version of Mom is taking some getting used to."

Chapter Eleven

The conversational roar of more than fifty people greeted Sara and Jenny when they arrived at the church, indicating how popular these society meetings had become. The crowd waited to hear Dr. Price Gorman, the guest speaker, retired from academia and presently the darling of the talk show circuit, and author of *We Know You Are Out There*. Clover met them at the door and led them to a table set up with urns of coffee, iced tea, and several plates of cookies.

After introducing Jen, Sara said, "I didn't realize metaphysics was such a popular subject. I'm amazed to find a goodly portion of the town's population present. I met some of these people at Adrienne Fowler's party last week. I wouldn't have suspected they were interested in tonight's subject."

Clover's tolerant smile made her realize how judgmental that sounded, which gave her a moment of guilt. The young woman was probably used to people regarding her as a little 'off center,' but not from Sara, supposed to be her friend. Those East Partridge prejudices had a way of sneaking up on a person.

"Many of the members of our local theater group are regulars at these meetings," Clover said. "The one you've been asking about, Steve Costner, is over there with Binki Wagner."

"How did you know I've been asking questions about Steve?"

Clover shrugged. "Everybody knows you're interested in his insurance plan. They can't help but wonder why."

Damn small town serendipity. Steve wouldn't welcome me prying into his business. This was not good. He'd already made it apparent he didn't like me.

"Clover, glad you could come, friend." A young woman dressed like Clover in sandals and a flowing dress, her hair worn long and loose, came up and hugged her. "Did you notice Binki? I'm really worried. Her aura has grown much worse."

Clover nodded toward Sara. "This is my friend Melanie, the one I told you about who reads auras. This is Sara Burkhart and her daughter, Jenny. They are living in the Stuart house for two months."

"Oh, hi, Sara," Melanie said, clearly distracted, and continued, "I wish Brian would take my warning seriously."

Clover glanced over to where Binki's husband, Brian, stood next to her, glaring at Steve Costner, who had assumed a proprietary stance by her side. Brian looked angry, in fact ready to explode and Steve appeared to be enjoying the moment.

"You do what you can, Melanie," Clover said. "He doesn't believe. His jealousy blinds him to everything else."

Sara had caught the remark about Binki. "What did you mean, her aura's getting worse?"

"There's so much black and dark blue. She is suffering great psychic pain and is very unhappy. It is not a good sign. She should have help before she harms herself."

Sara took a good look at Binki and noticed how she huddled, with her arms wrapped around her shoulders. She looked tense and drawn. With all her obvious insecurities, it couldn't be easy for Binki, living with a control freak like Brian who hovered, looking for the slightest mistake, expecting, at any minute he'd call attention to some inadequacy. Sara recognized the type, an extreme version of Richard, bordering on abuse. Her complaint about her own marriage dimmed by comparison.

Binki appeared lonely, standing there, like she needed a friend. Sara decided she'd find a way to talk to her this evening.

Cora approached with Henry in tow. "Well, look who's here. I didn't know you were interested in metaphysics."

Sara shrugged. "It's lately become an interest of mine. I think living in Stuart House has something to do with it." She glanced around the room. "It looks like a lot of the Village Players are interested too."

Cora frowned and changed the subject. "Living in that house can get spooky at times, but it's a wonderful vacation spot," she said, ready to defend her property.

Henry nodded, agreeing. "Things happen around here that are hard to explain, the weather, for instance. Ain't behaving as usual. There are lots of sudden storms that don't come from the usual places. Things don't feel right. Rumors say the house is right in the middle of it."

Sara frowned. This was the first she'd heard that, but now was not an opportune time to pursue the subject. Cora and Henry were looking at Clover and Jen with interest, reminding her she hadn't made introductions. Cora's short lecture when she picked up the key to the house reminded her that additional guests would cost extra. "Cora and Henry, meet my daughter, Jen, who is with me for a few days, and my neighbor, Clover and her friend Melanie," she said. "We were discussing auras. Melanie thinks Binki is unhappy."

"Humph." Cora threw a disgusted look toward where Binki stood. "If Costner doesn't stop hanging around her, that situation is going to turn nasty. I don't know what he's thinking. Steve keeps sniffing around her like a dog in heat."

"Plain to me what he's thinking," Henry muttered.

Sara nodded agreement. "Steve and his wife remind me of a couple I know at home. They could sense a marriage in trouble and liked to meddle, I think, to create dissension. They got off on seeing other people fight."

Jenny, eager to get back to the subject of Stuart House, asked, "How can a house cause storms?"

Clover responded, holding her hands as though enclosing something round. "The vortex of powerful energy centered there has increased in the last months. It has attracted the notice of others. The woman with our speaker tonight is from further south, a location in the South Carolina hills. She's here to investigate because they've detected the increased energy."

"Oh, no," Sara said, "Does that mean we won't be discussing parallel universes? I came to learn something about the subject."

"What are parallel universes?" Jenny asked.

Melanie smiled, ready to explain. "There is a belief that time, as the fourth dimension, is split into many planes, each with its own space in the millennium. A duplicate of this one exists, with life going on just as it is here, but ahead or behind us in time, only we don't usually connect. There could be another alternate universe beside us, in this room, without our knowing it."

"So what does that mean?"

"It is believed that occasionally one will slip through a warp, to another plane and see themselves in another time."

Jenny looked first at Sara and then at the rest of the group, obviously not buying the explanation. "You all believe this?" Sara didn't respond because Clover had taken her hand to lead her to the front of the room.

"Mr. Gorman," she said to the speaker, "here is my friend, Sara Burkhart, who lives in Stuart House."

"Welcome." He replied, and indicating his partner, said, "This is Elizabeth Van Dorn, an expert in astral phenomena, from South Carolina."

Before Sara could respond, his female companion demanded, "How did you come to be in the house? What have you felt since you've been there?"

Sara stepped back, alarmed by her intense gaze. "I'm here by chance. I wanted to rent a beach house for a vacation and this one became available."

"There is a strong imbalance of energy near that house. The vortex is reaching a critical mass."

Elizabeth Van Dorm definitely personified spooky. Sara didn't want to get into her beliefs any deeper. Thomas provided all the unease she could handle. "Call me anytime," she said, to forestall the conversation. "Come by for a visit."

"Would you please be seated?" Without any further discussion, the hostess called the meeting to order and, after a brief introduction, Dr. Gorman began by asking, "Who here has had a paranormal experience?"

Sara was surprised when a shy, elderly woman, dressed in jeans and a t-shirt, appearing very average, and not the least bit 'odd,' or prone to flights of fancy, raised her hand.

"Uh, I'm visiting and not from around here," she began, "but I heard about this meeting. I had a strange thing happen to me last week and it sounded like some place I could come and talk about it without anybody wondering if I imagined it. Maybe you could help me understand."

Gorman's welcoming smile could be likened to that of a TV evangelist at donation time. "You're among understanding friends here," he said, "so tell us about it."

After hesitating a moment, she began, "I'd just finished up dinner." She paused. "I live alone, and my thoughts were of my brother and his wife. The light dimmed and I realized I was with them in their living room in Oregon, a thousand miles from my home, and they were talking about her being pregnant, and then they were gone."

The room remained hushed, the audience caught up in the story. "The whole thing lasted about thirty seconds, then the light brightened, and the image faded. That was it. The next day I called. They'd just found out they were having a baby."

Gorman beamed with approval. "Many of the people I interviewed while researching my book reported similar experiences. I believe you passed through a time portal into their universe, happening at the same time. You're sure you weren't dreaming?"

"Absolutely not."

Jenny, fascinated, asked, "How can that happen?"

He acknowledged her question. "It happens all the time. If our minds are not open to the possibility, we think we dreamed it. There is evidence to suggest that whatever exists in this time also is existing simultaneously in another time, or parallel universe."

Sara shook her head in denial. No way did she think she dreamed that dockside tavern. She asked, "If it's possible to see the future or the past, is it possible to go there?"

"You're referring to time travel, which is a little different, where you are not merely observing an event, you are actually there. I have no knowledge of this happening, but I won't discount the possibility."

Sara waited. If someone else believed in this, could it be true?

Okay, I'm ready to admit it really happened. I know it did. What about the sand on my feet? The splinters? The smell on my clothes? Have I been traveling back in time, and if I did it again, would it ever happen that I couldn't get back?

"There is a theory," Gorman continued. "If man could travel at the speed of light, time would stand still and when he slowed down, he would be in a later time than when he started. He would end up sometime in the future. Since no one has ever gone that fast, we don't know. That is an oversimplification but we're not here seeking the technical or the scientific explanations. We'll leave that to the physicists while we explore our experiences with these inexplicable happenings."

"What about wormholes?" The voice came from the back of the room and, although Sara had never heard of a wormhole, she realized, from the nodding heads, that some of the audience had.

"Some theorize that wormholes are vortexes in the time-space continuum, open at either end. There is conjecture that if one were sucked into a wormhole they could possibly emerge at the other end in another time or place. In other words, there are portals to the past or the future through which you might travel in time and return. There is no limit to the possibilities, or to the size of what is being transported. Whole worlds could disappear."

"It could explain how whole civilizations could have vanished without a trace," a voice from the back of the room offered, "or maybe showed up someplace in another form."

Sara recognized the speaker as someone who had been at Adrienne's party. Her mind reeled. Could it be? Could that explain the disappearance of an entire town? She raised her hand.

"Then what you are saying is that time travel, if conditions are right, is possible? I mean to go back or move forward in time?"

Gorman smiled at her, showing his delight in her interest. "Ah yes, but you wouldn't want to go back. Too dangerous."

"Why?"

"The *Grandfather Paradox*. What if you accidentally killed someone—say, gave him or her a fatal case of the measles? If that person were destined to be your grandfather, you would never be born, wouldn't exist, therefore you couldn't get back to your time."

The spirit she'd encountered had urged her to help. What if she changed history? Fear of the unknown consequences held her in a cold grip.

"Well," someone commented, "we can't travel at the speed of light."

Gorman smiled. "Wrong. There is something that already does. Thought. What if thought could be projected through a wormhole?"

The audience stayed silent, considering. Sara's imagination hummed.

"I have another question. What if one of those people from the past came here?"

Elizabeth Van Dorn intervened. "There is speculation that if that should happen and a traveler should meet himself living in another time, the time/space continuum would be shattered and they would both be destroyed."

Another member asked, "Has it ever happened that a whole group of people moved from one dimension to another?"

Wow. Where did that come from? There's someone else in this room that suspects it's possible.

"Do you mean," the professor asked, "simply vanished?"

Elizabeth Van Dorn eagerly jumped into the discussion. "There are accounts of this happening, especially in Europe. There is a record of an entire village disappearing in Italy in the seventeenth century, and other similar accounts in France."

"Brigadoon," a voice murmured.

Sara suddenly remembered Henry's account of the people of Port Kensington gone after the hurricane.

"What happens to them? Do they show up somewhere else?" The same voice from the audience called out. She heard murmuring throughout the room. The subject apparently had caught the interest of the crowd.

"Wouldn't they know where they were?" Another spectator queried.

"I can offer a theory," Miss Van Dorn replied. "It is thought that they have new identities, perhaps replacing the spirits of those who have vanished in some disaster that precipitated the event. They have those genetic memories, unaware they belong to someone else, so they appear perfectly normal. Some theorists have even suggested that they change gender, the men coming back as women, and so on."

The room exploded in excited conversation. Sara was stunned. She needed to think about it. She'd never been so intrigued.

Dr. Gorman raised his hand, begging for attention. "Our time is up for this evening. Please, partake of the refreshments."

The evening ended to enthusiastic applause, and Sara and Jen rose to leave.

"Mom, do you believe this?" Jenny looked at her, doubt and excitement mingled in her expression. "I've read about time travel but always in fiction. One of my favorite books is about an English doctor who finds a thing—I'd guess something like a vortex—and she can enter it and go back hundreds of years to the Scottish Highlands."

"Yes, I think there is some truth to it. I'll tell you about it when we get home."

"Oh, wow. What if it's true? How dope is that?"

Cora interrupted before she went any further. Sara sighed with relief. She wasn't ready to explain her trip to the 1800s.

"Sara, there is a gathering at Adrienne's house tomorrow night. Some of us are meeting to start putting together a music show for the holidays. You're invited, and Jenny too, of course. Colin is going to be there."

"Colin?" Jenny asked, her interest unmistakable.

"Yeah, he plays a pretty good guitar and everybody knows him."

"Please, Mom, could we go?" Jenny pleaded, apparently interested in being anywhere with Colin.

"Sure, why not? We'll meet you there."

Although Sara had decided to take a chance that her daughter would think she'd lost it by telling her about her time in 1860 New Kensington, it was not to be. She needed time to herself to explore her thoughts. Jen chattered all the way home like a squirrel on steroids, and didn't stop when they reached the house.

"Mom, you said when you were at the library the librarian told you that most of the members of the local theater group came to town at the same time."

"Oh, come on, Jen. You're letting your imagination run away with you."

"Yeah? What if there's a group here, and Thomas is one of them? What if he's from the past and he's been living here in another body? He could be a woman."

Dear God. What if? Her daughter was mirroring her own thoughts. "Jen, stop it. You're letting your imagination run away with you. If I'd thought you were going to freak out like this, I would have never brought you along. The same cold that had enveloped her at the meeting was back. It was too frightening to believe.

"Jen, stop. I'm not going to talk about this anymore tonight. Go to bed."

"I'm going to tell Colin. I'll bet he knows more about it."

Sara sighed, watched her daughter head for the upstairs, and followed her, first making sure there weren't other presences in the room.

Chapter Twelve

By the time Sara and Jenny arrived at Adrienne's the next evening, quite a crowd had already assembled, enjoying themselves in the living room. Some of the people who'd been at the cast party last week were there. A large number of locals, including teenagers, lounged in chairs and occupied most of the floor space. Judging from the enthusiastic discussion of the proposed Christmas program, they shared a common interest in music and theater, and were clearly comfortable with each other. Colin sat with a group congregated in one corner, and Jenny immediately left to join them. Though Sara told herself she understood Jen's need to be with people her own age, there was some hurt there from being dismissed. Apparently hanging out with mom was not cool.

Georgia caught Sara's eye from across the room and came over to stand beside her. "The teens were part of the cast of last year's production of *West Side Story.* We're thinking we can do highlights for this variety show." Sara noticed, with relief, that the hosts were not serving alcohol, probably because of the young age of some of the guests. She didn't know if her daughter drank.

"We have some talented blues artists here, too," Bob Fowler, Adrienne's husband, remarked, coming up behind her. "Glad you could make it, Sara, and bring your daughter. My wife says you're really settling in, getting to know people."

Did she detect disapproval in his tone?

"Your daughter and Colin look like an item."

Surprised, she glanced at Jen and Colin. They were caught up in each other.

"She's helping him with his speech." Bob didn't need to know the boy was staying at her house. It was none of his business.

Bob glanced beyond her. "Oh, damn, here comes trouble. Brian is looking for Binki, who's standing over there with Steve."

Sara remembered Cora's critical comment about Brian's jealousy of his wife. The stress signals emanating from that young woman were so obvious she didn't have to read an aura to know she needed to be rescued. "I saw Binki at last night's metaphysical meeting and didn't get a chance to talk to her. I think I'll go on over."

"You've got guts, girl," Georgia said. "Those two men look like they're ready to kill anyone who comes near, but I wouldn't worry about Binki."

"Why?"

"Well," Georgia said, "we all know her. Today she's been happy. She told me that she has everything worked out. She's decided not to care what anybody thinks and be at peace."

Georgia's choice of words got Sara's attention. A sudden shift from severe depression to euphoria was a red flag for attempted suicide. Sara had taken a course on the subject when she'd volunteered for a hot line. Alarmed at the possible significance of the remark, Sara asked, "At peace? Isn't that a strange thing to say? It could be a sign that she'd made a decision to end the problem."

"Yeah, it was a little odd, but look at the hostility between those two men. Maybe she's finally decided to leave Brian. She's wanted to have a baby for a long time and he won't hear of it. Says he likes her figure just the way it is."

"Poor kid. That alone is reason enough to leave him."

"Don't get involved," Georgia warned. "He has a mean temper."

"Okay. It isn't any of my business, so I'll stay out of it, but when someone is as obviously unhappy as that woman, and suddenly insists that she's okay—well, that can be a bad sign."

Sylvie Costner's strident voice took command of the room. ""I thought we were discussing a music program for the Christmas show. Could we get on with the discussion? I don't have all night."

"I s-sing." Colin's words brought stunned silence to the room.

Sara glanced at him, his face flushed, sitting shyly beside her daughter. Reactions from the crowd were mixed between discomfort from the adults and cheers from the younger bunch. His handicap was common knowledge, but it seemed his friends knew better.

"Oh, please," Sylvie said, her voice full of scorn, "How can he sing? He stutters." Silence deadened the room, instantly ending all conversation. The guests, embarrassed at her rudeness, stared at the floor.

Jenny broke the silence coming to his defense. Her gaze was fixed on Colin's face. It showed love, and support. "Sometimes people who stammer find singing easier than talking." She took his hand, ready to do battle.

The look of near-worship on Colin's face when he looked at Jen, shook her. They undoubtedly had a connection there. Oh, Lord, Jen had grown up when she wasn't looking.

I'm not ready for this. Where have I been while this was happening right under my nose?

Just as she and her daughter were developing a relationship, she was losing her to a boy.

"I've heard of that," Cora said, attempting to soothe the waters. "I read somewhere that people with a stammer can sing because the words come easier."

Sara nodded. "He's been working with my daughter and making progress."

"Butt out, city woman," Sylvie exploded, her face twisted with hate, "We don't need outsiders telling us what to do or what to think."

Sara stared, speechless with shock. Sylvie had turned on her with a reaction totally uncalled for; her anger seemed directed toward something else.

Bob Fowler intervened. "I say we give the kid a chance. Back off, Sylvie," he added, the warning in his voice unmistakable.

There were murmurs of assent from every corner of the room.

"For crying out loud, Sylvie," Georgia said, "Can't you get your mind off yourself for even a minute?"

Adrienne jumped in, clearly alarmed. "Sylvie, that was uncalled for. We've all known Colin most of his life and we love him. He's one of ours and he's just given us amazing news. I, for one, want to give him a chance."

Jenny said, "We've been practicing his speech when we're alone. The singing was a surprise, but he's very good."

"Can you sing something for us?" Bob asked, glancing at his wife with a silent message.

Sara caught the look. *They know I've been nosing around and they're worried. Sylvie's anger is directed at me.*

"Go on Colin, " Jenny said, "sing our song. You can do it."

"Please," Adrienne pleaded.

Colin smiled at Jen; his expression so trusting it brought tears to Sara's eyes. He pointed to a friend's guitar, which was handed over to him without a word, and he sat in a chair, the instrument in his lap. The room was silent, everyone holding their breath, some clearly worried that he might embarrass himself. Sara prayed he'd be okay.

After a little experimenting with chords, he began. His beautiful baritone voice caressed the words softly, adding a Southern twang, much like Randy Travis in his prime—pure magic. It held the room in thrall.

"How will I tell her that I love her,
When I know the words won't be there?
How can I tell her I need her,
Let her know how much I care?
I pray to God that for a little while,
She'll understand
How very much I love her, when I hold her hand."

The last chord of the guitar faded, and he gently leaned forward and caught the tear on Jen's cheek with his thumb. For a moment all in the room were beyond speech.

Sara watched through her own tears, resigned that yet another complication had entered her life. The total devotion mirrored in the eyes of the two teenagers hit her like a sledgehammer. Blindsided by the intensity of her reaction, she was at a loss, for a moment, to identify it. Then it hit.

I'm jealous of my daughter, jealous of her relationship with Colin, and grief-stricken at the thought losing my newfound closeness with her.

A special kind of loneliness engulfed her. She wanted someone to share her life and her thoughts. For the last few days Jen had been hers to enjoy. Now all that belonged to Colin and she was alone again. The depth of her loneliness, and the anguish at her loss, threatened to bring her to her knees, weeping. It was simply too much. The divorce, the trip, the house, and the ghosts we're robbing her of her sanity. She was going crazy.

How had it happened that she'd become so needy? She'd always disdained suddenly single women who couldn't handle being alone; who settled for the first man to show an interest in them, ending up in a miserable relationship they couldn't get out of. She'd had feelings, however tentative, for Galen and even Thomas. What did that make her? No way would she succumb to "desperate woman syndrome." Nope, she wouldn't go there. She was stronger than that.

Georgia broke the silence by exclaiming, "Colin, you're awesome. That sure trumps my 'Adelaide's Lament'. We have a new star in our midst." The room erupted in applause.

Colin, smiling widely, said, "T-t-thank you."

"That just about done me in," Cora said, blotting her eyes with a tissue. "What say we call it a night and take up our discussion later in the week?"

Jen approached, Colin in tow. "Mom. Can I have the keys to the car? It's early and we want to hang out with the other kids."

"I'll drop you off at the house, Sara," Cora volunteered. "You're looking too tired to walk."

Still struggling with her emotions, Sara managed to say, "Sure." Maybe it was out of line, because they were both old enough, but she couldn't resist being a mom. "I know it's Friday, but not too late, 0kay?"

Jen rolled her eyes as she took the keys and walked away, leaving Sara resigned to spending the rest of the evening alone.

Cora patted her on the shoulder, saying, "They all have to grow up someday."

Chapter Thirteen

Sara watched, from the driveway, while the taillights of the Arthur's car grew smaller and finally disappeared. Stuart House loomed in front of her, filling the sky. Its windows, like so many black eyes, stared vacantly, telling of the emptiness within. The wash of white light from the rising moon did nothing to soften the forbidding darkness. She was alone again.

A great wave of despair washed over her, and with it reminders of the last remnants of everything in her life that she'd lost in the last months—memories too much to bear.

Hanging on to her composure by a thin thread, she gripped the rail for support, trudged up the stairs, and entered the house to seek the refuge of the porch, where she let the tears come. With a mournful cry she grieved for the home she'd had, the familiar comfort of her old kitchen, the lost loyalties of friends, and finally, desertion of the worst kind from the man to whom she'd given twenty years of her life.

"Women's tears?" The male voice taunted her. "What disaster could possibly warrant this display of emotion?"

Thomas stood on the porch, legs spread, arms folded across his chest. His amused glint regarded her; his lips lifted in a fond smile full of sensual promise. He looked very much like the master of a sailing ship. At that moment, with her emotions in such turmoil, she needed comfort and reassurance so badly even a ghost would do, if he had enough substance to hold her in his arms.

"Thomas." She didn't care if her glad cry disclosed her need. It happened so fast. Without appearing to move, his strong arms wrapped around her, holding her securely. She feasted on the warm comfort of his rock-solid chest and drew on the strength of his body. He smelled of the ocean, and salt air, mingled with the pungent scent of tobacco; familiar odors that pulled her out of her misery, comforted her, and protected her from the fierce wind that suddenly gusted onto the porch, bring with it salt spray.

"Come now," he crooned, placing a soothing kiss on her cheek, tasting her tears. He became every romantic fantasy she'd ever had about a desirable man.

His voice whispered in her ear. "Tell me all, Dearling. I've seen appalling destruction, experienced unbearable agony, and witnessed obscenely cruel death. Tell me what distresses you enough to bring tears." He held her, offering her all his strength.

Emotions, long buried and almost forgotten, surfaced, ravaging her senses. Her heart hammered. Her nerve endings tingled with sexual attraction until, finally, the shock of what was happening, hit her. This wasn't real.

Comfort from an apparition? How crazy was that? While her mind denied it, her soul yearned for it. Emotional needs created the fantasy of this scene.

Reason returned in full force, but still she held on. Unconditional support such as Thomas offered, had never been given to her, even in the darkest moments of her marriage. Richard had no tolerance for female tears. At the first sign of emotion he'd get angry and denounce her for trying to manipulate him. She'd always had to be the strong one; it was her job to endure. It was expected of her, her assigned role.

The temptation to yield was too strong to resist. She relaxed against Thomas, allowing him to support her weight as she struggled for control. There was so much of him. His strength surrounded her—keeping her safe from collapsing, weak-kneed.

Go with it, her inner voice urged her. Worry about sanity later.

"Ah, that's better," he murmured, while his lips roamed along the curve of her chin. "Your body is learning to trust mine." He took her hand and led her to one of the lounges, seated her gently, and returned to the porch rail. As suddenly as he left her, the wind ceased, and quiet returned.

"Sara, Dearling, tell me what plagues you?" His voice gentled to tease her. "I'd have thought women of your time were a formidable lot, rarely afflicted with bouts of female emotion."

The jibe was enough to restore her balance. She took a deep breath, grabbed for a tissue from the covered box on the table beside her, and regained control, embarrassed because she had to blow her nose. Hardly a romantic thing to do, but she felt better already, and a little foolish about such a display.

Determined to free herself from this emotional tangle, she said, "Forgive me for subjecting you to that. After all, you're a stranger. I don't really know you."

His expression shuttered. He gripped the porch rail, as if angered. Stunned at his withdrawal, she wondered how to get him back.

"Forgive me my presumption, Madam. Your demeanor and your style of dress led me to believe, in your time, that familiarity between a man and woman would be welcome."

He'd just called her a 'loose woman.' He really thought she was coming on to him? Not ready to give up on the moment, and figuring she had nothing to lose, she spoke what was in her heart. "No, Thomas. Your . . ." she searched for a word to replace familiarity, came up empty, and began again. "I felt some sort of friendship to you, as though I know you. Your . . . caring was most welcome."

"Sara, I'm a man of the sea, with no time for a wife and marriage." He voiced cold disapproval of her behavior. "I have women, of course, but only for pleasure, and I try to give some in return. This is of no consequence."

Well, wasn't that a bucket of ice water? She felt more the fool every minute.

"Sara, I know not what devilish mischief brought me here, some fey bit of witchery, no doubt. I know that I am drawn to you."

She snorted, indelicately. A pick-up line, Victorian style. "You expect me to believe that?" Eyeing him doubtfully, she continued, "You're a handsome man and I'm guessing rather well off financially. I don't doubt there are women in your life from your own time. You can't stay under the radar forever."

"Radar? What is this radar you speak of?"

"Never mind. It's too complicated to explain."

"You are known to me, yet I do not know you," he said, "for we've never met in my time. I do not understand how this is possible. This connection confounds me. I want to know what deviltry is afoot." He paused, returned to sit beside her, and took her hand in his.

She held on, surprised that his fingers were warm where she had expected a spirit to be cold. "In my time, we call it an emotional meltdown," she said. "I came home to an empty house, and realized I was entirely alone. I had no one in my life. This is a new thing for me. I used to have a husband and a family. Having you here makes it all seem so trivial. I don't imagine sea captains, with all their responsibilities, ever experience that kind of loneliness."

He regarded her thoughtfully. "I am a man of the sea. I speak in terms of the sea, a life strange to you. What know I of aloneness? How will I give voice to this?" He paused, rose, walked to the porch railing, and turned, regarding her as though considering his next words.

"Imagine being alone in a very small boat in the middle of the ocean with no land, no ship in sight, nor any sign, or even memory, of a human presence—or the possibility of it—any time soon. It will be years before you will feel land beneath your feet. The worst of it is that there is no sound to recall other life. All you hear is the water caressing the side of the small craft. Endless darkness below—perhaps a thousand feet before any hint of solid bottom, and lurking there, in the black, watery depths, are any number of un-named demons rising to the surface to devour you. You are engulfed in an isolation so deep it tears at your soul."

Shocked at the picture he'd painted of life at sea, Sara said, "Your description makes my outburst absurd. I stand corrected. I felt nothing to compare to it."

He nodded with satisfaction, indicating clearly he had, once again, taken control of the situation. His arrogance returned.

"You possibly have another question, Madam?"

Now was her chance to learn something about him. "Thomas, when we were last together you made a reference to Felicity. Who was Felicity?" The grief on his face warned her that something terrible was coming.

"She was my sister. We had a fondness for each other and she trusted me. I failed to protect her."

"How so?"

"I should have seen it. She was such a vital person, but so restless and discontented, demanding that my brother give her a place in the business; so unlike her sister, Mélange, who was so fearful of our involvement in the war and what it would mean. Our last evening together, at a family gathering, Mélange argued bitterly against a venture I was pursuing that, although risky, would increase our fortunes considerably. I had kept the plans secret. She was afraid the plan would be discovered, and there would be disastrous repercussions."

Irritated, he continued, "Her concerns were inappropriate for a female. Women should not concern themselves with manly matters. They are born needing no more than marriage and children.

"Felicity never accepted her marriage, which my parents arranged when she was still a child. The man was a tyrant, and twenty years her senior. I was at sea for years at a time, so I didn't realize how unhappy she was until my last visit home. I should have heard her desperation. She felt her marriage was a prison from which there was no escape. I was her last hope."

"What happened?"

"One evening, shortly before I was due to leave on another voyage, the family, as was our custom, gathered with friends for a social evening. I could see all was not well between my sister and her husband. She pleaded that I take her along when I set sail on what would be an absence of at least two years. Indeed, she appeared most desperate to escape her circumstances." He paused, frowning, regret showing on his face.

"In truth, the idea was not without precedent. For women to accompany their husbands to sea was an accepted idea in our circles, although life aboard a whaler was too harsh for most women. Some wives of sea captains traveled with their husbands constantly, but a separation of this sort for Felicity, leaving her husband, was unheard of. She would be ruined socially. I denied her. I will never forget the look she gave me as her irate husband drew her away."

A chill crept through Sara's bones—foreboding of what came next. How could she know anything of an event that happened a hundred and sixty years ago?

"I had no idea my denial would be the last straw, the one that almost destroyed her."

He paused. The anguish on his face chilled her heart. "I should have realized, from her cold, resolved demeanor, that my answer was unacceptable." His voice caught. His eyes glistened with tears held firmly in check. "Felicity left the room and, in the ensuing hours, tried to take her own life with a heavy dose of laudanum."

Shocked, Sara quietly gave him a moment with his grief before she spoke. "Oh, Thomas, I'm so sorry."

"As luck would have it, she didn't quite succeed. The scandal ruined her, of course. I learned, when I returned from sea, that her husband denounced her. Cast her out. My mother took to her bed. It took months for the family to recover.

"Maybe you could have delayed your departure to give her time to understand?"

He stood, his face twisted in a scowl, and returned to the railing to pace.

"No. Not possible," he said, dismissing her concern with a disdainful glance. "I had to leave. The timing was everything.

"Whaling is in my blood, it is who I am, as it is with all of us who ply the trade. I cannot stay away. I crave the excitement of the kill. Even a few weeks on land gives rise to restlessness. I live to be at sea, hunting the leviathan. It is the measure of a man."

The graphic pictures of whale slaughter were too fresh in Sara's mind. His declaration struck her as selfish. "Proving your manhood? That's what driving to extinction those magnificent creatures is all about?"

He stared at her, affronted, before answering. "I am a very wealthy man through my endeavors."

Sara sighed at the all-too-familiar, typically male response. Regardless of his romantic origin, he disappointed her. "But that isn't the thrill, is it? Why whales? There were many ways to become rich in your time."

He smiled, tolerant, willing to forgive, as though she were a small child who needed a pat on the head. "You have never known the triumph of besting a bull sperm whale."

He was not only disappointing, but also patronizing. This interlude was turning sour. Right before her eyes, Thomas was rapidly losing his luster, proving to be simply another man.

"You cannot ken its size. They weigh upwards of fifty tons. You must see it to believe such a creature can exist, up to seventy feet long—longer than this house—his head nearly a full two stories high. He is a demon put in the sea by God to test man." His expression took on a fanatic glow. "Indeed, the Bible tells us to go forth in the name of God to slay the dragon that is in the sea."

When turned toward her, his expression was one of a man caught in an evangelistic fervor. "The creature's death throes can go on for days, until finally, when he surfaces to sound, there is blood in the spout. It is time for the harpooner to strike the killing blow." His voice shook with anticipation.

Sara clenched her teeth to dispel the nausea that lurked, seconds away. The man she'd begun to admire was obsessed with killing for the thrill of it.

"Thomas, what joy can be had in slaying such a beautiful creature simply to prove your manhood?"

Head raised, nostrils flaring, he reacted to being challenged and, with an arrogant sneer, demanded, "What is there in your time? What test of courage is there? What acts ensure the making of a man?"

Richard's words echoed in her mind. *I want to do it all over again. The struggle. The uncertainty. The excitement. I want taking risks, not knowing how it'll turn out. Damn it, Sara, I want to feel young again.*

Thomas had the truth of it. In her time there were no more mountains to climb, no seas to conquer. Was that what a man's life was all about?

"You're right, you know," she said, finally understanding. "Odd that I should learn that from a man who possibly might not even be here. Are you a figment of my imagination, something I conjured up to satisfy some longing in my life?"

"Figment?" Thomas roared, his voice charged with anger, body straightened, ready for battle. "I am no figment, Madam. I am a man."

She shrank from him in fear. Apparently he couldn't tolerate being criticized.

Rapidly he closed the distance between them, took her shoulders in a bruising grip, and lifted her up. When her face was level with his, he shook her, his anger palpable. "By God, Madam, you will show me some respect."

This was another Thomas, frightening in his fury. "You think I am not aware of your attempt to undermine my plans? Your sympathies may not lie with the South, Mélange, but your loyalties should be to this family."

What was this? His mind was elsewhere, in another conversation.

"You're meddling in something you don't understand. You are a simple female, caring only about your creature comforts, with no comprehension of how the world works. Whatever it takes to survive, I will do, and you and my brother can both rot in hell for interfering."

She tried to find her voice, but her mouth was as dry as dust. Because of some stupid, romantic fantasy she could be dead in minutes.

"Thomas," she managed, barely. His grip was like iron. "You're hurting me."

Her plea was lost in the return of the wind that rose suddenly, battering the house until it shook. A lamp overturned and shattered when it fell to the floor.

Caleb, thank God. Caleb was here.

She felt the anger engulfing Thomas, who dropped her, staggering in a fight for his balance. He writhed against the force of it, becoming transparent, struggling, as he faded, in the grip of an awful, howling rage. His last words were an angry shout.

"No, damn you, let go. Leave me be."

He vanished, leaving Sara in a frightened heap on the lounge.

Her heart pounded so hard; it was difficult to draw breath. Her arms would show bruises tomorrow. For sure the fantasy of a romantic liaison with a handsome ghost had vanished along with the man.

Through all this, one thing had become clear. Thomas was fanatically obsessed with some illegal activity that made him dangerous if crossed. But how did this concern her? Was it because she happened to be here, in this house, and therefore available?

She felt it somehow involved the present-day residents of New Kensington. Without a doubt, her questions about the Ventures Foundation had triggered their alarm. A fragment of memory teased her—something about this part of town being wiped out by a hurricane—everything gone, with only Stuart House left.

Soon after, New Kensington Estates came into being and Costner and his friends moved in. A hundred years before that, a hurricane had wiped out Port Kensington. Those people had vanished, down to the last man.

Oh my God.

Her mind reeled with the possibility. No, it was too far-fetched even to imagine, but what if . . .?

However impossible, the idea nibbled at the edges of her mind. What if the vortex Clover told of really did exist? What if there really was a wormhole? What if some of the people in this town were re-living a former life? Not so far-fetched, considering everything else that had happened.

The next idea followed, logically. What if the event her house ghost kept referring to was some mistake from the past, and the survivors of that event were trapped in a parallel universe, reliving history in modern terms, over and over until it finally destroyed them? Is that what Caleb had tried to tell her?

You must stop them.

Was that what the message on the glass was about?

What if Thomas were here to prevent her from getting involved? Is she a perceived threat?

The thought completed itself and brought cold fear to her heart.

If that's the case, then her life was in danger and she'd better find out what is going on in her own time if she wanted to survive and go home. There was no escaping this force.

An awful stillness gathered around her. The ocean calmed, rippling like a placid lake. The air chilled. She felt another presence and knew it was Caleb.

"That's it, isn't it?" She knew he listened. "You want this to end, don't you? You want it to stop, here and now—the whole thing—the re-living over and over again. But, I don't know how. Help me. If you brought Thomas here, you owe me, damn it, for that if nothing else."

No reply, only the sighing of the wind and the whisper of the waves.

Tiredness such as she'd never known stole over her. She had to sleep. Her last thought as she climbed the stairs to her room was, maybe tomorrow, after a trip to the library, she'd understand.

Chapter Fourteen

The moment the warmth from the morning sun touched her pillow and awakened her, Sara knew she was not the same person she'd been yesterday. Too much had happened to bring about a change within her. The Metaphysical Society meeting and the subsequent revelations, the meeting at Adrienne's house, Thomas and her awareness of Caleb had all filled some empty place inside her, encouraging her to evolve into a different woman, secure in knowing what she had to do before she could grant herself permission to get on with her life. She had to solve this mystery. She had a purpose. It felt good.

When she opened her eyes, the first thing she saw was a rose lying on her bedside table—not any rose, but a deep pink, fully blown cabbage rose she recognized as an antique variety still prized by collectors. The flower's rich perfume enchanted her.

"Thank you, Caleb," she said to the empty room, with a smile of feminine pleasure. She knew she was being played. The house and its ghost were using her, but she could play this game too.

New thoughts formed along with her new persona. Her being here was no accident; it was preordained, as she'd first suspected. Something coming in her future was meant to be. Excitement coursed through her. Exhilaration. She could remember, exactly, how she chose this location for her getaway from East Partridge, and it wasn't by chance.

The first order of business: to find out what circumstances had brought Caleb Stuart to New Kensington-by-the-Sea. Knowing that might give her clues to her role in this eerie drama.

Without bothering to get dressed, she searched the Internet for information on Massachusetts' role in the Civil War. The bits of information she'd picked up so far convinced her Thomas had some scheme going that involved the War and The Confederacy. If the scheme were discovered it would result in arrest and possible prison for other male members of the Stuart family. She had to know what he planned.

Although Thomas's display of temper had effectively destroyed any romantic illusions she might have had, her involvement wasn't going to end there. She'd never be rid of these ghosts until destiny had been played out. They could follow her home. She had no doubt Thomas was capable of murder.

"Hey, Mom. What's up?" Jen came from the kitchen, a glass of orange juice in her hand. "I borrowed one of your sweat suits, okay? It's cold out and I want to go beach walking. Mine are at home."

Sara looked up, chagrined when reminded that she and her daughter wore the same size. "As long as it isn't my new Jane Lynch, which I intend to wear to the library."

Jen approached the computer screen. "What are you looking up?"

"The Civil War and Massachusetts. I'm trying to find out more about this house. Remember that strange man you saw in the kitchen?"

"The one you said was a ghost?"

Sara nodded. "He was here last night. I thought he was just, you know, not a threat or anything, just something to talk about when we got home."

"And now he isn't?"

"No. He's dangerous and he's related somehow to Caleb, the other ghost haunting the house. He threatened me."

Jen's disbelieving expression challenged her. "Mom, get real. You fell asleep on a chair and dreamed this."

Sara slipped her robe off her shoulders to reveal nasty bruises on her upper arms. "This is where Thomas grabbed me, in anger, when he took exception to something I said."

"Geez. What did you do? How did you get away?"

"I yelled at him and I think Caleb intervened, because there was this cold wind and Thomas started to disappear, then he was gone."

Jen, pale faced and shaken, sat in a chair, her arms hugging her shoulders. "This is getting way too weird. Don't you think we should get out of here?"

"I don't believe you have anything to be frightened of," Sara said, "I'm the one involved, but you have a right to know the whole story."

She wasn't ready to discuss the time travel, and hopefully, Jen would never have to know. She began her recitation with finding Thomas washed up on the beach and ended with last evening, voicing her concern that if she didn't find out what these ghosts wanted from her, they'd never leave her alone.

Once Jen accepted her story, her natural curiosity took over. "You think you knew Thomas in a past life? Like a reincarnation thing, or . . . "Stunned, realization dawned, showing on her face. "Like there's a wormhole around here someplace? Like they said when we were at the meeting?"

"Whoa," Sara said. "You're way ahead of me. I might be able to believe that he lived here at one time and somehow, some of him has been left behind."

"Mom. You must remind him of Felicity or he wouldn't have mistaken you for her. What have you found out so far?"

"For one thing, Felicity was Thomas' sister and she tried to take her own life."

"Oh, geez. Why? Did he say?"

"He blames himself. She was young and unhappy in an arranged marriage to a much older man. She wanted to go along with Thomas on his next voyage, something the wives of ship captains in Port Kensington did frequently."

"Thomas didn't agree?"

"Remember this was the 1800s. Taking his married sister along would have created a scandal, and besides, he believed women didn't have the brains for business. They belonged at home making babies."

Jen nodded. "Some things never change. Sounds like our Thomas was an arrogant, sexist bigot." She shrugged. "Typical."

"He wasn't quite the hero figure I thought at first." Sara didn't realize how deeply her disappointment was reflected in her voice until she caught Jen's speculative gaze, and said, "What?"

"Oh, Mom." Jen came to her and gave her a hug. "I didn't realize how alone you are. You lost everything when Dad booked—your friends, your whole life. I'm sorry."

Sara smiled, grateful for Jen's understanding. "In an unguarded moment, I may have been attracted to him, but I realize it was simply a romantic fantasy. Maybe someday I'll be ready. Not now. Besides, I've discovered I have a pretty wonderful daughter. I'd like to spend more time with her."

Jen, in thought, studied her hands, then said, "I've got to say something that's been bugging me." She frowned, considering, then continued. "I'll admit that when we were all together as a family I behaved like a spoiled brat a lot of the time. When I look back on it, I don't even recognize, sometimes, the person I was. Thank Colin for that. Knowing him has changed me." She paused, her jaw clenched in frustration. "This isn't coming out right, but, like Colin, I don't have the words to express myself."

"It doesn't matter. I can hear the words, even if you aren't saying them. We're both growing into different persons, and the new versions are going to be better than the old." Sara smiled, moved by the moment, while Jen retreated to her chair.

"So, back to our ghost and what he's up to. Any ideas?"

"Well, I've discovered that Massachusetts, in the middle 1800s, was a manufacturing center for guns and weapons. The Springfield Armory was a major supply center for the Union forces during the Civil War. The fighting never reached that far north, but the state, along with New York, sent fighting units to participate. They were definitely for the abolition of slavery and fielded a black regiment to fight the war."

"Well, that's a beginning, but it doesn't suggest anything criminal involving the Stuarts," Jen said.

"You're right. That's why my next stop is going to be the library. I'll let you know what I find out."

"Cool. I'm out of here. Later I'm meeting Colin and we're going to hang out. I'll be home by dinner."

After Jen left, Sara stayed at the computer, still searching, until she heard knocking on the kitchen door. Now what?

In no mood for interruptions, she decided if she ignored the sound, they'd go away, but the visitor persisted. Resigned, she hit "save" and went to answer.

She didn't expect to find Galen, looking devastatingly handsome wearing only swim trunks and sandals, and she certainly didn't expect what he held in his arms. Galen? What in the world? A nearly grown kitten, black as a midnight sky, desperately thin, and covered with sand and probably fleas, complained piteously at being restrained. She appreciated how gentle Galen's hands were while he foiled the kitten's efforts to escape. He had beautiful hands with long fingers. She imagined them roaming over her body and shivered at the thought.

He stood there, a sheepish smile on his face, as though not sure how she'd react, but he must have read something encouraging in her expression. His green eyes softened to a knowing look. He gave her a tentative smile.

"I met Jen out walking. She found this little guy on the beach and said you'd know what to do, and I should bring him here. He looks like he's been on his own for a while, and not making out too well. He's certainly smaller than he should be."

"He needs a meal and a bath." The pathetic mewling of the animal softened what little resistance she tried for. "I thought about getting a cat. I even mentioned it when I was at the library, but Emily told me that I didn't need to look for one. It would find me." Her heart went out to the miserable creature, shivering in Galen's hands.

"Oh, the poor thing." She took him gently, careful of his bones sticking out, and carried him into the kitchen. She laughed. "She said cats knew where they were needed and one would come along."

Galen grinned like a co-conspirator. "I think you're gaining a reputation as a soft touch for needy strays." His knowing look warmed her heart.

The kitten mewed piteously, kicking her mothering instinct into overdrive. "He's starving, Galen. What do cats eat?"

"Damned if I know. I've never owned a cat."

"Neither have I, or a dog. My mother insisted she had allergies and my husband didn't like animals underfoot." She frowned. It made her sound deprived.

With the kitten securely held on one arm, she searched the fridge.

"We have milk," she muttered. "Kittens are supposed to like milk. Strawberry yogurt? Probably not. Aha. Turkey lunch meat, and ham."

Cats probably ate cereal, but sugared oat clusters? No way. While Galen watched, amused, she put the kitten on the table, and started with a bowl of milk and some shredded meat, which it attacked voraciously. Fascinated, she watched, as its scrawny body seemed to fill out before her eyes.

Galen looked at her with a knowing grin. "I've heard that if you feed a stray cat, he's yours forever. So I guess you'll keep him?"

She smiled back, delighted. "Of course I'm keeping him. He's a gift. Since he'll be the house cat, I'm going to call him Caleb."

She wasn't prepared for the stunned expression on Galen's face.

"Where did you come up with that name? What does it mean to you?" His reaction was way over the top. What was that all about?

"It's the name of the man who built this house. It seems appropriate. What does it matter to you?"

He tried for casual, but didn't quite pull it off. "I don't know. It doesn't, really. It's an odd name name for a cat, that's all."

She didn't buy it. His expression told her there was a lot more to it than that. She wanted to know a lot more about this intriguing man.

"Well, you don't get to vote, unless, maybe, you want to take him back." She'd already decided Caleb was hers.

"Uh, no thanks. Forgive me for reacting. Maybe I'm jealous. I thought there might be another man in your life."

"That, Galen Andrews, is a crock, but I don't have time to pursue it. I have to get dressed, go shopping for cat food, and stop at the library." She turned to the kitten, which had finally had enough to eat, and was starting to groom himself.

"Thanks for the cat," she added, dismissing him, and brushing Caleb gently, with her hands, before he swallowed all that sand. She should have known it wasn't going to be that easy to get rid of Galen.

"Hold on. I'm responsible for bringing the cat here, so I have an interest in his welfare." His eyes gleamed with amusement. "You go do your shopping; I'll get cleaned up and meet you at the Fish Shack about noon. We'll have lunch and discuss Caleb's future." His wink suggested he had more in mind.

No man should be that aware of his appeal. Before she could respond, Galen opened the door and left, leaving her wondering why Caleb's name had garnered such an extreme reaction—as though it had some significance, but how unlikely was that? It was from another century and certainly not common today. She was missing something. She'd find out at lunch.

Chapter Fifteen

"So, how did it go at the library? Did you find what you needed?"

It was after noon when Galen joined Sara at the rough, wooden table outside the Fish Shack, and placed a plate of tacos and fries in front of her.

"I wasted the whole morning. I'm used to a larger library with online access to a statewide system. I know Massachusetts had an important role in the Civil War, which is why I expect the Stuarts were involved in something, but what?" She glanced at him, waiting. "Aren't you going to ask me why I'm so obsessed with this?"

He grinned at her, indulgently. "No. You don't like it when your motives are questioned, and we started out the day on good terms. I don't want to spoil it."

His intense green eyes caught hers in an expression of understanding so brief it vanished before she could respond; leaving her with a strange sense they'd had this conversation before.

"Why did you react when you heard the name Caleb?" She wasn't going to let this go. There were too many mysteries surrounding this man, in addition to the feeling that they'd met before, and she knew that hadn't happened.

"The man who built the house you rent was named Caleb. It isn't a common name, so you must have heard it somewhere. You're sure there isn't another Caleb in your life?"

"I've been looking into the history of Stuart House and the name came up."

His penetrating look said he didn't quite buy that, but he let it go. "How is our cat doing, by the way?"

Sara laughed, and confessed, "Caleb will be the best outfitted cat in New Kensington. I had no idea there were so many things I needed. Besides the latest in organic cat food, we needed a litter box, bowls and a brush, and…"

"Galen, you got a minute?" Vinnie had come up to the table, his face flushed, showing a lot of stress, and his eyes filled with worry. "I know you're a lawyer and everything, and I could use some help with this."

"Sure, Vinnie, all the time you need," Galen looked as concerned as Sara felt. "If I can't help, I'll fix you up with someone who can. What's the problem?"

The usually ebullient Vinnie wedged his large frame onto the bench opposite Sara and Galen. His bushy eyebrows knit into a frown as he explained. "You know I have this insurance policy that Steve Costner got for me, the one that will take care of my daughter when me and her mother are no longer around?"

Sara's heart sank. She knew there was going to be trouble here, someday. Costner was committing some kind of fraud on his unsuspecting clients and Vinnie was about to get burned.

"Yeah, sure," Galen said. "It was an annuity type in the neighborhood of a million dollars, right? Your daughter was the beneficiary."

"Yeah. Last week I needed some information for some forms I had to fill out for Social Services and I called them." He paused, his face crumpled in distress.

"Yeah, so?" Galen said.

"Well, they have no record of the policy. I've been paying the premiums for about ten years, and they have no records."

"What did Steve say when you called him?" Galen asked.

While Sara watched Vinnie's expression, her anger built. "Did he have an explanation?" She knew he wouldn't, but she had to know.

Vinnie's mouth sagged in defeat. "Neither Steve nor Sylvie is in town. I called Adrienne and she said she doesn't have anything to do with the insurance business, even if she is on the board, so I'll have to wait until he gets back next week. Hell, Galen. I can't wait. I have to know what's wrong. Those premiums take all our extra cash every six months." He looked ready to cry. "Who's going to take care of my girl?"

Sara's temper erupted. "Damn him."

Vinnie's startled glance reminded her that nice ladies didn't swear, but she was no longer a "nice lady." She was Sara. "I knew he was into something crooked the minute I heard about the tax deductions. That rat should be in jail for this."

"Now hold on, Sara." Galen's voice was conciliatory. He glanced at Vinnie, who had turned white. "We don't have enough information to go off half-cocked. Vinnie, surely you have receipts or cancelled checks for your premium payments?"

"Oh yeah, I'll bet he does," Sara said, her voice shaking with outrage. "All made out to that phony foundation Steve manages along with Adrienne and the rest of his relatives."

"How do you know that?" Galen's alarmed reaction warned her to reply cautiously.

"Because I've been looking into it. I couldn't let it go. I even talked to the F.B.I."

He slammed his fist on the table. "Dammit, Sara. After I told you to stay out of it? You have no business getting involved in things you can't understand. Leave it alone. Let somebody else handle it."

The fear in Galen's eyes made her heart leap. What did he know? Was he involved in robbing innocent people of their life's savings?

"Don't yell at me. This is none of your business. You do not tell me what to do." She paused, suspicion growing. "You knew there was something illegal going on, didn't you?"

The anger on his face shifted to guilt, then alarm while he looked past her, not meeting her eyes.

She stared at him, not caring if the pain of disillusion showed on her face. Something good had been lost here. Trust. She'd really liked him, more than a friend. He was so easy to be with. His male sense of humor was a new experience for her, a big difference from Richard, who didn't have a humorous bone in his body. She'd begun to entertain the notion that Galen could be a real friend, an adult male with whom she could share her thoughts. What made her think he was different from any other man?

Her hopes died a quiet death. He sat there, demeaning her because she was a woman, and therefore couldn't possibly know anything about how the world works.

He showed no respect, patronizing her by treating her like a recalcitrant child unwilling to acknowledge male superiority. He was a modern version of Thomas. Well, that was maybe a little harsh, she admitted to herself.

"Sara." Galen took both her hands in his. He must have read her thoughts on her face. "Don't go there, where you're headed. I swear I'm not in on this. I know Steve is hooked up with some very heavy hitters in Atlantic City. I warned you, if you got in their way, they'd do you some real harm. I don't know what is going on here, but it involves big money. These guys aren't small players."

His voice pleaded with her. "Please. Hold back until I can find out more. I care for you, Sara, and I'm afraid for you. Maybe you don't know me well enough to trust me, but I don't want you to get hurt. You've become important to me."

Too many things were happening at once, including the thrill that caught in her throat at that last statement, and the realization that there were layers to Galen that must be worked through before she knew the man.

Her fanciful imagination likened him to an ice cream bar. The outer, bittersweet chocolate layer must be demolished delicately, one small bite at a time, before claiming the first sweet lick of the creamy vanilla goodness inside. An unwelcome surge of sexual awareness blasted through her. It would have to wait. She saw Vinnie, a broken man, seated at the table, huddled into himself. His love for his handicapped daughter defined his life. He glanced up, his heart in his eyes.

"I know I'm not a smart man. I can't keep up with what's going on in the world, what with computers and all that, but I know I'm being done wrong. I have to fix this so my daughter will be taken care of. Please, help me."

"Of course we will," Sara said, "won't we, Galen?" Her glance said maybe she was willing to trust him again.

"Hell, yes," he said, winking at her, and then turning serious. "So tell me, how did you pay these premiums?"

"I make out the check to the foundation as a donation for more than the amount owed, and Steve pays the premium and keeps the rest as commission. He sends me a tax-deductible receipt for the whole amount."

Sara nodded, understanding. "So there's no paper trail when you do your taxes, except a record of the charitable contribution. Simple but clever."

"How many are involved in this?" Galen asked.

"A lot of the folks who live in the housing development and a couple of members of the theater group, that I know of."

Galen asked, "You never got a copy of the policy?"

"Yeah, the first year, but I can't find it. After that Steve lets me know when a payment was due."

Sara stared at him, realization hitting her. "Then you don't know who the current beneficiary of the policy is." Her mind moved at warp speed. "I'll bet it's Costner, and I'll bet he's become a very rich man from this, if many of his clients have died."

"It could be," Vinnie said, "About a dozen of them people moved into the development at the same time, and most are clients."

A chill crept through Sara. At the same time? Coincidence?

"I gotta go. I got customers. You'll look into it, Galen? See what you can do?"

"You bet, Vinnie. Don't worry about it. I have some people I can call." He nodded and left.

"I hope they're mob hit men," Sara muttered.

Galen smiled, and raised an eyebrow in disbelief. "You have a strange idea of the life I lead. Believe me, my clients might be colorful, but I'm not."

"You are to me."

He regarded her, clearly speculating on the meaning of her remark. Uh oh. He thought she was coming on to him, acknowledging what he'd said before, about her being important to him. She'd better clarify before he read too much into her words.

"Don't take that the wrong way. I'm not looking. The failure of my marriage left me feeling a little raw. It lasted twenty years and it's been that long since I've thought about another man. I don't know the rules of the game, so don't misunderstand."

And then, because that seemed so presumptuous, she added, "I feel so comfortable with you, a familiarity, like meeting an old friend after many years and taking up where we left off. That's the only way I can explain it, but that doesn't mean I want to take it further."

He took her hand, which she hadn't realized had been clenched into a fist, and gently straightened her fingers. "Okay, as long as we're being honest, be forewarned. I want you, Sara, very badly, and I'm going to have you—in my arms, in my bed, and in my life. What do you have to say to that?"

"Uh." Say? She couldn't even think.

"Oh, come on, Sara. Surely you've picked up on the signals. That night at your house, after dinner, you must have known how I felt when I held you and kissed you."

Well sure, she knew he was turned on, and she was excited by it. Giddy, really.

Giddy? I'm melting inside like a lovesick teen with a bad crush. Is this kind of excitement a possibility at my age? Is there still a chance for romance in my life?

In a sudden moment of clarity, she wondered. Was that what her interest in Thomas was all about? Could she be so needy she'd even respond to an apparition?

It took all her courage, but she had to know. "Galen, every day, you see desirable, beautiful women who are attracted to you. They're yours for the asking. You have it all—handsome, rich, and unattached. How could you possibly want a middle-aged, recently divorced mother of two teenagers who has never been anywhere or done anything but be a housewife?"

The wonder on his face was gratifying; the anger that replaced it alarming.

"Dammit it Sara. Don't demean yourself like that. You're everything I want."

"You're imagining me to be what you want."

"You are a woman in every way a man wants a woman."

He took both her hands in a firm grip that confirmed the determination in his eyes.

"You're what a woman can become when she matures. You're the finished product, ready to be some lucky guy's lifelong companion. You're done with the motherhood part, which is good, because I've never wanted children. You've been through the self-involved, my body is my temple part, and moved on."

He paused, running his hands through his hair, showing utter frustration.

"Do you know how hard it is to find a woman who is aware of what's going on more than ten feet away from her exalted self?"

His lethal description of the women he knew brought a wry smile to her face, but he was too intent to notice.

"You're living your life, not just passing through. You can talk about what's going on in the world. You read books and belong to the library. You care. You rush to the defense of abused boys and abandoned cats. You endanger yourself, butting in where you don't belong, because an almost-stranger is suffering."

She smiled, humbled. "You make me sound like a paragon of womanhood."

"Damn. That idiot you were married to really did a number on you, didn't he? If I had him here I'd knock some sense into him."

She glanced down, unable to meet his eyes, but he wasn't finished.

"I don't know by what twist of fate you came to be here, but I feel we're somehow connected. I think I was born looking for you, but I'd just about given up. Hell, maybe it's genetic, and goes back a couple of generations." He pulled her hands to his lips for a gentle kiss and continued.

"All I know is that I was in a room by a piano, entertaining a bunch of friends by singing an old love song, when I saw you standing there, and I knew. You were the one."

He was making love to her with his eyes and wreaking havoc on her emotions. The heat of hormonal rush awakened yearnings long denied. Barely remembered passion, not felt for years, flooded through her, making her heart stutter. What happened with Thomas was happening all over again, but this was way more. Her control, held back by a mere breath, threatened to let loose. She wanted him, physically, every way possible. She was very close to abandoning the carefully constructed person she'd become and not look back.

"Galen, stop what you're doing to me. It's too much. You're seeing someone who isn't here."

His expression was so autocratic—so sure he was in command. She'd seen this expression before, from similar green eyes. Again, that feeling of déjà vu.

Standing, he pulled her to her feet and into his arms. The intensity of his gaze held her spellbound.

"Sara, you're what I want. Come be my love and let me take you to magical places you've never seen. We'll play in the Southern seas, and visit the pyramids, and make love on a boat floating the Amazon."

What man talks that way? It was romantic dialogue out of a Regency romance. Shaken, but thrilled by it all, she leaned into him, surrendering to the truth in her heart. He was a man she could give herself to. If only she'd believe in the impossible, she could give him the love waiting in her soul.

Reacting to her surrender, his arms tightened around her.

"Ah, Sara. I'm so filled with need for you. I could make love to you right here, to seal the deal, but I've enough sanity left to know that a derelict dock, next to a decrepit walk-up food shack, right in front of God and man, is not the place for what I want to do to you." His body shook with wry laughter.

"I want you so much it hurts, but you're not ready. I'm taking you home, and even though I'll be in a hell to rival Dante's *Inferno*, I'm going to leave you to think about us the rest of the night. Tomorrow I have to be in Trenton to handle a dispute over one of the casino's leases, but I'll be back by Friday. Let me take you to dinner before we drop in at that party at Adrienne's house. We'll stay a short while then I want to bring you back here to show you my home. That sound like a plan?"

She knew her sigh of relief disappointed him, but he deserved every bit of it for doing this to her.

She nodded agreement and with a gentle push, backed off. "I need time. I believe I might be in love with you, but the idea is so sudden—not the way I usually do things."

"Whatever you need, sweetheart, as long as I get the girl in the end." He dropped his arms, finished for now.

She had to smile at his reference to a love story. "Its the strangest thing. I have a feeling we've met before, but that's impossible. You might be right about this being predestined. Be patient with me. Please?"

She walked with him to her car, weak from the emotional turmoil. She needed to be back in her house, where things, if not normal, at least offered peace and space. He left her to drive home, but any hope of peace faded when Sara pulled into her driveway. Something was not right. Colin confirmed her fear when he met her in the kitchen, pacing anxiously. Caleb was mewling in distress, reflecting his mood.

Sara gathered the cat in her arms, crooning to calm him. Filled with concern, she asked, "Colin, what's wrong? Why are you so anxious?"

"Is Jen with you?" His speech was halted, but he got it out.

"With me? No, I haven't seen her since this morning. I thought you two had plans after school."

Totally stressed, he signed that they came home early. She was tired and went upstairs to take a nap. When he went to check on her, she wasn't in her room, but he hadn't heard her leave, and there wasn't a note.

"Does she answer her cell?"

He signed, no. Her phone is on her bed, but the bed hasn't been slept in.

Ruthlessly suppressing a suspicion that made her weak with fear, she put Caleb in his bed, and ran upstairs. She searched her room first.

It was gone. The scrimshaw tooth wasn't on her night table.

She raced to Jen's room, and there she saw it, lying on the floor, half under the bed as though it had been thrown.

Dread, a heart-stopping cramp in her gut, rose to her mouth to become an agonized scream. Jen was gone—taken from here. Damn it. This had to be Caleb's doing. He was holding her somewhere to force her cooperation with Thomas.

What if she's back in Port Kensington? Jen would be wild with fear, not understanding what was happening to her.

"Damn you, Caleb," she ground out, "What have you done? Give me my daughter."

The room began to fade, slowly. Cold surrounded her. In the distance a foghorn moaned. Her voice came in a desperate whisper, "Jen. Don't be afraid. I'll find you, baby." The darkness took her.

Chapter Sixteen

Though she held her eyes tightly closed, she could feel the heat searing them. Her body told her she lay huddled against the side of a building; resting on cold, damp dirt with some crushed, loose gravel bruising her skin. Searching hands encountered the rough texture of a brick wall. Cautiously she braved peering between narrowed eyelids, and saw an alley between two huge brick buildings, a street beyond heavily traveled, filled with horse-drawn wagons, and all manner of pedestrians. Their style of dress left no doubt she had returned to a past she had visited before.

Though entirely different from the last time, the scene nevertheless proved she'd once again been deposited in a seaport town. The unmistakable odor of ocean backwash tainted with decaying seaweed and dead fish filled the air, tempered by an occasional waft of a sweet, heavy odor she recognized as spermaceti oil. In the distance she heard the familiar random clanging of a large bell, a buoy, rocking restlessly on the water.

Noise generated by the human activity on the street deafened other sounds. Huge wagons rumbled by on iron-rimmed wheels, drawn by teams of draft horses. Men shouted orders, horns blasted, the relentless clanging of hammers pounding metal—all contributed to a mind-numbing roar. Apparently she'd returned to Port Kensington, but to the commercial district down by the wharves where the ships were unloaded.

Slowly she got to her feet, bracing herself with her hands on the rough texture of the brick, thankful that the air was warm. Her tracksuit, while not in fashion in Victorian times, would be sufficient protection.

Was she still invisible, like the last time? Remembering how that worked, she could remain that way, if she stayed calm, and kept her level of emotion low enough. Worry grew into a random shard of fear. Her control, so tenuous, like a teetering tower of stacked blocks, could collapse any minute.

The need to scream for Jen, to vent her rage, to become hysterical, had her fighting to remain calm. She had no time for any of that. Jen was here, somewhere, no doubt terrified, and without a clue what was happening to her.

I didn't ask for any of this. All I'd wanted was a quiet vacation by the sea—a time to get myself together and visualize a new life as a single woman. Instead I'm tangled up with some ghosts, and my daughter is an innocent victim.

"Think, dammit," she whispered through teeth clenched to keep her emotions in check. "This is Caleb's doing. What does he want?" She already knew the answer

He wants to know what Thomas is up to and he's threatening Jen to force the issue. My daughter is the lure. She has to be close to the scene. He must have her stashed somewhere nearby.

She walked to the end of the building and entered the main street, amazed at what she saw—frantic activity from thriving businesses, all along the crowded wharves down by the shore. Swarms of men unloaded cargo from tall-masted sailing ships, tied up in every available space along the docks, while another fifty or so vessels were anchored in the bay, waiting their turn. Rows of warehouses, their yards filled with stacked barrels and crates, were inundated by wagons waiting to be loaded.

Assured of her invisibility, at least for the moment, she started walking, weaving her way through a sea of humanity, and marveling at the mix of people—African, South Pacific natives, Portuguese, American Indian, and European. Nearly naked, tattooed, sharp-toothed Fiji Islanders, carrying harpoons, mingled with conservatively dressed Quakers, and elegantly attired, top-hatted businessmen conversing in groups. There weren't any women in evidence, but judging from the rough crowd, that wasn't a surprise.

Right in front of her she saw a huge warehouse with a sign identifying it as "Stuart Brothers, Importers." The activity at the end caught her attention. It encompassed several docks extending from the building into the bay. Three-masted whalers crowded against them, being loaded with freight, but the cargo didn't make sense. Teams of men, cursing and struggling, strained to unload large boulders from farm wagons and bring them onboard. Rocks? What possible reason could there be for shipping that many rocks?

She needed to get inside the warehouse to see what was going on, but how could she get that close to the workers? They might not be able to see her, but could they feel her?

Apparently not, but she could feel them. A dockworker came close enough to jostle her. She felt a jolt, and an eerie coldness, but he passed right through without a sign of awareness. Creepy, but it gave her the confidence to go on.

Inside the warehouse the light was so dim, she had to be careful, making her way back to a corner, out of the traffic pattern. She saw a large mound covered with a tarp. Curious, she raised one corner to reveal long, narrow wooden crates stacked six feet high, identified by the stenciled letters, "Springfield Armory," a name she knew from her research. The Armory stored munitions manufactured here. This was a cargo of arms and ammunition waiting to be loaded.

Going where? The Union Army was no further south than Delaware, easier reached by rail than ship. Was this the venture Thomas was pushing—smuggling supplies to the Confederacy in exchange for gold? She'd seen enough. It was time to find Jen and get out of town.

Her familiarity with the old maps she'd found at the library guided her along the single main street that ran parallel to the shore. In the residential area, on the left, private residences crowded on the hill rising from the bay, as close as possible to the sea to afford a view of the channel. Sure of her destination, she set out toward a row of large mansions right in front of her, sitting high off the road.

"Sara?"

A familiar female voice came to her from the hovering mist—the same one she'd heard her last time here. She saw the form of a young woman wearing a long dress and a cape, her head covered in a bonnet, in a style she had seen in films set in the American 1800s. The woman walked toward her, sure of her destination. For some reason, the scenario had changed. Sara was no longer invisible. That presented a new dilemma.

"Yes, I'm Sara. Who are you?"

"I'm Mélange. I prayed to God for help and my prayers were answered. I knew you would come from a far place to help me."

Mélange. A name Thomas had mentioned. "I'm here to find my daughter. She's lost and that's all I care about. Have you seen a young woman dressed like me?"

"She's safe, at Stuart House, but terribly confused. I told her you'd be coming to get her."

"Then take me to her. You'll get nothing from me until I've seen her."

The girl turned and started toward the largest house in the long line facing the sea. Sara followed, her stomach in a knot, afraid of what state Jen was in. Her anger at Caleb, the one she blamed for all this, was growing by quantum leaps.

"Wait a minute. When is this? What year?"

"The year of Our Lord, eighteen hundred sixty-one."

The wary expression on the woman's face reminded Sara of how she'd reacted when Thomas had asked that question on the beach. She'd better come up with some sort of an explanation. Oh sure, just spit it out.

"You already know, from the strange clothes my daughter and I are wearing, that we're not from anywhere near here. We aren't from this time. I can't explain how this happened, but we are from the future, the year 2015. It has something to do with Thomas Stuart."

She wasn't expecting the smile that appeared on the girl's face.

"I asked God for help with the danger Thomas has brought to the family, and he sent you. It is enough for me. Come, now." She turned and walked toward the house.

It would have been easier to follow the road, but Mélange chose the stairs leading up to the next level, which quickly brought them to their destination, a basement entrance to the mansion. Cautiously she followed her guide into the dark interior.

The light, from a single lantern was poor, but enough to reveal Jen, huddled in a corner, her arms wrapped around her knees. She raised her head, her eyes wide with fear.

"Jen, baby." Sara ran toward her and dropped in front of her, taking her in her arms. "Oh, honey, I'm so sorry. Poor baby, you must be so frightened."

"Mom, where am I? What's going on?"

"Remember when we talked about time travel at the Metaphysical Society?"

Jen pulled away, staring at her, her mouth open. "You mean we're somewhere else? We're not home? This isn't New Kensington?"

"Sort of. This is New Kensington, but the year is 1861."

Jen's voice rose, but at least she wasn't screaming. She was amazingly calm. There was more excitement than fear evident in her voice.

"You mean what the guy said, at the meeting? We're in another time?"

"We're at the original Stuart House, just north of town, in Port Kensington, Massachusetts, the town that disappeared entirely in a hurricane in the late 1800s."

Jen stared, her mouth open, stunned. Sara frowned, waiting. Jen should be totally freaked out. "Stay calm. Don't be afraid."

"Mom, I'm not scared. Remember, at the meeting? I told you time travel novels are my favorite kind of book. I never thought I'd experience it, though. Oh, cray-cray."

"You're doing a lot better than I did when it first happened to me."

"So why are we here and how do we get back? Can we go home?" Her voice trembled. She was not as calm as she seemed. "How do we get out of here?"

"I'm not sure. I suspect this is Caleb's doing and he has a plan. I should have told you all of it from the beginning. Remember when I said Thomas was suspected of something illegal that put the whole family in danger?"

"Yeah, so?"

"Caleb wants me to find out what so he can stop it. I have a feeling that this last move of the townspeople to New Kensington might be the end of all of them. The present players in this scenario are breaking some serious laws and are going to jail. It must all come to an end before that happens, and they are revealed, but first Thomas must be stopped from whatever he is doing in his time."

Jen was silent for several moments. Sara waited, praying she'd come around. "Then we have to find out what it is and get free of it, or we're going to get caught up in the end and disappear too." She frowned, and then brightened. "Okay, we're a team. So what do we do?" Mélange, listening until now, spoke up. "May I make a suggestion? This evening we are holding a salon here, at Stuart House. We do this often. The family members and townsfolk who are friends gather to discuss business affairs and other matters. You can attend and listen. You might learn what you need to know."

"The last time I was here, I was invisible," Sara said, "but you can see both of us. I wonder if we'll we be visible at the salon?"

"Uh, reality check," Jen said. She pointed to her tracksuit. "If they can see us, don't you think we'll look strange?"

"That does not signify," Mélange said with a shrug. "You won't look out of place. I have all the clothing you'll need to look the part, and we appear to be about the same size. Avoid conversing as much as possible. I can explain that you are newcomers.

I'll say you are an American widow and her daughter just arrived from the Cape Verde Islands where you've lived for many years. We have new arrivals by way of the Portuguese Packets all the time. Since you're new, you won't know of current matters. You'll just have to sit and listen. That will get you through the evening."

"That's very clever," Jen said admiringly. "You're very good at this."

Sara wasn't convinced. "Why isn't Caleb aware of what Thomas is doing? Doesn't he keep up with what is happening at the docks?" Her mind went back to the warehouse, remembering the cases of rifles.

"Caleb doesn't concern himself too much with that end of the business. He leaves it up to Thomas and Uriah. There are so many other ventures he has to see to, now that he isn't whaling anymore. Besides, Thomas runs with a younger, more daring crowd. They wouldn't discuss their ventures with Caleb."

"You'll be there?" Jen asked, "I mean at the party?"

"Of course. Oh, I beg your pardon. I didn't introduce myself. I am Mélange Stuart. Caleb, Uriah, and Thomas are my brothers. Caleb is the oldest, and by rights, runs the family since our father was lost at sea. I have another sister, Felicity, who is married. They'll all be there." She turned and started out of the room.

"Come. I'll find my abigail and see to your rooms. We have a few hours until the salon. Several maids in the house are good with a needle, and alterations can be accomplished swiftly. I'm sure I have something that will be stylish enough not to cause comment."

Chapter Seventeen

While Mélange sent for warm water to freshen up, they waited in her rooms on the second floor of the mansion. Her suite contained three rooms, one for dressing, with closets and clothes, one for bathing, with a tub, a shower, and a flushing toilet, Victorian style with a tank of water near the ceiling to accomplish the task, and a bed/sitting room. Sara and Jen watched her go through her closet, searching for dresses.

"My gosh," Jen said, viewing the dressing room, "You sure have a lot of clothes. There must be four dozen outfits hanging in here. Wow, every one a different color."

"It takes a lot of clothing." Mélange shrugged, noncommittally. "One dresses for morning. After that, a change is required if one is going shopping, or riding in the park. Then one must change into afternoon clothes to receive guests or to go calling. We dress for dinner, of course."

"Oh, look at this." Jen pulled a pale green dress out of an armoire. "This material shimmers, but it's almost transparent, and such a beautiful, soft color. It must take yards of fabric to make all those tiers of ruffles in the back."

Mélange nodded. "It is chiffon satin. The color is Willow Green, in the current style. The narrower skirt, Empire waist, and bustle are positively in the first stare of fashion. Wide crinolines have gone out of favor with the younger crowd. I've only worn this dress once, so it might do for you." She eyed it critically as Jen held it against her.

"It's too long," Jen said.

"We can shorten it, but let's wait until undergarments are added," Mélange said, searching in the closet. "This is what you would wear under it, normally, but I'm afraid you don't have time to learn how to move in this." She held up an oval contraption made of whalebone strips and covered with muslin. It was clearly intended to add bulk to a lady's derriere. "This can present a problem sitting or moving through doorways. We'll use a petticoat with a bustle." She turned to her maid. "Biddy, find underclothes and start dressing Miss Burkhart, while I attend to Madame."

Madame? Sara winced. The term made her sound so matronly. The next remark didn't help.

"I think I have something more suitable to your age and status as a widowed mother."

Startled, because she hadn't considered the need for a logical explanation for her being here without an escort, Sara watched Mélange disappear into the back of the closet and emerge with a grayed pink—almost mauve—dress in a fine silk, still with plenty of skirt made of rows of wide, fabric ruffles, trimmed in lace. A bulky gathering of fabric in the back, and a modest bodice, buttoned up to the neck and trimmed with a lace fichu completed the dress.

"This is one of Felicity's gowns from last year that she never wore. The color is better suited to a more mature woman. It's called *Ashes of Roses*. We can hide the fact that your hair is short by adding a bun in the back. Biddy can use a curling stick to frame your face with a lot of little curls. Yes, I think that will do."

"Mom," Jen said, "will you get a look at all this stuff women wear under their dresses? There's a camisole and long drawers, then a corset, and then this petticoat with ruffles all down the back that could be a skirt. It's a wonder I can move and I don't even have the dress on yet."

Biddy was standing on a chair; holding the dress up, ready to drop it over Jen's head. She let it fall and began dealing with the dozens of tiny buttons closing the back.

Sara eyed Jen's breasts, pushed into prominence by the corset. Disconcerted by the transformation of her daughter, she said, "My, isn't the neckline a little low?" The scooped neck, trimmed with green lace, went from shoulder to shoulder, with short, puffed sleeves. Her daughter had grown into a mature woman overnight.

Jen, enjoying the moment, laughed. "Oh, Mom. Get real. This is so dope."

"Dope?" Mélange asked, confused.

"Teenage slang from our time, Mélange," said Sara. "It means really nice."

Jen said, "I feel positively elegant, but I'm going to have to get used to all this dress bunched behind me." She glanced into the pier glass to get a look at the cascades of ruffles that made up her bustle.

"She will be wearing long gloves above the elbow," Mélange added. To Jen, she said, "Come to the other room. There is barely time to do your hair. I think you will look good if we do braids, curl them on the crown of your head, and add some hair pieces."

The salon was in progress when they entered, several hours later. Held in a large hall with French doors opening to a veranda, which provided a view of the ocean along one side, it easily accommodated the fifty or so guests.

Jen whispered to Sara, "I guess they have larger rooms because the women need so much space for their dresses. This many people would fit into Adrienne's smaller house easily, but not with these dresses."

Massive chandeliers, bearing hundreds of candles, hung from the vaulted ceiling, and gave off a soft, golden light. The cloying fragrance of the candles proved to be almost too much for Sara, grateful that most of the smoke collected near the high ceiling and was vented through the skylights.

The gathering was impressive, made up of elegantly dressed women and formally attired men, many with coats and breeches that appeared variations of naval uniforms. Women were seated in groups, and men congregated in clusters, all intent on conversation. A stringed quartet in a far corner played softly.

"First I must present you to my mother." Mélange said, urging them along toward a gathering of women, all at least middle-aged, seated in a corner. They were listening intently to a matron whose gray hair, piled high on her head, was adorned with black feathers and sequins. A deep purple silk gown, covered with masses of silk ruching enclosed her ample frame. Sara wondered at the number of petticoats it must take to fill out that wide skirt.

Mrs. Stuart, impressive in a gown of grey silk, the full, bell skirt lavishly adorned with several rows of ruffles and black lace, smiled a greeting at her daughter.

"Mama, allow me to present Mrs. Burkhart, whom I've known from my school years abroad, and her daughter, Jennifer. They will be visiting for a few weeks."

Mrs. Stuart nodded graciously. "I'm delighted to meet friends of Mélange. Won't you join us? Mrs. Oglethorpe is entertaining us with the description of a parade she witnessed not long ago in New York."

Sara and Jen eased into two chairs careful to manage the yards of bustle, and prepared to listen. They were near enough to the circle of friends to participate, but had enough distance to converse privately behind their fans.

"I was simply quite overcome with emotion," the matron continued, after nodding a greeting, and fanning her flushed face vigorously, "It was the most thrilling sight. I was quite all to the boughs. New York's Seventh Regiment parading smartly in step, down Broadway, dressed in their bright red uniforms with gleaming gold buttons, all done to a turn, while the band played such a stirring march." She leaned forward. Her intent expression heralded the telling of an important secret. "I'm told they take their own band with them wherever they go. Even into battle." She leaned back, enjoying the flutter of gasps. "Imagine how exciting that must be. Such courageous young men. They were on their way to Washington, to engage with the troops of the Southern Rebellion."

"Those brave men," one woman sighed. "So romantic."

A male voice intruded. "They have no idea what they're getting into. Damn waste of money." The comment came from a man standing nearby. His dress, in formal business attire, set him apart from many of the male guests, who wore variations of sea captain's uniforms. "So many young men will die for nothing. The rebellion can't succeed. It'll all be over in a couple of weeks." He glared at his rapt audience, daring them to deny his pronouncement. "Damn nuisance, them Rebels. The ninny hammers think they can secede from the Union and start their own country. Nothing wrong with what they got, I say. Why'd they want to do such a thing?"

"Why indeed?" A male voice, full of authority, joined the discussion. Sara stared in recognition at the speaker, resplendent in brass buttons and epaulettes, readying to offer his opinion. The voice and the patronizing tone were familiar. Thomas. Sara knew before she looked up into those green eyes. She sensed Jen, frozen beside her. What if he recognized them?

There was no sign of it when his glance wandered over Sara, but then, it was 1861. They hadn't met yet.

"Such a serious subject for gentlewomen. Good evening, Mother, ladies. Mélange, I haven't met your guests."

He smiled down at her, his interest most definitely including her daughter, which set off a whole other set of alarms with Sara.

"You must understand," he continued to the group at large, "war is a game, very lucrative to those with deep pockets who know how to play it. All it needs is an inexhaustible supply of young men foolish enough to put themselves in Harm's way in hope of securing testimony to their manhood. Tell them how brave they are, and off they go. Many of them might die, but they are expendable, since they don't figure in the grand scheme of things."

"Fustian, Thomas," Mrs. Stuart exclaimed. "You make it all sound so contrived."

"Contrived in the sense that there must be war to create a very profitable market for munitions and supplies. Those smart enough to play are always ready to fill the need. War is waged on borrowed money. How else would bankers make their due?"

"Them Southerners print their own money," a man said, outraged. "Even elected their own president. Nothing wrong with Lincoln, I say."

There were nods of agreement all around. Sara couldn't help but remember reading of the awful casualties of that war. She glanced at Jen, who was listening, fascinated.

"I say they are all balmy in the crumpet," the man standing beside the speaker remarked, with a nod toward Mrs. Stuart, "if you ladies will pardon the expression."

Mrs. Stuart nodded, smiling permissively.

"Thinking they can outlast the government," he continued, "when they have neither the guns or ammunition to fight a war, and no facilities to manufacture."

"Off their onion," another man said.

"They'll be done when they find out they haven't the means to equip an army. No factories in the South. Can't run a factory on slaves." There were comments of agreement all around.

Sara remembered the crates of rifles and ammunition stored in the warehouse. For whom had they been destined? Was this what Thomas was up to?

"My nephew has joined the Eighth Massachusetts Volunteers," one matron remarked, graciously accepting nods of approval from the women.

Jen leaned toward Sara and held her fan in front of her mouth so she couldn't be heard. "Mom, they're talking about the Civil War. It's just beginning. We studied this last year in school. They have no idea what is ahead of them. If this is 1861, the First Battle of Bull Run will be in July. It hasn't happened yet. Thousands of Union soldiers are going to die in a terrible defeat."

"Hush, Jen. We can't talk about this." Sara looked around to be sure they weren't noticed, but everyone was listening to the argument.

Determined, Jen continued, "Have you noticed something funny about some of these people?"

"No, what?"

"Look around you. I can pick out five or six that resemble people we met at Adrienne's. That short, fat guy over there—doesn't he resemble Caro's husband?"

Sara felt a chill starting at her feet and rushing to her head. Jen was right, but what did it mean? She was too filled with foreboding to consider it. "Not now Jen. We'll talk about it later."

She nodded toward Mrs. Oglethorpe who, angered to have her tale interrupted by male impertinence, said scathingly, "I for one will not gainsay the bravery of those young men, so handsome with those buttons sparkling in the sun."

"Humph," the man retorted, expressing his disdain for her admiration of buttons, "The Johnny Rebs will be so blinded by all the gold, they won't be able to see to fire their weapons." The remark was followed by a burst of laughter from the gentlemen, and greeted with a frenzy of indignant fan waving by the ladies. Sara thought a riot was imminent.

Thomas laughed, ignoring the women. "Well, Sister, what will it be? Must I go begging for an introduction?"

Mélange said, "Madame Burkhart, Miss Jennifer Burkhart, allow me to present my brother, Thomas Stuart, who has the instincts of a prize hound when a new member of the fair sex is on the block."

"Really, Mélange," Mrs. Stuart said. "That was most inappropriate." She closed her fan with a snap.

"Nay. Mama, Mélange has the way of it," Thomas smiled admiringly at Jen, including Sara in his glance.

Thomas had no idea of her identity. Well, of course not, at least for another hundred and sixty years, so what was she worried about? Jen was way ahead of her. Her face lit with amusement as she peered at Thomas over her fan. Clearly she was going to respond and Sara dreaded what might happen if she forgot where they were. A very beautiful woman, about Jen's age, dressed elegantly, at the height of fashion, approached, and grabbed Thomas' arm, interrupting him.

"Thomas, I need to speak to you now. It's most important."

Annoyed, he glanced at her. "Not now, Felicity. Whatever it is can wait until after the salon."

"No, Thomas," she insisted frantically, it must be now. I must speak to you."

Felicity? Oh, no. Sara anticipated what this was about. She remembered Felicity begged Thomas to allow her to go along on his next voyage, and he'd refused, with disastrous results. She reached for Jen's hand, with a telling look, because she'd told her the story. Jen returned her look with a sad nod.

"What bee does Felicity have in her bonnet?" Mrs. Stuart asked, watching Thomas being led away.

Before Mélange could answer, another young man appeared. "Excuse me, Mrs. Stuart, but may I beg to be presented to your guests?" He looked at Jen with great interest, prompting Sara to sigh with resignation. Apparently they were not going to sit quietly in a corner. Pride mingled with her resignation. Her daughter had managed to attract the attention of every eligible man in the room.

Mélange took over, prefacing her introduction with the story she'd invented of their arrival, and ending with, "Madame Burkhart, allow me to present the son of one of my brother Caleb's good friends, Mr. John Paul Lovett, and with your permission," she paused to prompt a nod from Sara, "to present Mr. Lovett to your daughter, Jennifer."

Awed by all this formality, Jen offered her hand, which the young man promptly took and executed a formal bow. "So delighted to make your acquaintance." With a nod to Sara, he added, "With your permission, Madame, might I escort your daughter to the buffet for a light repast?"

Jen threw Sara a look that left no doubt to her intentions.

Denying her anxiety, Sara said, "Take care, and don't be gone too long."

Jennifer placed her hand lightly on her escort's arm and glided gracefully away, managing the yards of bustle as though born to it.

"Oh, dear," Mélange said, watching Thomas and Felicity in the center of the room. "My sister's so impulsive. She has this idea to go with Thomas on his next voyage. I'm afraid Thomas will have no tolerance for her notions. He has little patience with women who try to step outside their bounds."

Sara, remembering her own reaction to Thomas' sexist attitudes, sympathized with the girl. "I don't suppose it is at all possible?"

"Of course not. She's a married woman, and although some wives do sail with their husbands, Felicity's spouse is not a sea captain, and is very set in his attitudes. The voyages take years. She can't leave him. She'd be ruined socially." She sighed, dismayed. "She is so unhappy in her marriage, but something like this will cause a scandal. Her wildly reckless demands will bring disgrace to the family."

Sara watched the scene unfold, fighting against the desire to voice a warning of the coming tragedy. She didn't dare. She couldn't interfere, but she could sympathize with Felicity's misery.

The fascinated audience followed the scene while an older, stern faced gentleman, his face red with anger, dragged Felicity by the arm toward the stairs.

Sara said, "The older man forcibly escorting her from the room, is that her husband?"

"Yes, and he can be very brutal."

"It can't be easy for a vital, young girl trapped in such an unhappy marriage."

Mélange nodded. "It is a most unfortunate alliance between two families."

Sara let her mind drift, allowing the soft sound of the string quartet to ease her fears for the unhappy woman. They played chamber music she recognized, by Joseph Hayden. Conversational music, it was called, referring to the way the instruments took turns with the melody, as though conversing.

Mélange interrupted her reverie with an exclamation. "Oh, here comes someone you must meet."

Sara glanced across the room. A very tall and imposing man, resplendent in a sea captain's uniform, approached with unusual grace in his commanding stride. He glowed with vitality. Unlike many of the men in the room, his face was clean-shaven, revealing strong bones and a firm jaw. Cloaked in such an unmistakable aura of assurance, he was undeniably one of the most compelling creatures she'd ever seen. His looks, however, weren't what caught her attention; it was her shockingly strong attraction to him. When his eyes met hers, her heart pounded.

This has happened before. Some other time, in some other place, we've seen each other, been together, but where and when?

His gaze, so gentle and kind when he looked at Mélange, sparked with interest when his eyes met hers. They burned through to her soul, stirring a powerful yearning for something she couldn't quite grasp. She wanted to be close to him, feel his strong body holding her tight in his embrace.

I've been waiting for this man my whole life. He is my soul mate, but how can that be when we are separated by more than a century? I know him. He's familiar to me, but how?

Dismayed, she caught hold of her emotions, realizing the significance of the dark hair and unmistakably emerald eyes. Oh yes, she knew this man, even though she knew him only as a spirit. There was no mistaking his identity. Recognition struck with elemental force. Her breath caught in her throat. Dear God. Her heart knew what her brain could not accept. She was looking at Caleb Stuart, alias Galen Andrews. He was one of the lost colony?

The irony didn't escape her. Why now, when she was in another lifetime? Did fate intend that she would meet her soul mate in a scene being played a hundred and sixty years ago, only to have him vanish in a few hours, and then, in another time, be lost yet again, forever? Could fate be that cruel? Absolutely.

He uttered an imperious command.

"Mélange, go to Felicity and see if you can calm her. She's dangerously distraught. Damn Thomas. He could have denied her in a gentler way." He glanced at Sara, a brief, curious look flitting across his face, then back at Mélange.

"Caleb," Mélange said in greeting, ignoring his command and not at all put off by his manner. "Meet my new friend, Madame Sara Burkhart. Sara, this is my oldest brother, Caleb Stuart. Sara and her daughter are visiting from the Cape Verde Islands." With a nod, she hurried across the room to seek her sister upstairs.

Sara held her breath, not knowing what to expect.

How did this time travel work? Would he know her?

There wasn't a flicker of recognition, but his inspection was so intent, it would have bordered on rude if it weren't for his devastating smile.

"Madame Burkhart, it is indeed a pleasure. You've just arrived?"

His voice invaded her senses, filling her with excitement. She drank it in like a dry desert bathed in cool rain. The tone was deep and compelling. His interest shone in his eyes when he took her hand and bowed over it.

Struggling to recall the question, she barely managed to find a reply in her numbed brain. "Ah, only last week," she managed, pushing the words past her fluttering heart.

"And how did you enjoy your sea voyage?"

"Uh, I've never been on a boat."

He looked at her with amusement. "Then how did you get here? Fly?"

What did she say? Stupid. Stupid. She'd blown it. Too stunned by what was happening to her, she'd replied as though she were home in the next century. Frantically, her brain groped for a response—something he might believe. If he was anything like Thomas, he thought most women were flighty airheads, anyhow.

She tried for a shudder of distaste and apparently pulled it off, because he looked intrigued.

"I'm sorry," she said, in her most judgmental tone, "but my trip cannot be considered a proper sea voyage, on a boat, in any sense of the word. I never saw the ocean. From the moment I stepped on board that miserable packet, I never left my bed. I was vilely ill. The weeks stretched into an eternity, though I'm told the nightmare lasted only 29 days."

She hoped by waving her fan vigorously, it would emphasize her distress at recalling the memory. She was on shaky ground here. The Victorians probably considered a public discussion of any illness far beyond the limits of polite conversation. "My poor daughter served as nursemaid the entire time." A swift glance told her he wasn't buying it, yet.

She added, "However, she tried to cheer me with tales of beautiful sunsets, and lovely nights, so quiet, with only the sound of the breeze in the rigging. Now that I've recovered, I hope, someday, to experience the sea as you do, no doubt."

He grinned sympathetically and she relaxed with an answering smile that begged for understanding.

"Ah, *Mal de Mer*," he said, using the French term for seasickness. "Some people suffer dreadfully their first time at sea. It will probably never happen again."

On firmer ground now, she gazed at him, saying, "Tell me about life at sea. Are you gone for long periods?"

He shrugged while taking her hand and placing it firmly on his arm. "I'm not gone at all, anymore. Come walk with me. The air in here becomes too heavy with all these candles. Though I no longer hunt the leviathan, I haven't lost my need to be outdoors."

She allowed him to lead her across the room, noticing, on the way, Jennifer in an animated conversation within a circle of men. Jen looked up, caught Sara's eye, and sparkled. Sara sighed. Jen had to be doing better than she was.

Caleb led her to a bench on a small patio and sat beside her.

"Tell me about whaling," she said. Anything to hear that wonderful voice. "I've read about it, and it sounds exciting, although from paintings I've seen of whales, they are frightening creatures. Hunting them is surely perilous business." The image of Caleb standing fearlessly on the bow of a boat, ready to hurl a spear, made her heart pound.

He said, plainly mocking himself, "My sympathy was always with the whale. There are no words to describe the sheer size and beauty of these animals—a true behemoth of the deep with a fierce will to survive. They fought so hard to escape the harpooners' shafts. When finally beaten, their death throes were heart breaking. After a few voyages, I decided there were better ways to improve my finances."

Recalling her conversation with Thomas on this subject, she couldn't help but compare the two brothers. Her attraction to this brother deepened by the moment.

He shook his head sadly. "I'm afraid, in a few years, they'll be gone. At one time the sea was full of whales. Now it can be days before one is sighted. Wholesale slaughter has driven them near to extinction.

"The whaling industry is less important since the discovery of petroleum in Pennsylvania, and not changing for the better. New harpoon guns kill more efficiently, and steam engines, like those on the Hudson River, are faster than sails." He shook his head. "My brother, Thomas, doesn't see this. He doesn't accept the inevitable. He is determined to continue whaling until he gets too old."

The pain in his voice made her want to console him. She felt his frustration more and more.

"And as head of the family," she said, "you feel responsible, and are trying to steer him into other endeavors. Your despair suggests he doesn't see it your way."

He gazed at her, startled. "You are a most unusual woman. I cannot ever remember having a serious conversation with a female. I can only think the citizens of Cape Verde raise their women differently."

"Not really," she said, in a teasing tone, "I think you American men must be too busy with manly endeavors to notice. Many of us have functioning brains. Some of us even want to make a difference that will be remembered before we leave this world."

While she waited for a Thomas-like reaction, she remembered being on a beach, making a similar statement to another green-eyed man.

Caleb threw back his head and laughed heartily. "Good Heavens. I'm talking to a Bluestocking. You are truly a delightful wordsmith, Sara Burkhart, and would make a good ship's companion."

He paused and took both her hands into his own. Her yearning caught in her throat as she reveled in the warmth of his expression.

Oh, Caleb. This is breaking my heart. We were so meant for each other, but it cannot be.

"There is something oddly familiar about you, Madame Burkhart. I know it is not possible, but I have the strange feeling that I know you; or perhaps not that, but a feeling that I have been waiting to know you for a long time." He paused, his brow furrowed, as though searching for words. "Forgive me for being too forward, but I have the most irrepressible urge to take you sailing. I'd like to show you the sea in all its moods—take you to magical places you've never seen."

The shock of his plea stilled her heart. She was treading in dangerous water here. She'd heard these words in another time, in another place, from another man. Groping for a response, she said, "Captain Stuart, please. Clearly American men are more forward than I could imagine." She hastened to soften the dismay on his face. "A woman my age—a widow, with a child, no less—is not in a position to go wandering the world." It was lame, but her mind was spinning—frozen in time.

He shrugged, throwing off her protest. "Too old? Hardly." Lowering his voice to an intimate level, he quoted:

"Love's not Time's fool, though rosy lips and cheeks
Within his bending sickle's compass come;
Love alters not, with his brief hours and weeks,
But bears it out even to the edge of doom."

"You read Shakespeare?" Her voice was an incredulous squeak.

"Madam, you have no idea how many hours are spent on a ship doing absolutely nothing. Time hangs heavy, and I must admit, my personal cargo included all manner of reading material."

Before she could reply, Mélange appeared, white faced and shaking. "Caleb. We need you. It's Felicity. I'm afraid . . . oh, dear."

Sara knew, because Thomas had told her of Felicity's attempted drug overdose when he appeared to her at Stuart House. "Go where you are needed, Caleb. Meanwhile, I must find my daughter."

She watched Caleb hurry off, trailing Mélange, but not without a regretful backward look. She dreaded the scene that would follow when Felicity's act was discovered. Her husband would be livid and make the rest of her days a misery. It was time to go. She glanced toward the last location she'd seen Jen and spotted her, still in conversation.

Approaching her daughter, she acknowledged greetings from the eager young men before saying, "Jennifer, something has come up that requires my attention. I'm afraid we must take our leave." Jen raised an eyebrow, questioning, clearly referring to the scene between Thomas and Felicity. Sara nodded and Jen's expression became grim.

"Of course, Mama." Turning with a reassuring smile to her little group, she said, "We are guests of the Stuarts, so perhaps I'll hear from some of you tomorrow?" Heads nodded vigorously.

Sara pulled her along. "Really, Jen, did you have to be so obvious?"

"They were cute and so polite. Is this about Felicity?"

"I'm afraid so. We need to make ourselves scarce for a while."

"Well, I think I found out what Thomas is up to. Those guys were all talking about a *Stone Fleet*. They're real excited. It's the dumbest thing you've ever heard, but I can see where it's a perfect opportunity to make a bunch of money. I'll bet Thomas is up to his ears in it. Mom, when you were down at the docks, you said you saw crates of munitions waiting to be loaded. I think Thomas is smuggling arms to the Confederacy."

"What? That's treason. If he's caught the whole family will be disgraced."

"Well, he's such a dork, he doesn't care about that. He's so into himself, all he cares about is getting enough money to upgrade his ships so he can go on whaling. He wants to outfit his ships with steam to make them go faster."

"That costs money. Caleb won't help him. He believes whaling is dying."

Jen looked at her, surprised. "Well, you've been busy. You met Caleb?"

Sara acknowledged her query with a nod, but cared more about Jen's news. "How is he going to get away with this? Won't the dock workers know what he's loading onto his ship?"

"No. The town has sold a bunch of these old broken-down whalers, not worth repairing, to the government. There's thirty or so of them. They're going to load them up with rocks to make them heavy. The U.S. Navy is paying the owners for the ships and the farmers to bring in the rocks. They're calling it "The Stone Fleet.""

Sara thought for a moment. "That explains what I saw when I was down at the docks earlier today."

"Thomas has a boat in the fleet. He'll mix the munitions with the other cargo. Some of the crew will be in on it."

"Won't someone catch on to the smuggling?"

"Not if they load at night."

"So after they're loaded, then what?"

"The fleet will sail down the Chesapeake to Charleston, South Carolina, where the ships will be sunk, blockading the harbor so the South can't get supplies from Europe. They're going to do the same thing to Savannah, Georgia."

Sara gasped. "But how will Thomas avoid being sunk?"

"I'm guessing the Southern navy will know how to recognize his ship, and they'll capture him and take possession of the cargo."

"I've never heard of The Stone Fleet. How come this isn't in history books?"

"It must be, somewhere, but it's such a crazy scheme, I have a hunch things went wrong and it didn't work out. Anyhow, I'm going to look it up when we get home."

"And since we don't know when that will be, we'd better get down to the docks and check this out, to get the proof Caleb needs. Come on. Upstairs. We have to change into our modern clothes."

In a short time they were helping each other undo all the buttons and ties required to secure their elaborate dresses. Jen sighed with regret. "You know, it was fun dressing up like this and having all those guys competing for my attention. Victorian women sure were a pampered lot. At least the wealthy ones."

"You'd enjoy living this life?" Sara asked.

"No way." Jen shook her head. "It was nice, but not worth giving up my freedom. Poor Felicity, stuck in that marriage to that guy."

"Somehow," Sara said, "I don't think Mélange will find herself in that situation." She bent over to finish tying her shoelaces.

"Mom." Jen's expression was pensive. Something bothered her.

"Have you noticed something else in the room seemed familiar?

Chills made Sara shiver. Jen's observation lent truth to her own sense of de`ja`vu. "Familiar how?"

"Well, Felicity reminded me of Binki Wagner, and Caleb Stuart, if that's the guy you were talking to, looked something like Galen."

"I admit, I've noticed. When I came here the first time I was in a tavern, The Sounder, and I could have seen Thomas and Caleb." Could the arrogant sea captain abusing the boy have been Steve Costner, and the boy, Colin? No, not Colin. That was coincidence. He was born in New Kensington. It was too much to wrap her mind around.

Jen was way ahead of her. "If some of these people are part of that colony that disappears every hundred years or so, they'll be gone again, like the man said at the meeting."

"It's something to think about, but not now. Come on, let's get out of here before somebody notices we're missing. We're going to the warehouse to see what's going on."

"I just pray we don't get caught," Jen said.

Chapter Eighteen

It was near midnight when they reached the Stuart Brothers warehouse. The streets, dimly lit by occasional oil lamps, were deserted. All was quiet, except for activity at the very end of one of the docks where a tall-masted whaler was berthed and being loaded quickly and quietly by a few dockworkers.

"Be careful," Sara warned. "We're wearing dark colors, so we should be hard to see, but they can still hear us."

"The Edwina Louise," Jen read, eyeing the nameplate behind an elaborately carved female figure on the bow of the ship. Beneath the name, the words, Stuart Bros., New Kensington, Massachusetts, appeared in smaller letters.

Sara grabbed her shoulder. "See those crates? They're the same kind I saw filled with rifles. We're going inside to check it out."

Though Sara's eyes had become accustomed to the darkness, the inside of the warehouse, blacker than the night, had them carefully picking their way. The major light source, with the exception of an occasional lantern, filtered from outside streetlights through the closely spaced double hung windows placed high up, on both sides right under the roofline. The building was at least the length of two city blocks, filled with thousands of barrels of whale oil. She could tell by the sweet odor. They were stacked in endless rows with narrow aisles between.

Jen whispered, "This is the kind of place you find rats." They listened for the slightest rustling, ready to move.

Right in front of them, a huge pile of securely nailed wooden crates was stacked. The words *Springfield Armory*, stenciled on the sides, barely discernable, identified the contents.

"Well," Jen said, "there's our proof." She shrieked. "Oh, geez, something ran across my ankle."

"What's that noise?" A voice boomed out of the darkness. "Avast. Who goes there? Intruders. Sound the watch."

Within minutes, men carrying lanterns swarmed inside the building. There were probably only a few but panic destroyed Sara's reason. How would they get out of this if they were caught, or explain their identity, or where they were from? She followed Jen, pounding down the aisle in front of her, the sounds of pursuit getting closer with every step.

A cry, unmistakably from a cat, came out of the darkness. Really? Well sure, for the rats. Glancing up, she saw a black cat standing on top of some barrels stacked against the wall under an open window. Yes! Escape was possible.

"Jen, this way," she whispered, and started climbing, Jen close behind, until they reached the top.

Panting with the effort, Sara paused by the open window and leaned out, seeing the ground below. "We can get out this way. It'll be a drop of about twelve feet to the ground, can you make it?"

Jen went to the window, looked down. "Sure, tuck and roll, just like the obstacle course in gym. Come on, Mom. You're not too old for this. Be sure to bend your knees when you land, but that gravel at the bottom is going to hurt."

Sara's voice caught as she realized her daughter's courage. "Jen, I couldn't do this without you."

Jen went first, landing without incident, and waited for Sara, who took a deep breath and leaped when she heard a voice yell, "Up there."

Her leg twisted under her when she hit the ground. Pain shot through her knee. She wasn't going to be able to run far.

"What now?" Jen asked.

Struggling to her feet, Sara said, "Head for the water. We'll jump in and hide under the pier. We can submerge when they go by."

Jen shivered. "There's stuff swimming around in there and it smells filthy."

"So if we make it home, we'll dose on antibiotics."

"Over here," a voice, way too close, shouted.

Grabbing Jen's hand, Sara clenched her jaw against the pain, limped about ten feet onto the dock, and jumped into the dark water. The cold shocked the breath out of her while they sank deep into the blackness. The fall was endless. How long before they hit bottom? Panicked, she started to kick, praying that Jen was following her lead. With their air about gone, they both surfaced.

Chapter Nineteen

"Where are we?" Jen gasped. "Where is the pier? Mom, I smell French fries."

Dazed, Sara peered through daylight with watery eyes, stinging from the salt, searching for a familiar landmark. Gradually, details became clear. They were under a wooden boat dock, apparently within twenty feet of shore, and, yes, the heavenly odor of French fries drifted on the air. They were back in the 21st century. She laughed triumphantly.

"We made it. We're home, and, I'm willing to bet, within hailing distance of the Fish Shack." She let her feet down and found bottom in waist deep water. "Come on. Let's wade to the beach."

They made it as far as the tide line before collapsing on the sand. Sara was more tired than she ever remembered being. Hot sun warmed her face and took some of the chill from her sodden clothing. If they stayed close to the shore, they could probably hike the short distance home without attracting notice.

Jen flopped down beside her. "If Vinnie's cooking, it must be around noon. I wonder how long we've been gone?"

"As soon as I get my breath," Sara said, "we'll walk on home, check the date, and get out of these wet clothes. I need a hot shower and a chance to brush my teeth. My mouth is full of seaweed."

"Yuck. I itch and I smell like dead fish," Jen said. "Maybe we should save these clothes as souvenirs. They're loaded with antique salt and sand."

Sara grinned at her. "I want to be there when you explain where the sand came from." She put her arm around Jen's shoulders. "Come on, let's go home."

Fortunately, they didn't see anyone along the way to question their soggy appearance. Sara was too tired and emotionally drained to handle any questions.

Within an hour they were showered and lounging on the porch, iced drinks in hand, nibbling on cheese and crackers. Caleb, purring like a motorboat, curled up contentedly on Sara's lap.

Jen watched him, deep in thought. "He was there in the warehouse, wasn't he? He was the black cat."

"I think so. I believe our resident spirit was taking care of us."

Jen sighed. "Freakin' crazy. I don't understand, really, how we got to the 1860s and the downside is, I'll never be able to talk about it with anyone but you because, who else would believe any of it?"

"Maybe Colin. He's more accepting than a lot of adults."

"I mean," Jen said, showing she wasn't sure she'd made her point, "did it really happen? I want to believe it did, but how? There's too much evidence to think we dreamed the whole thing."

"Just accept it, Jen. Once we are out of this house, it will never happen again. There aren't vortices or wormholes everywhere, if that theory is to be believed."

"I keep thinking about all those men. I mean those young guys I met at the party. So many of them are going to die in that stupid war, or maybe even worse, end up without arms or legs."

"By the time it's over, all told, some 650,000 men and countless women will meet their death because of that war."

They sat in serious silence, considering, until Jen spoke.

"You know, Mom, men have made a mess of this world."

Sara waited, wondering where she was going with this.

"Women are going to have to take over to clean it up, aren't we?"

Sara laughed, delighted. "I'm afraid so. Maybe within your lifetime."

"You know what? I'm changing my major this year. I'm going to study world history and government. And then you know what?" She paused and glanced at Sara, making sure she had her attention.

"I'm going into politics. I'm going to run for office."

"Good for you, Jen. And I'll be right behind you with the checkbook."

"No way. You're going to be my senior advisor." She stood, ready to go inside. "To think, all this happened in less than twenty-four hours. I have to find Colin. He should be getting out of school about now. Do you have something on for tonight?"

"Not me. I'm going to bed early. Galen's taking me out for dinner tomorrow night. He's been at the state capitol all day, today. Afterward we're going to Adrienne's for some kind of meeting, and then to his house. I'll be home late. Are you and Colin going to be out?"

"I don't think so. Colin's worried about the weather. He says there's a terrible storm brewing." Jan hesitated, and then asked, "Mom, what if he's one of them, I mean part of that group who disappeared after a hurricane?" Another pause, and then, "He might not be here too much longer."

"I don't think he's one of them. He didn't show up with the rest of them. He was born and raised here."

Jen frowned, not finding the words to say what she wanted. "You really like Galen, don't you?"

"I take it you've noticed his resemblance to Caleb?"

"Well, yeah, and the way you looked at him . . ."

"Yes. I didn't expect to be attracted to another man so soon after your dad, but Galen's special. I can't deny there's something there. I felt a connection so intense, I can't describe it." She sighed, not ready to share her feelings with her daughter. The possibility of losing him was too new. "Maybe, when I've had time to think, I can talk about it. If Caleb and Galen are the same, there is no future with either of them."

Jen stared at her, showing new understanding. Quietly, she headed back into the house. Emotion, so close to the surface, brought tears to Sara's eyes.

I am so proud of her. I might have struck out with my son; he's going to be a carbon copy of his father, but my daughter is turning out to be the woman I wish I had become.

She wasn't going to dwell on the conversation. The similarities of the New Kensington citizens in the 1800's to some current locals, and the idea they might be from more than a century ago, was beyond her grasp. When they moved to another universe, did they keep the same identity, or did some of the men reappear as women, or the reverse? Did some of them come back as animals? Distracted, she rubbed Caleb's head. "How does this work?" she asked the cat. "Did you break the rules by showing yourself to me in the warehouse? Does that mean you'll never be more than a cat? At the least, now she knew the man, Caleb, as more than a gathering of mist in the corner of a room. She knew what he looked like.

Mooning over a lost love that'd been dead for a hundred and sixty years was madness. She'd do better to think about her date with Galen, who was alive and available, at least for a while, and definitely interested in her.

"I don't really know about any of this," she said to the purring cat, but I think you saved my life today. Thank you." She held him close to cuddle him.

"Now, I'm taking a nap and I'd like to wake up right here, in this chair, with no side trips to anywhere. You think we can manage that?"

She laughed, closed her eyes, and drifted off.

Chapter Twenty

Six different pairs of earrings, and she still couldn't find the right look. Sara pulled the gold knots from her ears in frustration. She needed something red to go with her dress—a simple, sleeveless, print design with several widely spaced, giant red hibiscus blossoms on a white background. She didn't own anything colorful except the Mardigras costume jewelry she'd bought her first week here, but the dangling beads looked cheap next to the elegant dress. She pirouetted in front of the mirror, admiring the way the skirt flared around her knees. Her scarlet, high-heeled sandals set it off. Now if she only had the right earrings. Maybe Jen . . .? She sighed.

Why was she fussing like a teenager, making this date such a big deal? It *was* a big deal. She wanted to look special for Galen. She eyed her reflection in the mirror. A day's rest had restored her common sense, and cleared her mind of fantasies. For the first time in over twenty years she had a date with a handsome, available man. She wanted Galen. He made her feel young, and desired. The thought of being held close to his firm body, his hands caressing her, set her every cell vibrating with anticipation.

I need this, dammit, and I'm going to savor every minute available. I've been too long without—too long since I've experienced intimacy. She grinned at the direction her thoughts were taking her. *Oh, hell. Call it what it is, girl. You've been without sex too long.*

Her last years of marriage had no passion. If added to the shock of being abandoned, the stress of divorce, and the destruction of her self-esteem, she'd become vulnerable to any relationship offering some hope she might still be desirable. Thomas and Caleb weren't of this world—only her personal fantasy. Galen, however, *was* real and she'd resisted her attraction to him because she was afraid of looking like a pathetic fool. She didn't want to act needy. That fear had held her back from taking a chance. No more. Galen was willing. She hadn't been out of the game so long she couldn't still read the signs. She was available, so why not?

Earrings. Reminded, she headed for Jen's room, stopping when the phone rang.

"Hello?"

The male voice shouted at her. "Sara, God damn it, what is going on?"

Only one person yelled like that.

"What stupid ass thing are you up to now? Whatever, it is, you've got me involved. What the hell are you doing that brings the fucking government down here snooping around?"

He was yelling so loud, his voice so hoarse, she could only guess. "Richard?"

"Who else would it be? You have some low life bastard hanging around?"

Anger roared through her, like a massive special effects explosion in a Tom Cruise film. "Stop yelling at me, you insufferable bully. You've no right to insult me. Calm down and tell me what you're talking about or I hang up."

"I'll tell you what it's about." His voice was only a few decibels lower than it had been, but she let him go on. "The friggin FBI was just here, all over me, asking about some damn charity outfit of yours operating outside the law. Wanted to know what I knew because my ex-wife—" his voice dripped sarcasm, "was involved in some scam."   Damn. She'd never imagined Richard would be brought into the investigation.

It's making him mad because I'm doing something he doesn't know. Big deal.

She struggled to assemble her thoughts and buy some time. "Uh, the FBI?"

"So you do know what I'm talking about. They showed up here with a warrant. Wanted to see the financials on my new business."

"What grounds did they have for a court order?" This was getting weirder by the minute.

"Don't play stupid, Sara. They didn't need a court order. With the Patriot Act the FBI can write their own warrants."

Stupid? He called her stupid? Shaking with anger, in a voice leveled with deadly menace, she said, "Shut your dirty mouth right now. You've lost your right to talk to me like this. When I learn something, I'll let you know. As far as you and I are concerned, we're done. She hung up. Was he always like that and she simply lived with it? How did that happen?

Jen came into the room. "Was that Dad you were talking to?"

She breathed deeply, willing her nerves to calm down. After all, he was Jen's father. She, at least, probably respected him.

"Yes, and he was yelling his head off, so I hung up. Apparently the FBI was asking him questions about The Congressional Ventures Foundation, and it set him off. I didn't tell him anything. It's none of his business. He isn't involved."

"Yeah. He called me earlier. He sounded really ticked. I didn't tell him anything either, but Mom, if they're asking questions in Florida; they're doing the same around here. How bad is this going to get? You're going to have a lot of people mad at you."

"I'm afraid so. I know several members of the local theater group have these insurance policies. If the IRS does an audit, they are going to be liable for back taxes and hefty penalties, possibly thousands of dollars per person and maybe jail time."

"Wow. If our local time travelers are involved, they have to vanish, and soon. They can't stand much investigation. If Galen is part of that group, he'll soon be gone." She shrugged, changing the subject with a grin of approval. "Hey, you look really hot. That dress is mad. I have some earrings to go with it. They're little red stones that dangle. I'll get them."

A few minutes later a knock sounded at the kitchen door. When Sara opened it, she saw Galen, looking drop-dead handsome, in a dark blue suit that fit him like a glove. Well, of course. Everything about him was first class, top-of-the-line, making her wonder again, why he bothered with an ordinary ex-housewife.

Don't go there, her inner voice warned. *You're not going to let self-doubts ruin your evening.* Considering there might not be many more, she might as well enjoy every minute.

His obvious approval made all the angst she'd suffered over her appearance worthwhile. "Looking good, pretty lady," he said, and winked. She beamed at him, handing over the knit wrap she'd brought because of the cool onshore breeze. He placed it on her shoulders, lingering a bit, eyed her shoes, and with an amused grin, took her arm to aid her progress down the back steps. "Careful now."

What? He didn't like her shoes? "Thank you. I wasn't sure how casual this was," she said. "You clean up pretty nice, yourself."

"I had plans to get you alone on my boat for a moonlight cruise, but the weather looks too chancy to risk it."

"I would have loved it. I've never been on a boat."

For a moment he faltered, giving her a puzzled look.

She'd said the same thing to Caleb at the salon. Could some sort of genetic memory be at work here? More than her shoes were making her unsteady. More like treading in mental quicksand.

"Plan B is a little restaurant a few miles down the coast that is famous for grouper stuffed with crabmeat."

"Wonderful. I'm going to miss the fresh seafood when I go back home." His car was a gleaming, sleek, midnight blue Corvette convertible. "Wow. What a gorgeous vehicle. Now I feel underdressed."

"If you're impressed, it's done its job." He helped her settle into the tan leather seat, soft as butter, enjoying her reaction. "Here's to a pleasant evening. Do you mind if we leave the top down, at least as long as it isn't too windy?"

"No. Driving under the stars, along the ocean, in a classy convertible, is every woman's teenage fantasy."

"With the beautiful woman seated beside me, my own fantasy is complete, but with this wind, it might not last too long. There's a Nor'easter coming in."

Their corny dialogue could be out of a very bad movie. Something was wrong. They were sparring like two virtual strangers on a first date. She missed the easy camaraderie, and wanted it back. Suddenly she realized—he knew. *This is about my snooping around.*

"The pleasant evening might be over once we get to Adrienne's," she said. "I'm afraid I've caused some trouble. The FBI has been asking questions of those who might be involved with Congressional Ventures."

"Yeah, I know. Found that out yesterday in Trenton." His lack of comment didn't bode well. A brief glance told her he was upset.

She might as well reveal the rest of it. "They've gone so far as to contact my ex-husband in Florida. He called this evening, screaming at me."

"I warned you to back off." Galen shouted, furious, talking over the wind. He slowed the car, and pulled over to raise the cover.

She sat, not saying anything, until they were out of the weather and back on the road. When he spoke again, he was calmer.

"You're getting in over your head. This whole situation is going to get nasty. There's a lot of money involved. Steve's been at this about ten years, under one name or another, and into a lot of marginal deals nationally."

"What do you mean, one name or another?"

"Congressional Ventures has been under investigation before, under other identities, same organization. Steve is well connected in Washington, which makes it easy. When the law gets too close, they dissolve the corporation and start up under another name—same clients, same board of directors, new non-profit exemption. The family members simply change job titles."

She already knew that. "So there really is something illegal going on?"

"Oh, yeah. But I don't think Steve Costner is the brain behind this. Someone else is pulling strings, and cooking the books. You were right about the insurance policies. He buys them for the families, listing the premium as a charitable donation; the organization is the beneficiary of the policies and the clients never know that they aren't going to collect on the insurance until someone dies. The family gets nothing. Unfortunately, this has happened in a few cases and there have been inquiries."

"That's terrible. So Vinnie's daughter isn't covered? How many clients are there?"

"I don't know, but the Costners have been mining the local theater group for clients for the last ten years, and enjoying the income from the premiums."

"And since nobody here has died yet, nobody knows," she said. Caleb's little group was on borrowed time. It was worse than that. When the colony moved on, Congressional Ventures would go too. The money couldn't be traced. Jen was right. They all have to disappear soon, including Galen. She swallowed her grief, refusing to think about it.

The conversation stalled while they sped along the highway. The night sky, and the stars, appeared less bright, and then the car swerved violently when caught by a sudden gust of wind.

"I don't like the looks of this weather, at all. It's getting worse." Galen said. "This storm has been building for days. The barometric pressure is nearing a record low. NOAA predicts we're in for one mother of a storm, to hit sometime late tomorrow. They say it'll be worse than anything we've had for the last century."

"Are we in danger?"

"The predictions are for a storm surge of possibly twenty feet, which means major losses and severe flooding. It's going to affect the Atlantic Coast from here as far north as Maine."

"Do you think we should move to the mainland? Caro told me New Kensington was entirely destroyed about a hundred years ago by a hurricane. Could it happen again?"

"We're long overdue. NOAA will know more by tomorrow morning and call for evacuation if it's advisable. It shouldn't take you much time to clear out if it becomes necessary. Let's hope it doesn't." He reached for her hand, his mood softening, to her relief. "I'm selfish. I want to keep you here."

She loved him and she was going to lose him. She couldn't keep the thought out of her mind. The storm that would end it all was fast approaching. This would be their last night together. She determined she'd savor every hour to the maximum—live in the moment as though it were her last.

The car slowed and turned into a parking area fronting a low slung wooden building at the end of a pier, partially supported by heavy piles extending out over the water. It looked very old, like it had been there beyond living memory. The wood siding was weathered grey. Black streaks from the constant soaking of high tides on stormy nights marred the patina. Intrigued, Sara eagerly anticipated the interior. She waited while Galen parked the car. Dodging gusts of wet wind, he guided her through the low-hung entry to the restaurant. She jerked to a stop, frozen.

What? This couldn't be happening.

Fighting off shock and fear, she stared at the sight of the familiar interior. Time held her suspended a century and a half into the past. Harpoons and antique whaling paraphernalia hung on the weathered wood tavern walls, highlighted by modern recessed lighting. Round, heavy wood tables set with linen placemats and crystal, and surrounded by sturdy, wooden armchairs, filled the space. A long, polished bar graced one side of the room. It lacked only a whale jawbone framing it and the eclectic clientele from another era—the odor of unwashed bodies and the crush of exotic foreigners—to be a modern replica of The Sounder Inn. With her sudden stop Galen ran into her back and reached to steady her. "Hey, what's the matter?"

She fought the threatening surge of nausea, the dizziness, and sense of unreality; she reeled while the thought hammered at her brain. No, this was not 1860. She was mistaken. This was 2015.

"What is this place?" Frightened, and a little frantic, Sara took a deep breath to gain some control. "It looks like something out of *Moby Dick*."

He laughed. "You look like you've seen a ghost from the past.

"Yeah, it's unexpected, to say the least."

He responded to her genuine distress with a worried frown, and hastened to explain. "You're not far off. The former owner was a history nut and whaling enthusiast. You might say a regular Ishmael out of Herman Melville's novel. The antiques are all his, from a lifetime of collecting, left for the new owners to enjoy." He paused, gave his name to the hostess, and steered Sara, following in her wake, to a table in a secluded corner.

"Your waiter will be with you shortly." The woman removed the other two place settings off the table, and left menus behind.

Embarrassed by her stunned reaction, and even worse, disoriented, Sara tried for a return to reality and a more normal tone while Galen seated her. "The scene startled me. For a minute there I thought we'd gone back in time to nineteenth century New England—you know, parallel universes and such."

"Oh, come on. The last thing I would expect from a modern uptown woman like yourself is mention of the paranormal, and stuff like time warps and other dimensions."   Was he patronizing her or calling her dumb? "What do you mean, like me? Why can't someone like me believe in time warps?"

"Whoa, hold on. I wasn't insulting you. Somehow I'm swimming in deep water, and I don't know why. I simply meant parallel universes don't usually figure in normal conversation." He looked at her, wary of having offended her.

She shouldn't have come here tonight, not with her memory of him in another time still so intense. Absolutely, this man was Caleb Stuart, destined a century ago, to be the lost love of her life, and without a clue that he was about to lose her again.

Sara breathed a sigh. Did it ever happen that two people who failed to connect in one life got another chance in another century? Does the longing carry over, one generation to another, until it is finally fulfilled, or was her romantic fantasy an exercise in futility? If she didn't stop, she'd ruin the evening. She managed a small laugh, while she tried to calm her nerves in an impossible situation. How could she act normally with a man she'd met for the first time two days ago, a hundred and sixty years in the past? She needed to say something, no matter how stupid.

"Sorry. All this talk of hurricane disasters has me on edge, and this place kind of threw me. It's unexpected."

Galen lost his wary expression and relaxed. She sighed. It was okay.

"Meeting a woman who has read *Moby Dick* is even more unexpected. It's one of my favorite books. One more thing we have in common." The waiter arrived to take the drinks order, interrupting his thought.

"Scotch with water back. How about you, Sara?"

"Rob Roy on the rocks." When he glanced at her, surprised, she said, "This place is a shock. The atmosphere requires something substantial." After the waiter left, she added, trying to lighten the mood, "I like my scotch with a little vermouth."

Galen gazed at her quizzically. "Aren't you supposed to order white wine?"

"The better to keep my wits about me?" she teased. "Now you're being sexist."

The waiter returned with the drinks, and announced, "The 'Catch of the Day' is fresh-caught Atlantic Grouper, stuffed with Maryland Crab, sides of baked potato and steamed broccoli."

At Sara's nod of approval, Galen ordered for the both of them. "Two specials, no sides, Asiago Vinaigrette on the salads, and tell the chef we'll be splitting a chocolate soufflé later."

"You've been here many times, I take it."

"Yeah, there's something about this restaurant that makes me feel right at home." Thoughtfully, he studied the room. "I'm drawn to this place. I must have some seafaring ancestors in the family."

She shuddered, studying the weapons on the wall. "I wouldn't have liked living in a time when whales were hunted.

Those harpoons are instruments of torture. From what I've read, it was indiscriminate slaughter."

"Yes, a brutal business. Sometimes, they took days to die." He paused, and smiled grimly before adding, "Once in a while, however, sweet justice prevailed, and the victims were avenged. There really was a Moby Dick, you know. He was a gigantic bull sperm whale, almost eighty feet long. He used his huge head, the size of a two-story house, as a battering ram. They called him "Mocha Dick because he was first sighted near Mocha Island off the coast of Chile about 1810, and he wasn't white. He was a sort of light tan in color."

The waiter arrived with their order, a grilled fish filet with a crispy brown crust, resting on a mound of crabmeat, lemon wedges on the side.

"Then there was truth in Herman Melville's tale?" Sara asked, sampling her entrée.

Galen's voice took on a reminiscing quality that sent cold shivers through her. She imagined his features changing, becoming sharper, more hardened to life in a bygone era—a talented actor about to tell a story.

"For near thirty years Mocha Dick roamed the sea lanes, a predator on the hunt, attacking ships in the Pacific. One year he showed up near the Falkland Islands in the Atlantic, quite a feat when you consider he had to travel around the tip of South America to change oceans. His hunt for victims was unceasing."

"You speak of him as though you've seen him." She was baiting him, wondering if there was any genetic memory. She wanted to keep him talking. "You mean he deliberately hunted whaling ships? He sounds humanly smart."

"He had uncanny intelligence—a true avenger with a passion for destruction. At the time he met his death, sailors counted at least nineteen harpoons embedded in his hide."

She sighed with satisfaction. "You tell an intriguing story. I can see the ghost of Mocha Dick roaming the seas, still searching for retribution."

"You're a great audience. You make it easy." They finished the meal in companionable silence. Galen glanced up, caught the attention of their waiter, mouthed the word, 'dessert,' and glanced at Sara. "We still have to stop by Adrienne's, briefly, then I have plans for the rest of the night. We'll go back to my place. I've been waiting for an evening alone with you for too long."

Her heart gave a leap. She imagined his beautiful hands stroking her body, and shivered in anticipation.

"Let's get out of there as soon as possible," she said. "I don't think our hostess nor any of that group are going to be pleased to see me." Without thinking she said, "Another hour won't matter. We've been waiting a hundred and sixty years."

He looked stunned, puzzled. "What? What do you mean?"

She recovered quickly. "Oh, nothing, really. This restaurant, the easy conversation and a wonderful dinner have made me a little fanciful."

"Sara, you entrance me. You have a romantic soul and I can't wait until I have you where I can explore it further."

Well, that was plain enough. In the past hour she'd come to realize there were forces at work here she'd never comprehend. Her dinner companion was Caleb, transported from another era, and they were caught in some kind of a time loop, playing the same scene over again with the same inevitable result.

Has he been a ghost in that house for a hundred years waiting for me to come to him? How long will we be together? Please let me have more than a few hours.

She loved this man like she'd never love another. She'd take what she could get. When the storm hit, history would repeat itself, and she'd lose him. The thought plagued her. She couldn't shake the feeling of dread.

The pain is going to be unbearable, but I'll get through it. In exchange for a few hours of being loved by this man, I'm willing to live on memories for the rest of my life. Maybe the next time around we'll connect forever.

With all the love in her soul shining in her eyes, she said, "Sounds like a plan to me. We've had a connection since the first night I saw you and heard you sing that love song."

He reached for her hand. "Here's to one of many evenings to come."

The waiter arrived with dessert, a dark rich mound of whipped chocolate, piled in a white ramekin, two plates, and two spoons.

Galen winked. "Chocolate is supposed to be very stimulating to the libido."

The sexual tension ravaging her nerves caught up with her. She gave an uncharacteristic giggle. "Then let's dig in."

Chapter Twenty-One

The hostile reception expected at Adrienne's house became reality the moment Sara and Galen followed their hostess into the room. Conversation faded while twenty or so people turned to watch Sara's progress; not everyone was ready to welcome her. She appreciated Galen's steadying hand at her waist.

"We're glad you could make it," Cora said, the note of apprehension in her voice unmistakable. "What with Binki and all that trouble, neither her parents nor Brian will be here, and with the storm coming, about half the guests stayed home to get their places secured."

"We were going to finalize plans for the Christmas show," Adrienne said, "but I guess we'll have to put it off for another time, and I have all this food." She glanced despairingly toward the lavish buffet in the dining room.

"What do you mean, about Binki?" Sara asked, foreboding creeping over her, remembering Felicity at the Stuart's house.

"I guess you haven't heard," Cora said, approaching them. "Binki overdosed on sleeping pills and ended up in the hospital yesterday."

"Oh, no. Did she . . . I mean, is she okay? I sensed something wrong at the Society meeting but I didn't want to intrude."

Georgia joined them. "They found her in time, and got her to the emergency room. She's home with her parents, but they're embarrassed by the whole thing, and don't want company."

"Poor kid," Galen said. "I know it sounds odd, but she always struck me as lonely—as though she needed someone to talk to, but had no one."

"For sure not her husband. Brian's furious," Georgia said. "So are his parents. Her mother told me Brian said Binki took the pills because she wanted attention; that she was behaving like a spoiled little kid. It'll probably break up the marriage."

"Isn't he being a little harsh?" Sara asked, feeling the need to defend her. Binki had been trapped like Felicity, whose anguish lingered in her mind. "Maybe Brian had her caught in a role she didn't want to play." Galen's glance of approval gratified her.

"Divorce is the best thing that could happen, if you ask me," Cora said, the hostility in her voice unmistakable. She'd never liked Brian. "Poor girl was miserable, married to a control freak. She didn't try to kill herself for jollies."

Sylvie Costner joined them, not saddened in the least if the scorn in her expression was any evidence. "My, Cora, why don't you tell us how you really feel? She didn't look sad to me the other night. She looked pleased with herself, but then, she always did when she was chasing after somebody else's husband."

Outraged, Cora, snapped, "If you can't keep your hound dog of a husband from sniffing around, that's your problem."

Steve Costner stunned them all into silence by grabbing Sylvie's arm. He hissed, "Shut up. You've said enough." He turned his anger on Cora. "All of you. You're bickering like a flock of vultures around road kill."

The atmosphere turned toxic. Recoiling from the animosity, Sara glanced at Galen, but his attention was focused on Sylvie like a laser beam, sending her a warning. To Sara, it appeared two conversations were going on here, but she was only party to the first.

"Seems to me we're all a little on edge with this storm coming." Henry tried to smooth the waters. Sara breathed a sigh of relief. Bless Henry and his easy-going nature. "This could 'a been a tragedy," he opined, "but wasn't, so we all need to give thanks and move on. The woman has troubles none of us paid much attention to, except maybe Galen who, at least treated her like a grown woman and not like somebody's toy doll."

Henry's insight deserved respect. His feelings went a lot deeper than his sunny, overly casual disposition led people to think. "You're right, Henry," Sara said. "Nobody wanted her to grow up and she hated it. Brian treated her like a child. What grown woman wants to be called Binki?"

The guests paused and glared at her. The remark had landed like a bomb waiting to explode, leaving all in the room at a loss for words, except for Adrienne, who, glancing helplessly at the dining room table laden with food, cried, "Oh, dear," and covered her mouth with her hands.

Sara swept the room with a smile. Determined to rescue her distressed hostess from the disintegration of her party, she said brightly, "It looks like we're not going to accomplish much this evening so why don't we sample some of Adrienne's wonderful buffet she's laid out and make it an early night?"

The anxious hostess looked relieved, clearly grateful the evening had been brought back from the brink of disaster.

Galen winked at Sara. "Sounds like a plan to me."

But Sylvie wasn't finished, her well of venom not nearly exhausted. "Why don't you just butt out? This is our problem. You're not from around here but you show up and start messing in our affairs. Well, we don't need your interference, or you asking a lot of questions, poking your nose into where it doesn't belong. Get the hell out and go back to your sweet little house in suburbia."

"Sylvie." Steve's voice thundered loud enough to shake the walls. "Shut your damn mouth or I'll shut it for you." Shocked silence once again changed the mood. Cultured New Kensington society apparently frowned upon such outbursts. Sylvie tossed her head in defiance. Turning her back on all of them, she sauntered over to the bar where she began making herself a drink.

The surreal atmosphere invading the room should have been fair warning to Sara, but battle-trained by rigid East Partridge social conditioning, she once more tried to restore ambiance. "I'm sorry if I've upset you, Sylvie. This is about the insurance policies with Congressional Ventures, isn't it? I wasn't trying to make trouble. I simply had some questions because I know something about tax laws. I've made some friends here and I care about what kind of trouble they could be in with illegal tax deductions. I didn't want to start any trouble."

Steve fixed her with a hostile glare. "Sorry, I just don't buy it. Calling the FBI was more than casual interest. You were looking to do some real harm here. What you outsiders don't get is we're happy with the way things are and have been for years."

Not everybody, she thought, thinking of Caleb, but she didn't voice an opinion.

"We don't need a morality check from a woman who has never had to make it on her own."

There it was again—the suggestion she'd been some naïve, kept woman for the first half of her life. Her temper started to heat. Social mores be damned, she didn't have to put up with this.

"I didn't mean any harm. I've made friends here I care about," she said, anger apparent.

Surprisingly, it was Adrienne who turned on her, eyes wild with hatred, prompting Galen to come to her side and put an arm around her waist, as though protecting her. What had she started? She braced herself.

Ugly red splotches marred the woman's cheeks. Her mouth twisted in a sneer. She laughed—a demented sound on the edge of crazy—and pointed at Sara. "You don't understand anything. You can't be bothered with how the rest of us struggle."

Her distress went beyond mere anger. Her voice escalated, laced with fear and pain. Sara regretted what she had set in motion, but her decision to become involved in the world around her was not negotiable. She'd come too far to stop caring.

Adrienne raged on. "You only care that your checks don't bounce. You're perfectly happy with your mediocre middle-income life. You and your friends lunch your way through your secure existence, caring only about your creature comforts. You've no comprehension of how the world works.

"Well, that's not good enough for the rest of us. We want it all, and we'll do whatever it takes to get it—whatever it takes to survive. You can rot in hell for interfering."

Bob Fowler broke the spell holding the rest of them frozen.

"Addy, Honey," he said, his voice pleading, "Your accusations are uncalled for. Sara doesn't know anything. She's become involved in something she should've stayed out of."

Rot in hell? The words were familiar—hurled at her by Thomas, standing on her porch, ranting. Sara watched Adrienne's features change, coarsening, while her voice deepened. Her eyes flashed a familiar green. With growing horror, she wondered if it was possible. Thomas? Could this woman be this century's version of Thomas?

Adrienne's demented rant held the room spellbound. "We take what we want, while the rest of you haven't a clue. People like you need to shut up. Be satisfied with your pitiful piece of the pie.

The world belongs to the rest of us—those of us who know how to play the game. "

"Enough! " Bob's voice threatened murder. He grabbed his wife by the shoulders, shaking her into silence. "Galen, take Sara home. She doesn't need to hear any more."

Cora rushed up to her, wringing her hands. "Sara. Please forgive her. I don't understand why she is behaving this way. I'm so sorry. I think Binki's attempted suicide has upset all of us."

Galen nodded. Nothing he could do but accept Cora's apology. Sara, too numb say anything, allowed him to lead her from the room to the outside.

"Well, that went well," he said. Stunned into silence, she let him help her into the car. The wind had died down. The sky lightened. The storm had given them a few hours of respite. "It looks like we might see the moon tonight."

"Do you have some mysterious power over the weather?" she teased, determined to lighten the mood. No way would she allow Adrienne's vindictive rant ruin her evening. "It has calmed down considerably."

He grinned, grateful for her mood. "I commanded it," he replied. "It'll only last for a few hours and I'm planning for a relaxing interlude on the outside deck at my house. We'll watch the moon rise over the ocean."

She wondered if it were possible, remembering the way the wind had suddenly torn at Thomas when he raged at her. She gave a nervous laugh.

"You don't appear affected by Adrienne's anger." Of course, he hadn't seen the change in the woman's face, or recognized words spoken in another time. As far as he knew, it was simply a catfight between contentious females. "You knew they weren't going to take your interference without reacting."

"I'm not ready to hear 'I told you so,' Galen, so back off. I'm tired of being dismissed as an airhead because I care about what happens to people I like. Why can't men give women credit for having a brain?"

"Hey, give me a break. Don't lump me into your 'all men' category. I tried to save you some grief by warning you. The men Costner and Fowler are involved with play hardball. I'm trying to protect your pretty little neck."

"See what I mean?" she said. "You'd never hear me describe your neck as 'pretty little,' a demeaning term applied only to women." She settled into the car and glared at him when he entered the other side. His worried frown shamed her. So maybe her bitchy attitude toward him was out of line. She tried making amends.

"Are we having a fight?"

"I sure as hell hope not," he said. "War is not on my agenda this evening."

She grinned at him. "I'm sorry. You're getting anger that should be aimed at Sylvie and Adrienne. So, tell me, what is on your agenda for the rest of the evening?"

His over-the-top, stage leer made her shout with laughter. "We're going to my place, where I'm going to ply your senses with an excellent wine, woo you with erotic words, and make love to you for the rest of the night."

"Oh. Ah, well, okay."

Chapter Twenty Two

Galen's home faced the ocean, behind a wall of glass, with bedrooms on the second floor. Both levels opened onto wide decks protected by an overhanging hip roof. On the lower level, the interior contained one large room with kitchen, dining, and sitting areas. A natural stone fireplace dominated the long wood paneled wall, sharing space with rows of books on shelves. The furniture appeared new, very modern, all leather, and linen. An open staircase ascended to the second floor.

"Wow. You really do things with style. I was expecting something sea-faring, or kind of nautical," Sara said. She sounded like a teenager on a first date.

He gave her a curious look, and laughed. "Like Moby Dick? Why would you think that? No, sorry, not a harpoon in sight."

"That was a dumb thing to say." She had to stop confusing Caleb and Galen. Caleb was lost to her, and Galen not far behind. She stifled the rush of grief. Grim thoughts would not interfere with tonight. She wouldn't allow it. The next few hours were for building memories.

Smiling, Galen took her hand and pulled her to him. "Welcome to my home, Sara. I'm glad you like it. I don't share my privacy with many people," he said. "You have the honor of being the first woman who has seen it." Before she could react, he took her in his arms and kissed her—a gentle, thorough kiss that had her heart pounding. His lips roamed lightly over her face, pausing to caress her mouth, gently searching for her acquiescence. He felt so good, his body's warmth pressed against her, his arms holding her closely. She stood quietly, absorbing his warmth, before she glanced up at him, smiling.

"I could stay like this forever, and never move." The words came before she thought. For her there would be no 'forever.' Soon she would lose him and be alone again.

He led her to the staircase. "You'll find the master bedroom on the second floor has a large bathroom. I've stocked it with everything you might need for an overnight stay. There's a nightgown, robe, and slippers, if you want to change those clothes for something more comfortable. When you're ready, come downstairs. We'll spend some time out on the deck, watching the moon rise." Clearly a man with a mission; he left nothing to chance, and did not expect an argument.

Sara shivered with pleasure. She was a ship being piloted through stormy waters by a determined captain who knew exactly where he was going—toward a memorable evening of seduction.

In her heart she knew, that somehow, somewhere, they would be together again in another life. What they had tonight would have to last her for a lifetime. The immediate future, however, loomed like a lifeless pile of sand.

Enough already. No more thoughts. This night is for loving.

She mounted the steps to the master bedroom, eager to see what was there.

"Wow," she muttered. First class all the way. The room was done in shades of blue with thick grey carpeting. The king size bed, covered in a navy blue velvet comforter, took up half the room. A satin gown, white terrycloth robe, and scuffs lay there. She laughed at the bed, turned down, ready for occupancy. Galen had put a lot of thought into this evening.

The master bath, in keeping with the owner's style, had a double size jetted tub, a huge shower, and a long marble vanity loaded with an assortment of toiletries bearing labels found normally in a luxury spa. Galen must have told the casino's spa manager to give him one of everything. She could have spent the next hour trying them all, but the bottle of lotion caught her eye. It was scented with Indian Champaca Flower, rumored to be an aphrodisiac. Smiling, she poured a bit of it into her hand, inhaling the sweetly seductive scent. With every whiff, her anticipation grew.

"I get the message."

Grinning, she slathered the lotion all over her body, then donned the gown, robe and slippers, ready to go in search of her quarry, but when she opened the bedroom door, Galen stood there, in his bare feet, wearing a robe like hers, his expression a whimsical plea for understanding.

"I couldn't wait," he said. "I've never wanted any woman the way I want you. This feels like the end of a long journey with endless time spent searching for you—waiting for you. I know it doesn't make any sense, but those are the only words I have to describe this longing. I ache with wanting you." He reached for her, his hunger desperate.

"Love me now, Galen," she said. "This night may be all we have."

When his arms wrapped around her, she sighed and rested her face against his chest, craving his warmth, absorbing his essence in her every pore, her passion rose with intensity unlike anything she'd even felt before—not even with Richard. Something new and different filled her now—emotions from a deeper place, sharpened with age, and honed with experience. Tonight she would have it all, the real thing, if only for a few hours, knowing how precious the interlude would be, and how suddenly it would end. She'd spend the rest of her life reliving the memory.

"Sara." His lips covered hers, soft and hungry; his eager tongue searched, intimately caressing her, determined to claim her.

His taste aroused her and stoked the fire raging in her soul. Warm moisture flooded between her legs. She was so ready to be taken by this wonderful man. Her need grew to an agony of desire. Their clothes fell to the floor when he lifted her in his arms and took her to the bed.

Passion consumed them with a force matched by the raging wind pounding against the glass, it's roar herald the imminent arrival of the storm. Roiling clouds darkened the room to a stygian black, dark as the deepest cave. It surrounded them, robbing them of their sight while protecting them from the fury raging outside.

"Galen, what's happening? I can't see anything. Why this awful blackness? It's strange, unnatural, beyond cloudy."

"Don't worry. It's the storm, my love." His voice calmed her. "The dark doesn't matter. We're safe here." His strong, hands roamed over her body, claiming her breasts. "Even if we can't see each other, I can taste you, inhale your essence, and learn your body with my touch."

She answered by nuzzling the hair on his chest, breathing in his scent. She stretched the length of him, melding closely, her heart lying against his. When had male sweat ever been so arousing? His lips caressed her breasts, pulling her nipples deeply into his mouth. The roughened texture of his fingertips, roamed over her skin, so sensitive with increased passion, exciting her beyond bearing, feeding her hunger for him. She needed more. She grabbed his hips with her knees, held him tightly, and brought his sex to her aroused core, trying to be even closer. Robbed of sight, her sense of smell became heightened. Inhaling deeply, she savored a special maleness no cologne could disguise—odors of salt, the sea, and pipe tobacco.

Wait. Rough hands? Salt? Pipe tobacco?
Though fogged with passion, her brain cleared for an instant.
Not Galen's scent. Not his hands. These were textured, work-hardened. Who?
 Her heart leaped. Though her eyes opened, the darkness kept him hidden, but the enhanced scent of his sweat couldn't be denied. Caleb. Oh my God, Caleb. She'd known, but now she was sure. Galen was Caleb. When his probing fingers touched her core she screamed her passion, felt her release coming.
"Sara, I can't hold back. Forgive me, Dearling."
He plunged; his powerful possession thrilled her, his essence flooded her womb. It wasn't enough. The ecstasy of his possession drove her to heights she'd never known. Though she clung to him with all the strength in her arms and legs, and gave him everything in her power, still, it wasn't enough.
"Caleb, my love. Oh, God, Caleb."
"My dearest, my beloved Sara. I've waited a century to hold you." He whispered to her, his voice husky with emotion while his lips roamed over her face and breasts. "I will love you forever, beyond this night, through eternity."
"Caleb, take my heart. I want it inside you, where it will live forever, no matter what happens."
"I will be with you always, my beloved Sara, until the end of time."
His words lay, like burnt ashes in her mind. For the next few hours they would have each other, then he'd vanish, and leave nothing behind. The winds of destruction howled their intent, shaking the house.
She whispered, "I love you, my darling, with all my heart, the rest of my life." With their hands, their lips, and tongues, they

loved each other. He took her again and again, while the storm raged outside their window, until exhaustion claimed them.

With one last cry, Sara lost consciousness. When she awoke, she was alone.

Morning had come; the rain continued, but the sky had barely lightened into day, with dark clouds shutting out any hint of blue. The worst of the storm could be no more than an hour away. The wind lashed the rain against the windows. She heard glass shatter somewhere downstairs.

Knowing she had scarcely enough time to get to safety, Sara still took a moment to savor last night, re-living it slowly, wanting to recall every moment of passion. She wanted it securely in her mind.

Rolling over onto the pillow beside her, she inhaled the essence of Caleb, and the merest hint of Galen's cologne. Did it matter? They were one and the same. She loved both beyond all reason. Though the bedside clock said 11:00 a.m., scant light filtered through the drapes. She stretched, feeling every sore muscle in her body. Galen was gone, but where was he? Surely not gone, as in vanished?

No. I won't think about that. We found each other, after waiting 160 years. I can't lose him now. I can't live without him.

She grabbed her robe from the floor, hastily pulled it on, and ran for the stairs. The lower level was deserted, but a note lay on the kitchen counter. She read it, smiling, while she ate the fruit and rolls Galen had left out.

My Dearest Sara,

I've gone down to the dock to secure the boat. The storm should make   landfall within the hour. We have to evacuate to the mainland no later   than noon. I've called Jen to come pick you up so you can finish packing.

I'll be back and we'll all leave together.

Love you.

She'd no sooner finished the note, than a car pulled up to the house. Jen entered through the front door exclaiming, "Wow. What a dope house. Galen must be awesomely rich to afford this." She glanced at Sara with concern. "He sounded worried when he called. How are you? How did last night go? Tell me while you get ready. We've got to get out of here now, before they close the causeway.

This storm is really bad. The weather service says it's the worst one we've had for more than a hundred years. Totally."

"This is it, Jen. The once-in-a-hundred-years storm we've been hearing about."

Jen paled. "The colony?"

"I think so."

"Where's Galen. Is he gone?"

"No. He's securing his boat." She paused, conquering the catch in her throat. "Jen, I'm so in love with him. How am I going to survive losing him?"

Jen hugged her, tears of sympathy showing in her eyes. "There's nothing we can do. You'll make it. Colin and I are with you. Hang in there, but move, Mom. We've got to get out of here. We maybe have a chance to make it off the island before this storm hits us. Come on. Get in the car. You can dress back at the house."

Sara followed Jen; glad she didn't have to drive. The sky was black, the wind howled in furious gusts, making it hard to walk. Though the storm surge hadn't peaked, Stuart House showed the effects of the battering sea. The increasing wind had thrown the furniture on the porch in a heap against the wall. Usually it escaped such damage, but this time the house wasn't going to make it. Clearly, in a few hours Stuart House would be gone.

Jen pulled her car behind Sara's SUV. Colin had begun loading boxes of food and bottled water. He'd dismantled the computer hardware and wrapped it all in a shower curtain to keep it dry.

"I have almost everything in suitcases," Jen yelled, over the sound of the wind. "Go upstairs and see what I missed."

First Sara needed to get out of her drenched robe and into dry clothes. Jen had done a good job of packing, leaving only a few things behind. When she looked under the bed, she found the whale tooth and, after a moment of indecision, put it in her bag. Without its magic it would still make a precious souvenir. She found another pair of sweats and changed, donned a pair of sneakers, and closed her suitcase, ready to take it downstairs. Her Jayne Lynch sweat suit was still in the laundry. Regretfully, there it would stay. Time was running out. The house shook with every blast of wind and water, making it difficult to drag her bag, bumping along on its wheels, into the kitchen and by the door, where it would wait to be loaded into the SUV.

Jen, busy in the kitchen, assembled the cat's things, and stacked his food dishes, blanket, and bed on the table, next to his carrier. Caleb, crouched inside the case, mewled anxiously, his tail flicking.

"Is there anything left in the living room?" Sara asked.

"No, I have everything. Colin put most of it in the SUV. I thought he could take my vehicle with the cat stowed on the back seat. You'll ride with me." The sound of a car pulling up to the house distracted her. "Are you expecting anybody besides Galen?" she asked, peering out the window, and groaned. "Oh, great. Just what we need. What's she doing here?"

"Who?" Sara glanced at her, puzzled, and cried out in alarm when the kitchen door flew open, and slammed against the wall. Adrienne entered the kitchen, with a rush of wind and rain, obviously distraught, wide-eyed, her face gaunt and drawn with panic, her clothes disheveled. She held a gun in her hand and waved it erratically, pointing it toward them.

Sara froze in fear at the sight of the weapon.

"Adrienne." She cried, "What are you doing with a gun? What's wrong with you?"

"Damn you," Adrienne yelled. "You're going to get what you deserve for meddling where it's none of your business."

The woman staggered drunkenly into the room, out of control, her face twisted with insane rage.

"Are you crazy?" Sara cried, eyeing the pistol, terrified. "Have you lost your mind?"

Her nerves screamed at her, *escape,* but there was nowhere to run.

"I'm going to kill you, Bitch. Finally, I'll be rid of you and your damn snooping into our business."

"Mom." Jen realized Sara's danger, grasped her shoulders, and tried to move her out of the line of fire. "Look out. Get out of the way."

Sara stared, unable to move, seeing only the dark hole at the end of the gun barrel pointed at her. "Adrienne, for heaven's sake, calm down before something happens you'll be sorry for. What do you think you're doing?"

Adrienne, her face wet with tears, her voice hoarse with hate, screamed above the howling wind, "What does it look like I'm doing? The police came this morning. They arrested Steve and Bob. Took them away. It's all falling apart because of you. You've ruined everything."

Dear God. Sara begged, but the deranged woman was too far-gone to listen to reason. "Killing me isn't the answer. Can we talk about this? Please, put that gun down before it goes off."

"That's the whole idea, you meddling bitch," Adrienne cried, screaming her frustration.

She doesn't hear me. I have to do something.

"Adrienne." Jen moved toward her, keeping her voice quiet. "Calm down. Think about this. You don't want to hurt anybody."

Jen's words forced Sara to action. She had to get her daughter out of the kitchen, away from the danger. Grabbing Jen, she shoved her aside. Her voice shook.

"Come with me, and we can talk."

Seeing Jen near the door, and not daring to get close enough to touch the raving woman, Sara inched her way backwards and turned toward the living room, praying Adrienne, clearly beyond rational thought, would follow. It worked. She came right behind, viciously jabbing the weapon into Sara's back, making her stumble and fall to the floor.

Glass shattered; the sound startled them. The gale's force had broken one of the windows. Waves slammed against the house, throwing salt spray into the room, soaking furniture beyond rescue. Sara struggled to her feet, fought for balance against the raging wind, and cowered against the wall.

Galen, his face pale with shock, rushed into the room. "What the hell? Adrienne, what in God's name are you doing? Put that down before you hurt somebody."

"Stay away from me, traitor." She turned on him, waving the pistol wildly.

Sara saw the muzzle drop, becoming heavy in her hand, and even more dangerous because soon, when Adrienne realized she was losing her grip, she'd pull the trigger while she still could.

"Mom." Jen screamed. She had followed Galen. "Mom, get away from her. Oh, please, don't shoot my mom."

"Jen, get out of here," Galen yelled. "Damn it, Adrienne, put that damn thing down before it goes off."

Adrienne, distracted, yelled at him, accusing him. "You. You've been in on it all the time. You had to help your whore snoop around. Ruin everything. You talked to the police, didn't you? Got your big deal friends in Atlantic City involved." As she spoke, her voice deepened, taking on a masculine tone. Her features began to change, becoming coarsened, more masculine, while her brow thickened and her body grew heavier. Hair covered her jaw. Rapidly, her appearance altered. She became a man, wearing seafaring clothing from another century.

Galen stared at her, shocked. "Adrienne? What's happening to you?"

"My God, Thomas?" Sara cried, terrified. "Thomas, Please stop. Don't shoot."

Adrienne, or Thomas, raised her arms, gripping the pistol with both hands.

Behind Galen, a cloud formed, spiraling from the floor while it took shape. Gradually, it solidified, becoming a human likeness. Caleb. He had come to take Thomas and put an end to the colony. No, that couldn't happen here, in this room, with Galen present. The lesson learned from the psychic at the metaphysical meeting surfaced in her mind. Caleb and Galen were the same. They could not see each other, together, in the same parallel universe. They would self-destruct.

"Damn you to hell, Caleb," Thomas roared at the shape behind Galen, "This time you won't interfere. I'll have my way." He raised the gun, his arm tensed.

"No," Sara screamed, and leaped toward him, but she was too late. A shot rang out. Blood poured from Galen's chest in an obscene flood. He fell backward, to the floor.

The wind howled like a living thing. The tide surged, the surf increasing in height with each wave, poured through the windows.

Caleb's arm wrapped around Thomas' throat, holding him in a death grip. "It is over," he roared, his voice lost in the sound of the wind. The remaining windows in the room shattered. In an instant Caleb vanished with Thomas.

Sara, heedless of the blood soaking her clothes, threw herself over Galen's body.

"No. Please God, no," she cried, her hands on the wound, trying to stem the flow of life from his body, even as she realized it flowed no more. His heart had stopped.

Someone screamed, the sound loud enough to override the raging storm surge; screams so loud and constant they made her throat raw.

"Come back," she cried, and blessedly, the screaming stopped. Numb with grief, she realized the voice had been hers.

Though his beautiful eyes stared at her, they whitened. There was no recognition, no life. She pumped futilely at his chest, but his flaccid body didn't respond.

"I love you. You know, don't you, that you'll be the only man I love for the rest of my life? You have my heart. Take it with you and wait for me, my beloved. "

She leaned over him and kissed his cold cheek, holding him in her arms, shrugging to escape the hands pulling at her.

From a distance she heard, "He's gone, Mom. There isn't anything we can do. We have to get out of here. The house is falling down around us."

The words forced from her throat, were raw with grief. She had to tell him—to make a promise.

"We'll be together, in another life; I promise. Wait for me."

Jen held on to Sara's shoulders, and pulled her to her feet, dodging debris crashing through the windows; the wind hurled boards, tore siding from the walls, while Stuart House slowly gave up the fight. They had to get out before it crumbled into oblivion.

"Colin," Jen's voice shrieked, out of control. "Help me. Help me get Mom out of here."

He appeared in the doorway, white faced, taking in the scene at a glance. "You have blood all over you. Where are you hurt?"

"It isn't hers," Jen said. "It's Galen's. He's dead. Thomas, or somebody who used to be Adrienne, shot him, and then disappeared."

Jen screamed in fear while part of the roof tore off, and fell to the ground with a large crash. Water dripped from the ceiling.

"We have to get out of here, now. Help me with Mom."

Colin, not moving, stared at the blood soaking her clothes. "Is she okay?"

"No, she's not okay. She's in shock. Colin move. Help me."

"I'll take her," he said. "If we can get her on her feet, we can put her in the van. You drive. I'll take your car. Follow me. I know how to get to the causeway without driving on the shore road.

Jen stood, and together they managed to pull a nearly catatonic Sara to her feet. Between them they got her down the stairs and into the vehicle. Colin ran back inside the house and got the frightened cat, escaping the kitchen only moments before the ceiling collapsed.

Jen, with Sara belted in beside her, backed the SUV out of the drive, and waited for Colin to stow Caleb. He backed out around her and took the lead into town, avoiding the beach road, which was beginning to flood. Strangely, once they pulled away from the house, the destructive force of the storm lessened, making it possible to navigate.

While they made their way, Jen glanced out the rear view mirror in time to see a massive wave deal Stuart House a killing blow. She watched it slowly begin to crumble to the ground. Soon there would be nothing left but the memory.

Chapter Twenty-Three

East Partridge, NY—two months later

Sara stood in her living room, surveying the holiday decorations critically, searching for some source of satisfaction, or some sense of pride in the green, red, and gold elegance the decorators had achieved. With money, she mused, anything is possible. She felt nothing. Since the escape from New Kensington to East Partridge, she'd been barely aware of the passage of time. Her mind had been floating, like being enclosed in a dark deprivation tank, shut off from feelings.

Suddenly the Christmas holidays were here, and too tired to resist, she'd allowed her friends to drag her into participating. Grace had badgered her into lending her home for her law firm's office party, hence the elaborate decorations. A huge Christmas tree, a perfect pyramid of artificial perfection, held court in the far corner of the living room, cloaked in the candlelight glow of a thousand tiny lights. She could have opted for a natural tree this year, since Richard was out of the picture—something she'd always wanted, but she never won the argument, but it didn't matter, although the presence of dropping needles would have represented a departure from the usual way of things. It was too much bother. She let Colin and Jen drag the tree box from the garage and patiently reconstruct the plastic wonder. Next year, by God, she'd be on a tropical island somewhere, away from this ritual madness.

Garlands of fresh evergreens, festooned in wide, wired red and green ribbon bows, hung in every room in the house—a total cop out on her part. She used to do all this herself; this year she called in a decorator to do the work. Fragrant boughs graced the fireplace mantel in the living room, covered the staircase bannister, and followed its graceful curve to the second floor. She'd always loved that staircase, and smiled at how she'd visualized her daughter coming down it someday in her wedding dress.

Dear God, how I wish I could find an excuse to go lie down and sleep. Jen would worry. I've been doing too much of that lately.

Caleb! Her mind cried his name. No, she wouldn't go there. The merest whisper of his name triggered her darkest thoughts. She would get through this party, by God, without having to endure the pitying looks from all her friends. No. She wouldn't allow any more melancholy. She'd put on her smiley face and do her hostess thing, even though it wasn't her party. She hadn't the energy to resist Grace's pleas to use her house for the annual reception for members of her friend's law firm.

"All the preparation would be done for you," Grace had declared. "You won't have to lift a finger. I've told the caterers to go all out, and gave the decorators carte blanche to achieve an over-the-top Christmas mood throughout the house."

The open house, presumably, was a favor for Grace, because "this house is so perfect for the occasion, so much better than renting a hall somewhere."

She smiled at the way it was presented to her. She recognized the ploy as another attempt by her friends to rally around her, cheer her up, and give her a purpose. Things had been this way since the return from Stuart House. Her friends had no idea what had happened there, only that a devastating hurricane had terrified her, destroyed the house and sent her home early.

It wasn't as though she had anything better to do. Her role in this evening's festivities was minor. She simply had to appear and be gracious to the guests. Out of habit, she would perform the expected hostess rituals because Christmas had always been a time for celebration. Fulfilling expectations was her job, and, if she was lucky, there'd be no memories to avoid.

Grace thought her melancholy was some sort of Post Traumatic Stress resulting from said hurricane and the trauma of divorce. Such a simplistic explanation for the last eight weeks and three days, ever since . . . oh no. She felt her heart start to pound and forced her mind away from the memory.

Oh please, I can't go there.

Her throat caught. Deep Breaths. She couldn't chance another anxiety attack in the middle of a party. It simply wasn't done in East Partridge society.

The memory of the scene she tried to forget, of the madness, the blood, and her beloved's eyes, whitened in death, rushed back like the storm tossed waves, swamping her in misery. She should have never left him. If she'd stayed, they would be together now.

How she'd fought for possession when Jen found the clothes, stained with his blood, and took them from her, although she knew how sick it was to hide them in her bed. She wanted that last bit of him. She wanted something left from their one night together. At least, she had the whale tooth. It took her weeks to admit the magic was gone. There was no going back.

From where she stood, she could see the table in the formal dining room, made festive by a huge holiday floral arrangement, and loaded with buffet food, featuring the sterling silver candelabra she treasured.

Richard had never appreciated the room's elegance, though he liked the impression of wealth it conveyed. He'd always complained it made him uncomfortable, and insisted they eat in the kitchen. Sara smiled at the memory, relieved for the moment, of the sadness haunting her ever since she'd returned from the Jersey Shore.

Nothing could help that. Galen, or Caleb, as she liked to remember him, was gone. Life stretched before her bleak and empty.

Life? What life? Without him nothing lay ahead. She was simply marking time until it was over. So why did she endure this waiting?

"Mom?" Jenny came in from the kitchen, an anxious look on her face. "I've been looking for you. How are you?"

Impatiently, Sara gritted her teeth. Another thing she had to live with—this need everyone had, whenever they approached, to examine her critically, assessing her state of mind.

"Just fine, the way I was the last time you asked."

Jen hugged her briefly, and then backed off. "Sorry, I know I'm being a derp again, but I worry about you. I'm in the kitchen, helping the caterers. Colin's doing door duty and taking care of the coats and stuff."

She hadn't realized people had begun arriving, but the house was filling.

Jen asked, "Who's coming and how many will be here?"

"Thirty or so law partners from Grace's firm and their wives or dates should be showing up, so we'll have a crowd, maybe sixty or so; at least until the alcohol runs out." She glanced over to the corner of the dining room where the bartender, hired for the night, was setting up. "Grace will be here momentarily, and I expect the rest to arrive with her, all at once."

"Why did it have to be here? They could have hired a hall."

Sara gave a wry laugh. "I have good, loyal friends. Apparently, they got together and decided the way to get me through my first holiday season alone was to keep me so busy I didn't have time to brood."

"Is it working?"

She fought to subdue the catch in her throat. "Oh, Jen, he's never far from me. When I remember the Caleb I met at the Stuart House in 1880, I wonder what he'd think of life in the twenty-first century; when I think of him as Galen, I relive our last night together and I just want to be left alone with my thoughts."

"Sara! Sweetie!" Grace called from the hallway and rushed into the room to embrace Sara. "Ohmigod. The place looks divine and smells heavenly with all this greenery. You've done a fabulous job, like you always do.

"Jen, you look gorgeous in red. Lordy, I wish I were young enough to wear that dress. I met Colin at the door. Way to go, girl. He's positively scrumptious."

She has to stop for breath sometime, Sara mused. When she did, she peered at Sara sharply, assessing her. Sara braced herself.

"How are you, Honey?" Her voice dripped sympathy. She glanced at Sara's dress, sighed, and said, "You've lost some more weight, but you look divine, even if you are wearing black. You doing okay? This isn't too much for you?"

Trying hard to avoid a grimace, Sara answered, "Just fine. Don't worry about me." She looked toward the crowd of arrivals at the door. "Let me greet your friends and get on with the evening."

"Uh, about that." Grace paused, her expression suspiciously anxious before she continued. "I've invited another guest. He's a lawyer I just hired to fill a spot we had in a new department we're setting up. His name is Andrew Pierce."

Fury shot from Sara's gut like a lava eruption. Not now. She couldn't do this.

"How many times do I have to tell you to stop trying to set me up with an available man? Just back off."

Her expression crumpling in the face of Sara's rage, Grace pleaded, "Sweetie, it isn't like that. He just got here two days ago.

He has no family. He'll be spending the holidays alone in a hotel. What could I do when the entire office was talking about the party? I had to extend an invitation, didn't I? After all, I'm the boss."

"Mom. Take it easy," Jen said. "There's no conspiracy. Grace is just being nice."

"Grace isn't being nice." Her voice turned grim. "She's determined to push me into my old role of happily married housewife so I'll fit in with our crowd, and an extra woman won't embarrass them. Right, Grace?"

"Sara, I'm sorry." Grace was near tears. "I had no idea you'd react like this." The front door bell chimed, interrupting her. "That's probably him now. I'll go greet him," she said, intent on escape.

"Just keep him away from me. I don't want to see him or talk to him. If he comes anywhere near me, so help me I'll lock myself in my bedroom for the rest of the night."

Grace fled, while Sara fumed.

"Mom, calm down," Jen said, her eyes on the door, curious to see who entered. Her breath caught; her eyes widened; her voice shook. "Who is that?"

Oblivious to Jen's reaction, Sara continued, "I mean every word I said."

"Mom."

"So help me, Jen. Don't argue with me. It's not negotiable."

"But Mom." Jen pleaded.

Sara paused in the middle of her rant to see what held her daughter's gaze transfixed on the door. When she turned, she saw a man looking at her intently, drinking her in like a desert starved for rain.

Stunned, she returned his gaze, taking in all six feet of him— his slightly long dark hair, the lock falling on his forehead, begging to be brushed out of the way.

Puzzled, she stood motionless, and watched him, cold racing through her veins, while he walked slowly toward her. There was something odd . . .

"Mom." Jen was white with shock.

"What on earth Jen? What's the matter?"

He stopped within a foot of her. She glanced up into eyes a shade of green she'd expected never to see again in this life. She didn't know this man—never met him, but the eyes made him seem familiar, even though it was apparent he didn't know her. Her heart rate increased along with her libido. The way she responded to him shocked her. What was happening?

My body wants him, even if my mind doesn't know him,

"Hello." It was all she could manage. "I'm Sara Burkhart, your hostess."

"Hello, Sara Burkhart," he said, a puzzled expression on his face. "I'm Andrew Pierce." Cautiously, he added, "You seem somehow familiar to me. Have we met?"

Oh, God. He had to say that. I need to remain calm, before I lose it.

She smiled, desperately trying for casual party small talk. "I get that a lot. I have a generic look about me. You are the new man at my friend, Grace's, law firm. Yes?"

He nodded. "Got here two days ago. I specialize in Maritime Law. The legalities of sea commerce are a new territory for them."

On firm ground now, she said, "Well, then let's get you settled with a drink, and we'll find a place to talk." She led him toward the bar. "Maritime law. That sounds like you have a lot to do with ships."

"Foreordained, I'm afraid. It's in my blood. I come from a long line of seafaring ancestors, whaling captains, and such, although the extent of my involvement these days is owning an ocean going sailboat."

Sailboat? Was it possible?

The thought stunned her. After what she'd lived through in New Kensington, could she even doubt it?

"Forgive me for making a pest of myself," he said apologetically, "but I have to ask again. Haven't we met before?"

Her smile was brilliant, blossoming with hope. "Not in this lifetime."

His mischievous grin acknowledged her joke. "In some other time, then? Another universe? I think I've suddenly become a fan of the supernatural. I'd like to know more."

"One of my favorite subjects." By the grace God, or by whatever merciful being, Caleb, the only man she would ever love in any lifetime, was here, alive. He stood before her, solidly real. Her heart swelled, too large for her chest.

"I have an idea," he said, smiling down at her with those gloriously verdant eyes. "How do you feel about boats? I'd like to take you sailing. Would you consider it?

"I could show you the sea in all its moods—take you to magical places you've never been. We'll play in the Southern seas, and visit the pyramids, and make love on a boat floating the Amazon. How about it?"

She knew the words. She'd heard them before—spoken to her in another time.

She laughed, barely containing the tears of joy in her eyes.

"I've never been on a boat," she said.